BE A TEEN GODDESS!

Other books by Francesca De Grandis

*Be a Goddess! A Guide to Celtic Spells and Wisdom
for Self-Healing, Prosperity, and Great Sex*

*Goddess Initiation: A Practical Celtic Program
for Soul-Healing, Self-Fulfillment, and Wild Wisdom*

*The Modern Goddess' Guide to Life: How to Be Absolutely
Divine on a Daily Basis*

Her Winged Silence: A Shaman's Notebook

Be a Teen Goddess!

Magical Charms, Spells, and Wiccan Wisdom for the Wild Ride of Life

Francesca De Grandis

CITADEL PRESS
Kensington Publishing Corp.
www.kensingtonbooks.com

CITADEL PRESS BOOKS are published by

Kensington Publishing Corp.
850 Third Avenue
New York, NY 10022

All Kensington titles, imprints, and distributed lines are available at special quantity discounts for bulk purchases for sales promotions, premiums, fund-raising, educational, or institutional use. Special book excerpts or customized printings can also be created to fit specific needs. For details, write or phone the office of the Kensington special sales manager: Kensington Publishing Corp., 850 Third Avenue, New York, NY 10022, attn: Special Sales Department; phone 1-800-221-2647.

CITADEL PRESS and the Citadel logo are Reg. U.S. Pat. & TM Off.

First printing: April 2005

10 9 8 7 6 5 4 3 2 1

Printed in the United States of America

Library of Congress Control Number: 2004116399

ISBN 0-8065-2651-3

To Kaya, William Winston, and Rachael.

This book is here should you ever want or need it.

So am I.

Contents

9 You Name It, We Got It: Magical Mystical Miscellany **235**

TABLE OF SPELLS

The following list includes spells, rituals, prayers, and the like. Fact is, in some ways all these terms are synonymous.

1 Make Sure to Read This: The Basics of Powerful, Safe Spells

This chapter explains spellcrafting basics—yummy magical lessons setting you up to use the rest of the book powerfully and safely. Then you have the right to wear a tall pointy witch's hat. Not! But you *can* then just about jump to any section in the book, read it to know what else is needed to do its spell(s) powerfully and safely, then use the spell(s). Whoo hoo! But do *not* skip Chapter 1 or you'll have lame spells that don't work, not to mention trouble on your hands.

And with that, let's jump onto our brooms, and get going. (Someday, I'll be sweeping the floor and, I swear, that broom'll take off!)

Wicca Is . . .

Wicca is the love of magic, the fellowship of Fairies, the touch of stars on my face.

Wicca is my laughter; Wicca is also knowing my giggles are a blessing on anyone who hears them—anyone who is open to the Mother's joyful touch.

Wicca is the sun, first thing in the morning, helping me feel I can have the sort of day—and whole life—I deep-down want.

Wicca is a refuge when I'm tired and sad. It is the rain pouring down, telling me truths—ones that are cleansing, joyful, or perhaps melancholy.

Wicca tempts me into goodness; it does not bind me with self-hate.

Wicca is my Mother's divine voice, guiding me through life's mazes.

Wicca is a mystery that makes sense, a house cat that teaches wisdom, a moment's hush then . . . all is right.

Wicca is knowing that every person is a God(dess), and learning to draw on that divine power in me.

Finally, Wicca is . . . you.

I've said what Wicca is to me, but what is it to you?

Let's talk . . . (so to speak): Get something to write on—your journal, a napkin, a scratch pad, whatever. Write down what Wicca is to you, because that's what it comes down to. This is a religion that, instead of *telling* you, helps you tell yourself—you get to trust your inner wisdom, make choices that are appropriate to your unique personality, and decide what special gift you bring to life's party.

If you don't already know how to do this, this book's type of Wicca will teach you. If you already know, you'll learn to do it better. But be patient with yourself: growth happens slowly, bit by bit. The first step—putting pen to paper: "Wicca is . . ."

You don't *have* to do this in order to use this book. But if you want to, here are some thoughts. And in any case, it's important you at least read all this. So:

Perhaps you write, "Wicca is something I know nothing about." Or "Wicca is something I'm not sure I want to really do a lot of, but I'd like to learn a bit." Or "Wicca scares me." That's all great! Because if we decide that *our* "Wicca is . . ." statements are not good enough, or are irrelevant, we miss the point: Wicca is *you*, whoever you are, right at this *second*.

Write!

Some witches keep a "Book of Shadows," making entries as often or as sporadically as they feel like. This is a journal of magical spells, spiritual insights, personal confusions, joys, ranting, ventings, victories, defeats, longings, frustrations, and anything else that is part of their journey. If you do this, it can strengthen your sense of who you are, not only as a witch, but also as a person. And as a God(dess).

"Wicca is . . ." statements are among the things that can go in this diary. It's up to you what goes in your magical journal. Perhaps *you* only put in your spiritual insights while another person might throw in *everything*, including a math quiz score and clothing budget.

Everything thus far in this chapter relates to powerful, safe spellcrafting: The better we know ourselves, trust ourselves, and express ourselves, the better our spells work. The more we deceive ourselves about who we are, suppress ourselves, dislike ourselves, the worse our spells work.

The book'll help you with all this, you betcha! Which will also help you be more *you*, and that is the ultimate goal, anyway. A witch is a dancer in the swirling dance of life; this dancer plays an individual part that portrays a unique, beautiful expression of commitment to living fully. The work in this book will help you dance your special dance.

So, read on. There's more introductory material to set you up for a great broom ride! (I swear, I am going to find a way to make that broom of mine rise up into the air.)

Wiccan Laws, Wiccan Opinions, Wiccan Contradictions

I believe in the role of the teacher. While Wicca has no repressive rules, it does have laws (which will be discussed throughout this book). These laws are not meaningless dictates that no longer have relevance, but are both magical and spiritual facts that even a tree or glimmer of starlight knows.

These laws do not oppress you, but help you be yourself. They help you fill yourself with joy, and heal your soul-wounds. These laws keep your spirit whole, your mundane life sane, and your magic safe. They help you see through your delusions and those of others.

So you have a choice, the choice all Wiccans make. Will you, of your own accord, accept me as your teacher, in order to learn the spiritual and magical laws of Wicca?

This book is my opinion, but it is based on many years of study. I've talked with a lot of trees, stones, ocean waves. I've listened to my own heart. I've studied with masters. Year after year, I've watched, psychically, to understand, and be able to create, rituals. I've learned from my mistakes, and made a life's study of magic and spirituality. I've taught zillions of students and learned by doing so.

Contradiction: listen to yourself, do what I say. Another contradiction: if you do what I say, you'll learn to be yourself. Can you accept those contradictions? This book is full of many others.

If you don't use my lessons as given, you might have more trouble exploring Wicca, and your life in general, than you need. Life has enough trouble, as is.

I'm not asking you to be a mindless sheep. I'm asking that you try on for size what I say for a while. Do the spells without adaptation. Use the rules for spellcrafting that are in this book. Try to live the high morals of Wicca as they're expressed throughout the book. Be Wiccan the way I explain it.

All apprentices have done this, throughout time. (And rebelled behind their teachers back! Let's face it, no one's perfect, I only ask that you try.)

I ask you to follow my lead because I want you to do *effective* magic; be safe during and after it; and have a fun, happy life on the mundane plane. (*Mundane plane* refers to the material world and day-to-day life in school, at home, and at the mall, as well as going to movies, doing chores, dating, studying, and so on.)

Back to opinions: There are as many types of Wicca as there are people. *Everything* in this book is *my* opinion. If you meet people who disagree with me that means you've left your bedroom—because you can't go anywhere without meeting a unique opinion. (That's a *good* thing.)

Almost twenty years ago I created and started teaching a system of Wicca. You could also call it a *tradition* of Wicca. The tradition's name is the Third Road®—a fancy term for stuff Francesca makes up. *Or* Francesca's opinion. Traditions of Wicca can be radically different from one another, for example, having different beliefs, goals, and magical styles. So don't be puzzled if stuff in this book—for example, definitions or the most basic premises—does not concur with other Wiccan sources.

The particular system of Wicca in this book celebrates and draws forth the enormous magical, spiritual, and mundane powers that are in you. This system helps you recognize them when you don't and use them better when you do. The methods of the Wiccan tradition herein offer you control over your inner and outer life. Enjoy the God(dess) you are!

Nuf said.

Except: despite all I've said, don't be neurotic or perfectionist about following my instructions and Wiccan laws, whether we're talking magic or spirituality.

In the following, we'll get more of the basics down, then it's spell-crafting time.

THE WITCH'S SPHERE OF SAFETY (THINK GLINDA AND HER BUBBLE)

Do the better part of your magic within a psychically protected space. The lighter-weight rituals may not need this protection—decide yourself what *you* need—but the rest of the time take two minutes to do the following before any spell:

1. Pray, "Mother, Father, guide, empower, and protect me in the work ahead." (This prayer is great before any nonmagical activities, as well.)

2. Imagine a sphere around you. Picture it as you will—perhaps like a soap bubble—and imagine it keeps you totally safe.

   If during your Wiccan practice, you are going to stay within, say, a room or home, make your bubble room or house sized, as the case may be. If you're going to travel about, then picture a small bubble about *yourself* and after step 3 say, "My sphere of safety goes where I go."

   If you're doing ritual with a friend, both of you imagine a bubble that you share. Three or more of you? Three people creating a bubble shared by everyone is probably strong enough, unless someone feels more protection is needed, in which case have more folks in the group visualize the bubble. If your group is wandering past a room or home, everyone should have their own movable bubble.

3. Imagine the sphere keeps out all negativity, yet allows all beauty, power, goodness, and love in. You don't want to be isolated. And you want *good* powers to feed your spell and whole life.

You needn't "take the bubble down" afterward. Protection is great to have for its own sake. In fact, this bubble is great to set up *whenever* you need protection on the magical or mundane plane, or just want some insurance.

When you first try this rite, you may not do very well visualizing the sphere. Don't worry. Keep practicing by doing it before each spell you cast. Practice is one of the main routes to good visualization. Just put up the bubble as well as you can before doing a spell and eventually you'll have it down.

If pets, family members, or anyone else walks into or through this bubble at any time, it is not a problem. Remember, the protected space taught in this chapter keeps out negative forces, so should a person other than the people doing the spell walk into the sphere, they'll do no harm.

What if the protection doesn't work? Spellcrafting is no more foolproof than anything else in life. This understanding, in itself, is an important lesson, so let's touch on it right now. It might be easy to think, "Since a spell is no guarantee, why bother?" Putting a lock on your door is no guarantee that an intruder won't get in somehow. Or that an earthquake won't occur. But it is important to use the tools God gives us—the ability to make locks and spells—then go from there. And as we use these abilities, even if we fail in our goals, we learn to make better locks, better spells. If you refrain from the locks and spells that are available, however, then how much *worse* harm might happen? In other words, if, for example, after a protection spell, harm still happens, remember that perhaps far worse would have occurred without the spell.

Witches are lucky. We get to use magic to keep ourselves safe and sound!

Navigating This Book

Wicca can give you some of the spiritual power and magical control you need to navigate the wild ride of youth. But first, you need to know how to navigate the Wiccan world, including theses pages.

In this book, *Wicca, witchcraft, the Old Ways, Craft, shamanism, Goddess Spirituality*, and similar terms are used as synonymous. By and large, the same goes for *Wiccan, witch, Pagan, priest(ess), magician*, and the like. Ditto *spell, ritual, rite*, and generally *prayer. God*

refers to God Herself, unless context shows otherwise such as a reference to our Pagan Father. Though, when you see any reference to the Goddess, I often am really talking about the God and Goddess anyway since they are so in love they never separate. More terms: Most people don't know that *Gods* is a gender-neutral term, refering to either or both genders. This book basically uses *Gods* to refer to the *Pagan* Gods—basically, for our purposes, that's the Divine Mom and Dad. Another term for them is *Old Gods*.

Wicca fits into your life. While you fly about, being your witchy self, think of this book as an ever-ready tool kit.

A thoroughly modern witch uses what's on hand instead of musty, outdated relics. Fact is, that's what ancient witches did as well—it's just that, what was on hand for them is an antique for us! Again, witches want a religion that fits into their lives. So the book's spell ingredients and magical potions are concocted from kitchen herbs, household implements, and the like.

Here's how to find a spell you need right when you need it: look at the table of contents and the Table of Spells in the front of the book. That might seem obvious but this book's Contents is extensive and its chapter and section titles are carefully designed. Same goes for the Table of Spells.

Wicca is practical. Magic and spirituality should be tools for *living*, something you can integrate into daily life, instead of something set apart. You can best learn to integrate spirituality and magic into what's going on at any given moment in your life if that's the way it is *taught* to you. So the Wiccan teacher instructs through practical application: after these introductory lessons, every chapter touches on a part of life—social life, or romance, or sex, and so on—and gives you spells and Wiccan spirituality that you can apply.

In some books, you have to read *everything* just to do one spell. In others, you can skip around, going right to the spell you want, but with no instructions for effective, powerful, and safe magic. This book will give you the instructions you need for the spells you need: each chapter contains a collection of sections, as well as a special introduction. Read that intro in order to use the spells in that chapter powerfully and safely. Then read all of the specific section a spell's in, then do the spell! This gives you a thorough, but easy, guide to spellcrafting.

So I did not organize the material as a front-to-back read, but as introductory info coupled with tailored stand-alone sections in each chapter. I hope this makes for a relevant and organic resource: you can jump around in the order that suits you as a unique person. This book doesn't make *ideal* sense if you read it in sequential order. This book's lessons come alive and make ideal sense if you read—and use—them in the order you *want*. Knowledge of Wicca is gained by application, not reading alone, and application that is relevant to one's present concerns, needs, interests, and desires.

A Wiccan teacher creates the lesson plan according to the individual student. As a witch, I trust *your* reasons for reading the chapter-sections in *your* order. If you go to, for example, a section in the chapter "Fashion Magic," because you hope it will be fun, then next you go to a section in the chapter that focuses on Witchcraft as a religion because you're curious or have questions about it, *that's* the book's order. So, again, look at the Table of Contents and the Table of Spells so that you don't miss out on anything you need.

Regarding chapter 6, "Magic Is an Inside Job: The Mystical Art of Inner Transformation": the more inner transformation you do the happier you become. Sure, you may be happy already. But why not become the happiest you possibly can? Besides, striving to be the best *you* gives enormous satisfaction not gained in any other way.

Also, we're put on this planet to grow. As well as to have fun (contradiction!) and unless you grow, the fun stops being much fun. Finally, when taking concrete measures toward a mundane goal that relates to your happiness and your standard is high—for example, the *best* date for Saturday night, *excellent* athletic skills, the ability to *really* make a difference—you're more likely to succeed if you also have a high standard for your inner being and pursue it. Not to mention that the greater your personal growth the more effective all your magic. So check out that chapter and use some of it!

While we're on the topic of spells working: some rituals work on the spot; others take months before you see their results. Don't keep repeating the spell or it won't have a chance to work.

This book has an initiation rite. But you do not need one to do spells or call yourself *Wiccan.* If you try to learn effective, ethical spellcrafting, as well as the Wiccan religion and lifestyle, you're a novice-witch! So you can jump in, and just start.

Here's another way to use this book as your "pull off whatever you want to achieve" manual. Most goals that you might have—financial abundance, popularity, safety, courage, and so on—can be reached by many different magical routes. If none of the spells obviously geared toward a specific goal you have seem right for *you*, then look at other spells herein. Usually, one will be just perfect if you put on your thinking cap: you'll likely find a spell that helps with your goal in a way that's different from what you have been considering. You can get people to laugh by cracking a joke, making a funny face, embarrassing them so they titter nervously, or tickling 'em.

You're a unique person with a unique life. You *can* find the approach that suits *you*. On top of the perhaps less obvious approaches mentioned above, you'll usually find more than one if not several rituals in this book overtly geared to help you achieve any particular goal. Choose whichever you want for whatever reason you want. At another time you may choose differently. You can even use several spells toward the same goal. Let's say you're training to enter a swimming match and you do the "Spell to Become (Or Remain) a Winner." Great! A straight-ahead spell for success. But if nervousness about the competition is keeping you from swimming your best, instead or in addition you could use the nostril breathing technique ("Waking

Up Magic") before swimming, which will calm you down. Or your nerves could be abated if you do "The Great Mother" rite the night before the match so you don't feel all alone. The ritual can really help you feel She's there with you, at your back. Therefore you'll have the serenity to win. Maybe you want to do all three spells! Here's a simpler example: you might prefer one of the book's protection spells over the others or need more than one working for you at a time.

I hope you enjoy this book. The Goddess and God are with us every step of the way, every step of our day, watching over us. And the following last few sections about starting Wiccan practices safely and strongly will help the Goddess and God do so. Or as they say, "Praise the Lord and pass the ammunition." It may not be a Wiccan expression, but it's totally to the point.

Use an Ax!

Live life! Enjoy it. A powerful magician never uses magic instead of living life or instead of taking relevant concrete measures, such as seeking adult help when it's needed.

With any spell, you also need to take practical action on the mundane plane. In other words, along with a protection spell, you might have to tell your parent(s) or a teacher if someone is being mean to, or endangering, you. (Sometimes the mundane act should be done *before* the spell.)

If you combine spells with down-to-earth action, magic helps you gain what you want and allows you to have full control over your life instead of merely being rituals that are an ineffective and inevitably self-defeating escape.

Yeah, we all wish a magic wand could help us escape the difficult work that life demands. But dig this, Wicca empowers that work, helps you to do it better, and makes it more likely to succeed.

If someone tells you that magic makes for a free ride, they are trying to take you for a sucker—at best—and could be really up to no good. Well, they might be a novice who is innocently misinformed. If so, help them out with accurate info. But otherwise, run as fast as you can from anyone who tries to take advantage of your problems by telling you garbage.

Don't get me wrong. Magic works! Miracles occur as the result of spells. A spell might be the very thing that makes a difference. Therefore, if you are in a desperate situation about which you think you can take no mundane action, a spell might change that. But one mustn't think a spell stands alone. If you want money for a concert, and your folks don't have it or think you should earn it, use a money spell *and* look for some odd jobs for cash.

Here is a story about that.

"A shaman taught a man a spell to kill an alligator. The student worked hard to master the spell, and the shaman praised him profusely, but then said, 'Wait, I'll be right back.'

"Upon returning, the teacher was carrying an ax and said, 'Now I'll teach you to kill the alligator with this ax.'

"The student exclaimed, 'Why? Doesn't the spell work?'

"His teacher responded, 'Not without the ax.'"

The lessons herein tend to offer spells accompanied by practical measures one can take toward the same goal. But don't leave it at that; think for yourself, in order to get what you need out of life. And if you need more than *that*, or don't know where to find the ax you have in mind, go to the non-Wiccan resource guide, Guide to Axes. It's, duh, full of axes!

You might also pray, "Goddess, please show me the ax." Then be open. Her reply might come as an idea that pops into your mind immediately or later, as advice (solicited or not) from a parent, teacher, or friend, or through reading a book or even a sentence about the matter at hand. As you'll learn in this book, the Pagan Gods are in everything, so *anything* might be used for guidance. Ever see a bus drive by with an advertisement on its side and that ad somehow gave you just the idea you needed? In the same way, you might receive the advice you pray for from a chance phrase you hear on a TV comedy, or maybe you'll realize that your pet is your perfect role model for, as an example, kicking back and letting love in. Be open to the myriad, endless ways Gods advise, whether it's regarding axes or anything else.

If you can think of no ax, do the spell anyway.

And with that, once we address the fear of witchcraft, we're on!

Afraid of Witchcraft?

Are you interested in Wicca but a little afraid? Some people have major misconceptions about it. Magic is no more dangerous than the rest of life. I ask the Goddess to protect me in my *whole* life. No fancy words, unless you want otherwise. Just "Goddess, protect me in all I do." Perhaps you could try that, too. First thing in the morning is good. That way you don't forget and it's easy to incorporate as a daily practice. You can also say it again, whenever you feel the need.

Do you have fears that magic is evil? Like Glinda in *The Wizard of Oz*, you can be a good witch. Just cleave to the magical ethics and other cautions in this text.

No one's ever too young to believe in magic. But watch what you get involved with. All that glitters is not gold; all that has glamour—in the old Scottish sense of *glamour*, which is a sort of magical Fairy glimmer—is not good for human beings. Especially not for beginners, no matter how great or painful their hunger for it. For now, pursue the rudimentaries (aka what's in this book). To become an adept one must have the basics firmly in place. Only then is one powerful and safe with more sophisticated spells. You can't do algebra without math.

And despite what Hollywood portrays, advanced work—which may demand sophisticated magical techniques, employ challenging powers, or move you into volatile psychic realms—basically should not be trained for, learned, let alone done, until one is eighteen, at the youngest. If you are cautious out of respect for yourself and the powers you seek, you can gain great power and joy in the magical realms.

Also watch *who* you do magic with. Stick with folks your own age unless your parents know them. There are many unethical practitioners disguising their ill intent with mumbo-jumbo talk and confusing pomp. I'm sorry to sound like such a stuffed shirt, but I have seen very sophisticated worldly adults get conned and really hurt. If you want info about avoiding practitioners who'll get you into trouble—this includes *young* Wiccan fools—see the section in chapter 7 titled "Celebrate an Initiation and Wiccan Secrets (Avoid Harmful Teachers and Damaging Cults")."

If a particular spell makes you afraid, and Witchcraft doesn't generally have that effect on you, maybe you should not do that spell. Maybe your fear is telling you something. Maybe that spell's not for you, or not yet.

Now let's talk about psychic evil as well as demons (and Fairies and bigots, oh my!). Religious bigots spread the antiwitchcraft lies that there are evil spirits and demons ready to pounce on anyone who tries Wicca. Wrong! But many Wiccans refute the lies by going to the other extreme, saying there's *never* a chance of a problem (and the magical realm is populated only by cute little happy bunny rabbits).

It's not that evil spirits have much to do with Wicca. Real Wicca is nothing like *Buffy* and *Charmed*. But the psychic realm is the same as the material plane when it comes to good and evil—they both exist. And some people who are really drawn to Wicca do not practice it because they fear or sense that in their case there *are* evil spirits and demons ready to pounce. Such people might be picking up something because they are particularly vulnerable. Thus their concerns might not be based in antiwitchcraft propaganda.

Bigots also say witches are in league with the devil and that all spirits are evil. Wrong again. Spirits are good, bad, and indifferent—just like people!

Don't get all morbidly fearful, or become an instant drama queen, rolling on the floor, crying out "A demon's got me!" That would be like being told, "Not all people are safe to hang out with" and deciding that everyone you have ever met is plain old evil.

The psychic realm, though, has its dangers. As does the baseball field. And the highway. Get it? And if you're worried or concerned, listen to yourself. Just as you should on the material plane. Everyone's different. For example, I didn't learn to drive for years because of trouble understanding spatial relations. I would have been a serious hazard to myself and others on the road. Fact is, someone would likely have been killed. In the same way I used to be more vulnerable on the road than most people, maybe you're more vulnerable to ill-intended spirits than your best friend is. (And maybe because of that, your friend doesn't understand your concerns and pooh-poohs them.)

 Don't practice Wicca if you think it leaves you too open to negative forces! Wait till you find a teacher who can guide you regarding your specific vulnerabilities. Or wait till you're older and see if the vulnerability dissipates. Or if certain (perhaps lighter) aspects of Wicca don't worry you, like "The Magic of a Woman's Hair" (in chapter 2), just do *them*. Maybe you're ready for Wicca, but not certain spells.

More on spiritual bigots. They'll tell you stuff like "If it isn't exactly what my church does, it's from the devil." Wrong once more! But if you've been raised by them, you yourself, though you intellectually know magic is not evil, might in practice have trouble distinguishing bad spirits from good ones. A wonderful fairy appears and you say, "Be gone, demon!" Or, in trying to be open minded and reject your folks' bigotry, you welcome the demon as a very odd, but interesting, fairy.

It can be confusing. Also, there are more subtle ways that the input of spiritual bigots or other circumstances can make a given individual susceptible to negative psychic events that might not be an issue for someone else. My motto regarding all this is "better safe than sorry." But again keep in mind that magic is a normal part of being human—it's built into human nature; we're born with it. Morbid or neurotic fear is not the same as healthy fear. Don't let unhealthy fear keep you from doing what you want in life, whether it's magic, skateboarding, scholastic excellence, or artistic expression.

If you ever need it, or think you're the sort who needs such info as a preventative measure, read "Protection Against Evil Spirits," in chapter 8 ("Protection Against Evil Spirits" is a subsection of the section "Protection" but stands on its own.)

One of your best protections against psychic evil: Don't do stupid magical things! Don't play around with suspicious spirits, or morally dubious texts of magic, or attend shady groups of practitioners.

If you however *do*, and get in trouble, get help. Look at Wiccan Resources to learn how to find someone who can give you exactly what you need.

This ends the introductory lessons. Everyone is different. So if you have needs or concerns not addressed already, and feel that you as a unique person need to deal with them before casting your first spell, look at the Table of Contents and Table of Spells. And should you in your pursuit of magic and Wiccan spirituality happen to run up against a magical or mundane problem, remember to look at the tables to troubleshoot.

"Afraid of Witchcraft?" has dealt with heavy stuff. But it doesn't represent the world of Wicca. Don't expect problems. Magic is fun. Wicca is about joy, freedom, and self-expression. And you can relax and enjoy all that because now you know you're covered. So, we're ready to go! Blessed Be. Let's fly.

2 Fashion Magic

Francesca's dictionary for savvy witches says "*Fashion magic:* spells focused on looking good; or the ritual use of clothes, accessories, and the like for any other purpose." And now, I hope you enjoy this chapter's following introductory material, after which you can skip to—and use—any section in the chapter.

Let it be clear: I'm a *Pagan*! As in I love a good time. And my Gods are Pagan Gods—they love fun themselves and bless spells that create merriment. (Of course, magic should never be trivialized by flaunting it. Show-offs end up in huge spiritual and magical tragedies.)

Have fun while doing magic that is focused on looking your best. Think of it like this: on the mundane plane, there's nothing wrong with enjoying nice clothes. Anyone in the fashion industry spends a *lot* of time on the art of looking good.

They also will tell you that if you squander all your time and money on it, current trends replace real confidence and you have no money for important things. Your mentality becomes petty and warped.

Avoid becoming obsessed with spells that focus on looking good. Don't use so much of your time and energy on it that there's none left for anything else; you lose the real you, have nothing but fashion going for you, and become, as I said, petty and warped.

And with that—onward, to be the divas and dudes of style!

You'll be doing the Pagan Gods a favor. They thoroughly appreciate modern adornments. Watching people run around in togas got boring after a few centuries.

Charmed Jewelry

We all notice the following: the flash of a thread-thin gold chain about a woman's neck; a richly colored fake tortoise-shell barrette, holding back stray hair with its coy and good-humored allure; a thick black strap studded with stainless steel, perhaps with a watch attached— worn around the wrist. Consider a single pearl dangling on a silver bracelet; or bone bead worn on a string; a macramé choker sporting a tiny rough chunk of rose quartz; a plain leather belt with silver-colored buckle; or wee bit of faceted red glass adorning an ear.

Human beings are drawn toward self-adornment, and have been forever. What's the charm, the draw? Part of it is charmed draw: a pearl can magically draw the moon's wisdom to you, helping you understand witchcraft better. An amethyst draws sobriety and balance, helping one become or stay sober instead of being alcoholic, drug addicted, or going on emotional benders. Jewelry, on the psychic plane, has the ability to either bring certain influences to you—the specific influence depending on the specific jewelry—or the piece of jewelry itself exudes an influence, again what influence depending on what jewelry.

I've mentioned pearl and amethyst. Here's more. Gold brings cheerfulness, and illuminates the mind. Silver helps you understand people better when they're speaking on a personal level. It might also help when they're discussing the impersonal, for example, a math teacher teaching her class. Steel adds vigor, passion, and determination. Diamonds help strengthen the healthy ego. Rose quartz brings self-esteem and self-love. Garnet brings zest and energy. Carnelian and turquoise are protective. Bone gets us in touch with the earth, feeding us its power, peace, and inspiration to get us through challenging times, as well as just normal everyday life. Today, using real tortoise shell will not bring you good energy; the earth will resent your using a product that threatens to exterminate a species. But the fake stuff has the same effect as bone.

If you cannot afford the real gem or metal, do not scorn the fake. And if you cannot acquire either, there's *always* another type of magic or mundane means by which to attain your goal, so no despairing—

instead, pray, "Mother, Father, bring me to my goal. By whatever means you choose, whether human intervention, divine inspiration, chance occurrence, blessed luck, or anything else, including a combination of many things, bring me to my goal. Help me humbly be open to your help so that I both recognize and accept it when it comes. Thank you." This is also an excellent prayer to say when we see no possible magical or mundane means to our goals, large or small.

As to the other stones, metals, and natural substances, if you're drawn to something, feel it out. Maybe borrow a piece of jewelry with a stone (metal, . . .) you're considering, and see how it feels for a few days. Notice how those days go. I don't, for example, wear black stones. They depress me. Except for obsidian—black, gorgeous, and my favorite stone. It makes me feel balanced, down-to-earth, and in touch with my magical powers. But I've heard that many people find it draws negativity!

Waking Up Magic

Stones and metals exert their psychic influence regardless of any effort on your part; however, the degree of their ability to do so may be minimal without an added bit of magic on your part. That's one of the ways witches are lucky. It also means often you needn't avoid wearing a certain piece of jewelry when you don't want its magic bearing on your self and life. Feel it out—there may be little effect

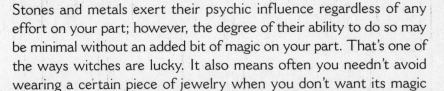

unless you add your own Wiccan touch to things. But should you want to bring that touch to bear:

1. For one full minute, breathe in and out through your nostrils, making each inhalation and exhalation as slow as you can make it and still have your body relaxed and comfortable and your breath natural and unstrained. This breathing technique can relax you; it also helps clear your mind, still your being, and thus focus, all-in-all making you a clear channel for the magic of the following steps.

2. If you feel particularly anxious about your spell, are enormously distracted, or are otherwise needing more work to focus yourself, take another minute or two for the slow nostril breathing.

3. Don't expect perfect focus. The important thing is to have settled down at least a bit. Or at least tried to. If you see no shift in yourself from the nostril breathing, keep on with the spell anyway. The more you practice magic, your skills, including focus, improve. It is in the *doing* that we learn to do better. In any case, holding your piece of jewelry in your right hand, raise your left toward the sky.

4. Whether aloud or silently, recite slowly, slowly, slowly

> *The powers of the Old Gods are mine.*
> *These powers flow to me,*

then, blessing, flow through me.
Then bless some more.

So now the Old Gods bless my adornment,
waking its powers, and making them enormous.

Thank you.

5. Now, bring your left arm down to a normal position, and transfer the jewelry from the right hand into the open palm of the left.

6. Tap the piece of jewelry nine times with your right hand.

7. Wear the piece of jewelry to reap its benefits.

8. Future uses: now that you've done the above, you've a powerful charm, the nature of which depends on what the jewelry's original psychic asset was to begin with, for example, if it's a silver amethyst ring, the silver's ability to help you listen, and the amethyst's power to bring sobriety. (This, by the way, includes the sobriety of not letting oneself be on an emotional roller coaster—a form of emotional drunk—because of a family member or other person's lack of sobriety.)

If you only want to empower part of the piece of jewelry, to use the last example, just the silver or just the amethyst of the amethyst ring, hold on to *it* during steps 3 and 4. If you accidentally touch other parts, or *have* to hold on to other parts of the jewelry to have a grasp, don't fret. With this spell, the exactness of the hold needn't be perfect.

When you want to wear the charm as sheer ornament, tap it nine times with your left hand while holding the charm in the open palm of your right. This "turns it off," or at least reduces its power to its innate amount.

Just hold it in the left hand, tap nine times with the right, to turn it back on. Whoo hoo!

If you feel the power of the charm weaken, do the whole ritual again. Trust yourself to know when or if to do this.

Charmed jewelry is subtle. Your social science teacher isn't going to send you to the principal's office because you're wearing a pentacle—a five-pointed star some Wiccans wear to bring them bounty, luck, power, and protection—or another overtly magical charm. In addition, you can wear the jewelry fashion styles that truly suit *you* and still turn them to your magical advantage.

And then you can go about your witchy ways, having your witchy way!

A last word on using the charm once you've "magicked it up." You might ask, "Now that I've charmed my pearl, how do I find the moon's wisdom?" Or, "What do I do once my amethyst (silver, whatever) is awake?" Just go about your business. There's nothing you have to *do*. The magic is there now, feeding you with its specific blessing. (Often, going about your business is the same as using your ax.) Here's the deal, explained through some examples:

Since pearl helps us gain Wiccan wisdom, just go about your witchcraft. After a while, or even immediately, you'll see an improvement in your ability to understand, or gain new insights. Be open to this shift. With the amethyst (sobriety) perhaps attend a meeting of Alcoholics Anonymous. See "Guide to Axes." With the bone (earth power), just go about your business and you'll feel empowered as you do so. In other words, use your ax, live your life—you've done the magic part already—and the charm will go about its business all on its own, taking its course, as long as you're open to change.

Go for it!

The Hidden Power of Red

The hidden power of red, of black, of white combined with blue—all these have special power for a witch.

There's a reason people associate black garments with witches! Wear black during your rituals to add power to the magic. Also wear black for an exceptionally powerful day. Wearing black also helps strengthen the ego, which not only gives you confidence about your magic—thus making it more effective than it might already be—but also is a good thing regarding your mundane activities. You can wear either all black or a single item—black T-shirt, shawl, tie, dress, pair of socks, or the like. How about a black ribbon tied about the neck like a choker? Adding a pendant to the choker makes it elegant fun. A black handkerchief tied about the ankle or wrist works well and looks interesting.

If you feel like adding more power to your black clothing, a blessing is below.

BLACK BLESSING

> *Night sky,*
> *Day's ground*
> *Power, power*
> *all around.*

As you recite the first line, hold the garment up as if showing it to the night sky. It's nice if you can actually do this rite at night, but a witch is practical—you do what you can. So if you have to do this blessing in the daytime, remember—it's always night somewhere. A witch is creative.

Then, reciting the second line, take your black article and lay it on the ground. Ideally, this should be actual earth, but the floor will do. A witch is flexible.

Then hold the item in front of yourself and say the third line.

Reciting the fourth line, turn in a circle.

Then wear your garment and enjoy the power!

You can wear the item afterward as a magical item or not.

Whenever you want to "turn it on high" again repeat the gestures made during the chant. The chant need never be said again. If the gestures are too obvious in a given situation, here's the stealth version: tap the object eight times with your right hand.

Watch out for the tendency to wear too much black. Yes, it looks witchy but if you wear it constantly, it may actually suppress power. It can have a dampening effect that might make both your magical and mundane efforts less effective. (Think of the Puritans' dismal black garb and equally dismal lives.) In addition, it can actually *weaken* your self-confidence. (And, of course, make your parents and teachers think you've gone over to Satan and are on drugs!)

Red is also an important color for witches. Like black, it is pure power. Red's power is the vitality of love, fire, sassy confidence, bold courage, humanness, and just plain old gobs of energy. By *humanness*, I mean red embodies our warmth to each other, the blood that flows in our veins, and the beating heart that both loves and longs for love.

Be absolutely clear: never blood-let in a rite. To learn why, see the section, "Taboos That Really Should Be Taboo," in chapter 9.

In any case, red clothing reminds us of, and celebrates, the power of our blood as life force and vitality.

Recap: wear red clothing in order to add sheer simple power to a rite or day. Or, wear red to add vigor and vitality when you're feeling tired or blue. Or wear red to give you self-confidence. Again, all red or a single item will do.

If you choose to add power:

RED BLESSING

> *Red of love*
> *Red of blood*
> *Red of heart*
> *Never part*

As you recite the first line, hold the red garment to your chest. With the second line, hold the item to your belly. Third line, return to chest. Fourth line, hold item against the upper stomach (so that it's between the chest and belly).

The enormous power of black and of red teaches us why moderation is useful: some things in life are so powerful (or so pleasurable, or so effective or so . . .) that one is tempted, and rightly so, to use them (indulge in them, whatever, as the case may be) all the time. But it's like food—it fuels you, is enjoyable, and great to share with friends; but if you ate twenty-four hours a day you would get oh-so-seriously ill. So we eat, then sleep, then work, then play, and all these things empower us. In the same vein, we can't always do the magical or mundane things that are most powerful or fun or effective or indulgent or . . . If we do, that power or fun turns on us. Which brings me to the following statement:

Blue and white in combination are also important for a witch, both magically and spiritually. This power is usually harder for new witches to understand than the power of black or red. Here's why.

In our repressive culture, both black and red symbolize a rejection of that repression. They shout vigor and confidence. They somehow embody the wildness of the Old Ways: feeling the wind against your face awakening your hope of living your dream life; respecting the beauty of your sexual feelings—not being ruled by them, mind you, unable to restrain yourself, but not being ashamed of them either. Wiccan wildness is also allowing yourself to feel the love, hate, pain, joy, sorrow, happiness, grief, and jubilation that is human (again, wildness does not mean we act uncontrollably because of these feelings, or even act on those feelings at all, but that we let ourselves feel them, guilt-free). Wildness is letting the spirit soar high, with belief in a good world and a better tomorrow.

We of the Old Ways are not wild like stubborn children, going on stupid high-risk escapades just to show "No one can boss *me* around!" Do that, and you're basically still repressed, because instead of finding the joy and health of *real* wildness—which I described above—you're buying into this culture's ignorant portrayal of wildness as irresponsible, arrogant, and blindly rebellious. Wildness is not a reaction to something else; wildness is something in and of itself, and is natural and innate in *all* people.

In any case, when you see someone in red or black coming, you might imagine them to be strong, assertive, and attractive to others— a free spirit. Someone wearing white and blue may seem more namby-pamby to you. It's hard to see that particular color combination as just as powerful as red or black.

But think the white of a snowcapped mountain and the pale gray-blue of the rest of that mountain. The mountain stands tall above the rest of creation—serene, immovable, untouchable. Or think of a bright blue sky during a chilling white, quiet snowfall. The snow controls *everything*, stopping all traffic, all commuting, all hustle and bustle to clear the way for the Gods' work. Think of the pure white and clear blue of an inner calmness that helps you withstand all difficulties and sorrows. Think of a white-and-blue force moving slowly, surely, serenely, inexorably forward, so indomitable that none can stand in its way or stop it.

Thus, when you wear the combo of blue and white, you have the white and blue power to rise above all. You also are immovable as well as able to more serenely handle problems. In addition, wearing that combo clears the way for you, moving through all obstacles, making you a victor in all things.

If you want your outfit to be all blue and white, wear an assortment of white items and blue items and/or items that in themselves are both colors; or just see that you wear *some* white and blue. Optional blessing:

WHITE AND BLUE BLESSING

> *The power that made all creation is the power of white*
>   *and blue.*
> *That power is unstoppable*
> *and that power is mine.*

With the first line, hold the item(s) as you turn in a circle, clockwise. With the second line, move slowly forward, holding the item(s) in front of you. With the third line, walk back to where you had been before that forward movement. Then kneel down, and bow your head.

   Afterward, as with the black or red items, you can wear your blessed clothing magically or not, and "turn them on high" the same way.

Blue and white combined symbolize many things, including acceptance and surrender, two virtues that have been misportrayed so much as a way to hurt people in this culture that we tend to reject them. We might mistakenly think that acceptance means not going after our dreams or tolerating rudeness, meanness, and even abuse. Many believe acceptance means not drawing on our fiery drive and desires to change our lives for the better or to fight the good fight, making a difference in the world. We might also think that, when life deals us a blow, we're supposed to not have perfectly human responses, like disappointment or anger.

But these are not true acceptance. Real acceptance is facing facts instead of pretending things are not the way they are. Acceptance is not approval or submission, it's just seeing what is true, *fully* seeing it. Only if we accept our reality as it is can it change. In other words, if you don't accept that, for example, prejudice exists, you can't fight it because you are pretending it's not there.

Acceptance also means acknowledging that you don't always get what you want and understanding that tragedy is an inevitable part of life. Acceptance even means coming to terms with awful, unfair, even abusive situations.

Abuse is *not* okay. Nor should you put up with disrespect, unfairness, prejudice, or any other mistreatment. You shouldn't even have to pretend it doesn't matter to you when life itself gives you a raw deal.

I want you to fight abuse—whether it's perpetuated on you or on someone else. If a parent is hitting you or being sexual in any way at all with you, I want you to never surrender in the sense of giving up. That's not what I mean by acceptance and surrender. In fact, please, *please* look through the Contents and Table of Spells for magical and material ways to end abuse if it's happening to you, and don't ever stop trying until you've become safe, happy, and free!

What I mean by acceptance of life's problems, from the small to the enormous, is, nevertheless, very difficult. And no one can do it well at all. But, you may have to try in order not to fall prey to resentments, despair, endless bitterness, or forever-loneliness.

Real acceptance of a problem means, first of all, admitting it's real. You may want to say, "It can't be this bad," or "So what if the other team won by cheating. I don't really care about the game anyway." Or "He wasn't really being rude, I just imagined it," or "My mother loves me, so it's not abuse. She's doing this for my own good." Or, "I must want this or it wouldn't happen. So it's not really abuse." Or any other statements that are refusals to face facts.

Saying "That's life," and not admitting to yourself when you're upset by the ups and downs life deals everyone is also not acceptance, because you're refusing to face the fact of how you feel.

We don't want to accept—note the word *accept*—that a person can't always have his or her way, or that life is not fair, or that abusive horrors are real, or that these things are happening to us. The human psyche recoils. So everything in us rejects the facts. In which case, nothing can improve! No facing facts = no changing facts.

Hard as it is to face up to reality, you can do it. Wearing blue and white helps. So does the prayer "God, help me overcome life's challenges." Serenity, courage, confidence, and victory ensue.

Acceptance of problems, even abuse, also means viewing it in the larger context of a loving God. It makes no sense that a beneficent deity would allow abuse. But by at least trying to believe that context, we can leave the abuse or other problems behind: the power of blue and white can work in our lives, for example, by giving us fortitude and victories.

Mind you, believing that God loves you despite, for example, the abuse is not the same as deciding *you're* bad and that's why She allows the abuse. Thinking that you're the one at fault instead of the abuser is, once again, thinking that the abuse does not exist. Apply this paragraph to *any* mistreatment, not just abuse; ditto the next paragraph.

You are not bad, you did not cause the abuse, you do not deserve abuse, you do not want it! *And* God loves you, She truly does.

And don't let anyone tell you that acceptance means that you did something so bad in a past life that you are making up for it this lifetime! That's still blaming yourself instead of acknowledging life's problems as real. Never, ever blame yourself for any mistreatment you're dealt, even through New Age nana such as I just mentioned, or any other New Age, Wiccan, Christian, or other claptrap.

Moving on: whether we're talking about abuse and trauma, or day-to-day setbacks, everything in the human psyche will strain against acceptance. It's one of our hardest spiritual challenges as human beings, one that we never have to stop facing.

Surrender is the same: every bit of intellect, survival instinct, and desire will fight against surrender. Yet to be fully happy we must continue to try to accept and surrender.

Surrender is not being a doormat to anyone or to the world at large; surrender is not thinking that you don't deserve the absolute best life (the same goes for acceptance). Surrender is not any of the things that repressive or misled people may have taught you.

The terrible, terrible misuse of these core spiritual principles—misuse by people who try to control others, misuse by people motivated more by hate than by love—adds to our rebellion against acceptance and surrender.

Real surrender is saying, "Okay this is the way it is. Maybe I can change it, but when I can't, I live with it with dignity, self-love, and respect for others."

Surrender is also about going with the flow instead of always trying to have your own way, and being a control queen about it. Surrender is also doing what you think God wants you to do, instead of always thinking you know better.

Since it is human nature to struggle against acceptance and sur- render, and the Old Gods love us for the humans we are instead of judging and loathing us for our humanity, I don't know why They would ask for acceptance and surrender. But without these traits we are eventually miserable.

With them, we have *the* tools to face the disappointments and failures that are inevitable parts of life. Sure, a witch often says, "I'll get it better next time!" And, with healthy determination, the witch strives for success and often does make it the next time. Oftentimes, however, it just won't work. When we face actual despair, failure, or tragedy, there comes a time where only acceptance and surrender will do.

In addition, the fiery, fierce, and beautifully proud attitude of a witch needs to be integrated with the white and blue virtues. Otherwise, one can become miserable, having lost any balance. For example, it is vital to learn, as a witch does learn, to trust one's own opinions, common sense, and intuitions. However, it is just as important to listen to others' input, and to realize that your intuition, common sense, and opinions are never 100 percent foolproof. Even when you get that little feeling inside that "always" lets you know that this time you're absolutely right, you can still be wrong. Some may think, "What's the big deal if I'm wrong sometimes and don't know it? At least that's better than not trusting myself at all." Nope! Either extreme is dangerous. Hitler had absolute trust in himself.

Here's another example of Wiccan life without the white and blue virtues. Wicca teaches us that it is good to go for what we want and that we needn't be ashamed of our desires. Let's call them red and black virtues. Great stuff! But, again, that can go to an extreme. We can become selfish, not to mention deluded, thinking we must have something that in fact we don't need, and hurt many people in the process. Or, in trying to fill a legitimate survival need, we might forget others are trying to do the same and that we all have to help each other instead of being in a dog-eat-dog world.

Surrender and acceptance bring balance to the red and black virtues. Lack of that balance may not seem relevant to you or in fact that dangerous, but I beg you to trust me in this because of the misery I have seen witches fall into because they did not learn surrender, acceptance, and humility, which is yet another blue-and-white virtue—and is also misunderstood. It is not about thinking that you're garbage or less than other people. Humility means having healthy pride. I hope you are proud of your accomplishments. There is nothing wrong with wanting, or taking, credit for what you can do or have done. But humility also means listening to others and understanding that sometimes someone else does know better than you, and acting accordingly.

So, when you wear white and blue together, the power that created all things will move through obstacles for you, and make the way smooth before you. But during this time, for the magic to work, you must try to be a student of humility, acceptance, and surrender, practicing these virtues. You may not embody them well at all. But that's why it's *practice*. Adult or teen, novice or adept, the power of blue and white is an enormously challenging practice.

If you tend to wear red and black often, balance it out by wearing the blue-white combination equally as much, or by adding something blue and white to your black and/or red outfit. White underwear is an easy way to add the white. (Black and red together make a great power combo. I use it and love it! Personally, I prefer to wear it with a bit of blue and white.)

This brings us to the issue of the witch's balanced lifestyle. Free yourself from self-doubt, shame about your desires, fear of a punishing, angry God who speaks of love but acts in hate, and any inabilities to express your unique self and to live your dream life. (Wearing red and black will help you to do these things.)

But don't focus only on such things or you'll just go to the opposite extreme: when we embody the opposite of something we are rejecting, we are, on a subtle and sometimes not so subtle level, becoming that which we reject. So balance your quest for freedom, fulfillment, and self-expression with humility, surrender, acceptance, and, well, all those Hallmark card virtues that can seem schmaltzy: kindness, patience, selflessness, restraint, self-control, and all the other white and blue virtues. To be only red and black or only white and blue is a miserable life. A witch learns to gloriously balance the two. (For more info about balancing the two, see Wiccan Resources.)

As you work on this balance, don't focus on one side and only try the other now and then. Constantly work on both. Then when all is said and done, you will be one unstoppable, successful, happy, and content person in everything you do. Your magic will give you your heart's desire and your day-to-day life will be fulfilling.

Whew! Heavy stuff. But we're dealing with real power here, and now you can use it—strong magic.

(A side note: "How to Find Magical Tools in the Mall," in chapter 9, has more ways to use colors for fashion magic.)

A Witch Is Beautiful

A witch is beautiful (or handsome, if you prefer). This doesn't mean you can't be a witch unless you're considered a beauty. It means that *any* witch can recognize that he or she *is* a beauty, inside and out.

When Frances was fourteen, she was considered god-awful unattractive by her peers. I knew that she was quite pretty, but the prevalent taste in her neighborhood ran toward petite, fair-skinned, snub-nosed Irish girls. She was tall, dark, and strong-featured. I gave her some of the axes below plus the magic and info mentioned at the end of "A Witch Is beautiful." By the time she was sixteen she was considered a real beauty. More important, she came to like her own looks.

This was not an easy process and she still has setbacks and often tends to dwell on her physical imperfections rather than overall appearance. But all in all she has matured into a woman who feels confident in her looks. The following are some of the axes that helped, and other axes that can help you feel good about your appearance.

1. *Learn fashion basics.* Read fashion magazines and books. If you like the way a friend or celebrity looks, analyze his or her outfits, hairstyle, and makeup, and figure out why and how they work. Take a class in makeup.

2. *Find your own style.* Most teenagers boast of doing things, and dressing, their own way. And these same teens are clones when it comes to clothing and behavior. There seems to be some pathology that strikes people from ages thirteen to seventeen, that makes them think individuality is the equivalent of following a trend.

I don't understand it, but . . .

At age fourteen my father gave me a pair of men's blue jeans. In the basement was an old button-down oxford shirt of my brother's. Putting on this ensemble, I felt comfortable in an outfit for the first time in my life. I am *not* young, so this incident happened before dungarees became a fashion staple. Heck, slacks on women were not allowed in school, and the parameters of femininity were strict and way too "girl." So my outfit was odd and definitely a gender-bender years before *gender-bend* was shown in any fashion magazine. I am not telling you this as a way to say, "Aren't I something!" My point is, I really did find my own style, so I finally felt attractive. My tall, muscular body didn't look silly the way it had in the overly fussy dresses and prim looks of the early 1960s (which were still hold-overs from the '50s, and not yet replaced by the sass and freedom of the styles that would appear only a few years later). The athletic way I moved and the strength of my features were highlighted by my tomboyish garb, instead of mocked and made ridiculous by 1950s styles.

Mind you, now I know that there were women's styles that would have suited, had I been better informed about fashion. But that initial breaking out of the mold that I *did* know helped me find my style, and therefore I was later able to acquire a more feminine style that suited *me*. If I had been afraid to choose what seemed right out of what was available, I would not have been able to do so.

Explore. Find your style. Then wear it cockily! Don't dress like Marcy, just because she looks fabulous. You'll look stupid and feel extra ugly because you look so bad in something *she* pulls off beautifully. Don't wear the same styles as Bob when he is broad shouldered and beefy while you are long and way lean. You're better off *accenting* your string-bean body.

Find what suits your temperament and activities with fashion books and magazines, online fashion groups, friends, or paid consultants. Through the same means, discover your body type—everyone has a basic shape—and what clothing styles best suit it. Example: My body is square. Much as I love romantically draping fashions made with volumes of fabric, they make me look fat. I need tailored clothing.

Also, find your colors. I love the fall colors of orange, brick, and bright yellows. But they make *me* look orange, brick, and bright yellow. Find *your* colors. You can do this via the same means you might find your body shape.

Store clerks can be a great help in all this if they're not too busy. Be extremely polite. Ask nicely if they have time to give you some advice. And request guidance only if you intend to purchase something at the clerk's store. It's one thing if you can't find something but another to take advantage.

Tell the clerk what sort of outfit you want (school garb, party clothes, outfit for the beach) and what you lack in fashion sense. Ask, "Could you help me buy the right thing?" Then explain: "I don't know what colors go with my skin tone" or "I need to learn the right styles for my body shape."

Don't descend upon the shop with a gaggle of your friends, or be loud. Loud is okay, but it has its time and place. Shopping is not a spectator sport, so stores are not set up to accommodate a large group there to support one or two shoppers. Go with one or two companions because you enjoy their company or need their input and moral support, but leave it at that. Moving on, here's more beauty axes:

3. *Get a makeover* aka have someone do your makeup for you. Go into a department store and approach one of the clerks at a cosmetic counter. Ask if and when they offer free makeovers. Tell them the look you want, ask if it suits you, and, if relevant, tell them what event you want to wear makeup to: school, recital, prom. Use all the guidelines I suggested with clerks (e.g., be prepared to buy, be courteous). However, don't feel you have to purchase everything used.

(And I myself am always hard pressed not to!) The results of a makeover are usually fabulous, so you want to own every last product used to get the same results. And it might be the only way to pull it off. I'm all for quality makeup when one needs it and can afford it. But you may be able to achieve the same goal with less expensive products or with what you already have. If your budget is not up to department store prices, ask the makeup artist, "I want to buy some of what you've used, but can't afford all of it. Which products are vital for this look, and what could I achieve with less expensive products?"

In any case, the younger you are, the less makeup you need or should wear. Until fifteen, lip gloss really is enough. If, during a ritual, you want a lot of makeup to get in the mood, that's great. But otherwise save it until you're older.

If you can't afford a pro makeover, ask a friend or sibling to do it or to give you tips. And read up on it.

Sometimes, I use expensive cosmetics. With my dark Sicilian coloring, I have a hard time finding the things that look good on me otherwise. But I will not spend money unnecessarily. A witch doesn't waste resources. To do so is to squander power. Here's what I've learned. Wet 'n' Wild, one of the least expensive cosmetic lines around, has the sort of fabulous colors that are usually only found in expensive brands. I'm not saying that all Wet 'n' Wild's colors are top notch. But a lot are! And they're inexpensive enough that if you err, it's not the financial loss a more expensive product would be. This

Mediterranean miss has found some perfect Wet 'n' Wild goodies for herself. And their lip liner No. 666 (I know, 666, but what can I say) is used by major makeup artists.

Search out this sort of thing. For example, Max Factor has killer lipstick colors.

4. *Learn proper hygiene.* This might seem like odd advice, but no one wants to sit next to someone who smells bad, and people often do not know they have hygiene problems. If you do not bathe regularly, brush your teeth at least once a day, use deodorant, or wear clean clothes, start doing so. If you suspect you have a problem yet are already doing these things, ask a parent, guidance counselor, or older sibling for input. Or go to the library, muster up your courage if necessary, and ask the librarian what book will help. You can also search online.

5. *Learn the rules of etiquette.* Beauty is very subjective and a group's *perception* that certain of its members are more attractive than others is to a great extent based in those "attractive" members' confidence and assuredness. Etiquette develops these traits.

6. *Be a good person.* Yeah, I know that sounds hokey. And if you watch your goofy brother and his friends, or the way some girls fall all over guys who are louts, it seems people's view of good looks is never based on moral considerations. Notwithstanding: your goodness shines through, and some people will find your physical being extraordinarily beautiful because of it. And this is a beauty they will never

stop seeing in you. Nasty motives also are apparent—they shape your facial expressions into an ugly mask that eventually leaves telltale wrinkles that speak of your inner pettiness and/or the like instead of the laugh lines and other wrinkles that confer dignity and charm.

Now that you know lots of axes, the following has spells and info that also helped Frances recognize her beauty, and it can do the same for you: "The Second Secret of Self-Confidence" (see chapter 6) and "A Spell for Beauty, Romance, and All 'Round Popularity: Adorning the Goddess You Are (Guys, There's an Adaptation for You)" (see chapter 4). The following info might also help:

Dieting

The Wiccan approach to dieting: don't. Food is not your enemy. Food is yummy, nurturing, fun, holy, sexy, delicious, and good for you. Your body is not your enemy. Dieting—the practice of eating insufficient food—hurts your body. Love your body: enjoy athletics; take bubble baths; eat lots of organic veggies, lightly steamed so they are a bit crunchy and fill your tummy with sunshine; admire your toes; pretend you're a cat chasing your own tail; rub a really good-smelling lotion all over your body.

If you do not like your body, get an objective, professional opinion. Body images tend to be skewed in this culture. Weight loss is a big

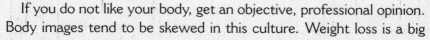

business that brings people big money, and a poor body image feeds this business. So much of what you read and see in the media is designed to make you hate yourself. Fight back by not buying into their sick messages!

If you need to lose weight, do it under medical supervision. And most professionals will tell you not to diet, because it usually doesn't help, and usually actually hurts. If you eat the amount of food that would maintain your ideal weight, you'll eventually get *to* that weight. However, if you get there by dieting, you will not learn the facts, skills, and lifestyle needed to keep you at that weight, and you'll either put it all back on or maintain the weight through self-abusive methods. To figure out the amount of food to eat to maintain your ideal weight, talk to a professional.

If you seriously overeat, it may be too hard to stop on your own. Ask for help. Do not starve yourself. That's called anorexia and it kills people. If you alternate starvation and overeating, then you are still anorexic. Do not throw up your food. It can also kill. If you starve yourself, vomit, and/or seriously overeat, and can't stop on your own, see Guide to Axes to receive the support you deserve. You are a God(dess) right now. Even if you don't believe in your divine state, you can act as if you do by asking for help. (Even Gods need support! A Pagan paradox.) When you let others in, it activates that awesome power within you, your divinity starts to work and you are a God(dess) who can pull off her or his wildest dreams and dearest schemes.

Food is sacred. It comes from our Divine Parents, and is filled with Their love.

And you, as a God(dess), are worthy of worship. A witch is beautiful! Or an oh-so-handsome fellow.

The Magic of a Woman's Hair

This is a woman's section.

I'm walking down the street, and my lipstick is half chewed off, my mascara is smudged so that it's down below my eyes, and my hair hasn't been washed in days. I'm funky! And guys are looking at me. It happens all the time. I have hair almost to my waist. Nothing else seems to matter to these men. It's magic.

Repressive religions may make their women cover their heads, but Wiccans use their hair as sacred offerings, magical ingredients, and sultry looks. Long or short, your hair really is your crowning glory. Celebrate it! And don't say to me, "But it's straight (curly, oily, dry, frizzy, thin, nappy, thick)."

Okay, you said it, didn't you? So, let's deal with that.

Have you ever noticed that the wonderful tresses on the beauties in pre-Raphaelite paintings are identical to the "before" shots in TV shampoo commercials? It's all a matter of attitude.

Find a way to wear *your* hair, as well as an attitude that helps you enjoy the particular magic of your hair.

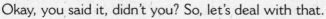

It's hard, I know. When I was younger, my hair was thick and shiny. Now it has become wavy, gets fuzzy if I brush it, and is a lot thinner. And some of my girlfriends tell me about their seriously nasty self-images regarding hair. For me, I had to get objective feedback from my friends, who said, "Your hair is fine! Yes, you can still wear it long." This input really helped. I also talked to other women who worship long hair the way I do. (If your hair is short, find women who celebrate *that*.) They helped me to see that *all* hair is grand long.

I also paid attention to photos and paintings of really long-haired women, until my measure of my hair was not a TV ad designed to make me feel bad. I watched women on the street with the same heartening results.

Beware when you go to hairdressers—if you like long hair, most of them are your out 'n' out enemy who want to cut it all off. They might even say you won't look good unless they shear. (Is this so they'll get repeat business?)

If you like your hair short, they still might want to cut it to suit themselves, instead of you. Go to a stylist who is recommended by someone whose opinion you value, be clear what you want, and make sure the hairdresser understands your instructions.

Anyway, yes, I wear my hair differently nowadays. I don't brush it into a fuzz. I let it dry naturally, then play with it, with my fingers, allowing its curls to blossom.

Hair magic helps you see and enjoy the beauty of your own locks.

A WOMAN'S HAIR SPELL

Ever hear of 100 brush strokes for hair beauty? I do that sometimes.
As I said earlier, I refrain from brushing because it makes my hair
frizz. Sometimes, though, the night before I wash it, or for some
reason I know my hair will suddenly look good brushed, I do the 100
strokes. It distributes the scalp's oil through the hair, a marvelous
conditioning.

And as I do it, I'm transformed. I don't need a chant or anything
else to make the magic happen. I know hair has power, and I let
myself relax, appreciating my locks—nothing else is needed. But if
you need an overt rite to be in the groove, or just want to have magic
fun, here it is.

If your hair is too delicate to withstand 100 brush strokes without
breaking, or if you wear your tresses in a fixed hairstyle—for example,
a weave, dreads, or braids—adapt the ritual. Instead of brushing,
stroke your hair with your hands, caringly, the way you would lov-
ingly stroke a child's head. You might put just the sheerest amount of
scent on your hands first. (If hair is delicate, more than a nominal
amount of scent that is, for example, oil or alcohol based can be too
much.) The pleasure of smelling something nice on your hands during
the rite can be oh-so-fine. In fact, maybe try a scent on your hands
even if you use a brush.

Brush, starting at the bottom, with short strokes. Once that little bit is tangle free, start your stroke a bit higher. (If you start high in the first place, you cause tangles.)

As you brush (or stroke with your hands), chant, "I am the Goddess" over and over for ballpark thirty strokes.

Then repeat, "I am a child of the Great Mother, I am a child of the Earth," again, about thirty strokes.

Next, "My beauty creates beauty," while doing roughly thirty strokes.

(You can do this with one-inch-long hair—don't argue with me!)

When you've hit approximately ninety strokes, repeat, "I am at peace, so mote it be," while you finish the brushing with roughly ten more strokes.

Then repeat that last line five to thirty more times as you sit restfully, allowing your spirit to settle peacefully. (This is a great way to relax before you need to sleep at night.)

Don't worry about *intellectually* understanding this ritual as long as, during it, your spirit bit by bit comes to resonate with it.

This powerful spell is subtle. It doesn't have a lot of outward bells and whistles, and it doesn't make you feel a lot of sparks inside. But it gives you the quiet confidence of a woman who is sure of herself, her desirability, and her independence. Instead of a brazen hyped-up pretense that you are hot stuff, you simply, gently know you are!

3 A Witch's Fab Social Life

Okay, *this* chapter teaches witchy ways to create your ideal social life.

Witches understand that everything is a weave. The whole universe is like a connect-the-dots picture, except that every dot connects to every other dot, and creates a picture so complex we can't even see it let alone know what it is. But it's there and after a while you learn to trust that it's taking care of you. You also come to understand that whatever you do in one area of your life—dot!—affects all other areas of your life—all the other dots!

So if you do anything in this book that improves something for you, it, perhaps invisibly, improves your social life. And sometimes it's not so subtle. For example, if you're not happy with what's going on academically—let's say you're flunking math—it's harder to enjoy yourself at a party. If your parents will even let you attend. So, finding peace of mind and success in other areas of your life helps you relax and be whole enough to have fun.

And there are even *more* obvious "dots" in this book that are not in "A Witch's Fab Social Life": tools abound throughout the text for creating a wonderful, fun, social life. For example, "Spell to Become a Bitch" releases you from the constraints of always trying to act like others think you should. And "Spell to Remove Inner Problems" can help you with shyness.

So enjoy the sections in *this* chapter—I had a blast creating them—as well as socially related spells elsewhere in the book. But remember the witch's weave, and be well rounded. Otherwise one's social life feels shallow and lifeless. And obsessive use of social magic—frantically making yourself miserable applying one spell after another to your social issues—messes up the magic. Don't focus solely on social magic—the other dots of life need to be connected for your social magic to work. (If you're obsessive or all you do is social magic for months, no problem. I'm talking years.) Enjoy *all* the arenas of life. Then you can also indulge in a real witch's fab social life.

Orange Crayons and Friendships

The following spell draws friendship and gives one self-confidence.

A Spell for Attracting a Friend(s)

When you are not feeling sure of yourself socially, or want a friend or friends, get an orange or yellow crayon. (No, I am not talking down to you by suggesting crayons. I *like* crayons.) Orange has the magic of healthy pride in yourself. And yellow is sunny, cheerful, and brave.

Draw a picture of yourself. It needn't be what others would call good art. It can be as simple and unskilled as what a three-year-old would do. A stick figure is fine. On the other hand, if you want to, you can make a very elaborate drawing of yourself looking very proud and free. When you are done with the picture, write these words somewhere on the paper: "I am a good friend."

Acquire Fairy dust. It's described in Chapter 6's section "You're The Best Thing Since Sliced Bread." Sprinkle one tiny pinch of the Fairy dust over the drawing then whisper,

Sprinkle, sprinkle bits of dust.
Goddess, make me what I must
be to be the best of friends.
And please draw the friendship in.
Once the circle holds the tribe,
help me hold it fast and wide.
Sprinkle, sprinkle bits of dust.
Goddess, help
the spell be cast. Goddess, help
the spell be cast.
Goddess, make the spell be cast.

Next, take four deep breaths, breathing in and out slowly with each of the breaths.

Then say, no longer in a whisper, "This is done, the way is clear. Thank you, Goddess, friend most dear. So mote it be!" Exclaim the last four words quite loudly.

Do whatever you want with the picture; for example, tuck it away in a drawer, give it to someone, toss it, or attach it to the refrigerator. I myself might tape the picture into my Book of Shadows, or draw it there in the first place.

This spell attracts friends in three ways. First, when we have self-confidence, as well as believe that we are a good friend, others will be attracted to us. Second, when we are a good friend, others will be good friends back. This sounds like self-help claptrap as if I am just giving you a pep talk and only pretending it's a magical spell. Or that I think magic's a metaphor for shifting your psychological mind-set. No. Magic is real! And this spell's real magic does a *third* thing: it straight-ahead draws friendship. La, la, la, wave your magic wands, girls and boys. (Umm, the spell doesn't use a wand. I was being figurative.)

Success in Sports and Everything Else You Do

This section's ritual is a straight-ahead spell for success! It will also help you overcome your inner blocks to success. This embodies a magical principle mentioned elsewhere in this book: If we are not inwardly ready to win, no spell for success will work.

SPELL TO BECOME (OR REMAIN) A WINNER

Let's start by seeing if you need to change your ideas of success: first of all, there is nothing unfeminine, immoral, or unfair about wanting to succeed in life. As long as one is willing to take the bad along with the good, there's no reason not to take the good. So if you believe otherwise, your attitude is going to keep you from winning.

Ladies, you can still be a lady and succeed. Healthy aggression on the basketball court is how you win a game and it's okay to sweat, feel fierce, and be proud of your body's power. If anyone tells you otherwise, stick one ladylike finger in each of your perfectly delicate and well-shaped ladylike ears while singing in oh-so-ladylike a manner, "Mi, mi, mi, mi, mi." This will block out all input from your not-so-genteel self-defeat coach. Okay, don't do that, it would be rude. Be courteous—blah—and sound like you mean it when you say, "Thank you for sharing that." Then, instead of arguing, which would prolong the boredom, change the topic (or vacate the premises) in a cheerful, pleasant way ASAP!

As to it being unfair to win, or having to stoop to unfairness in order to get "the prize," those are the beliefs of the insecure and/or angry. People who say, "It's always rigged. Only cheaters win and I

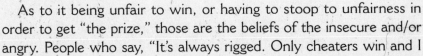

won't do that" might just be afraid to ever get in the game. People who don't play fair are often holding grudges, though they might be hidden ones. So if you think you have to cheat, or believe that even a legitimately won victory is somehow innately unjust, I hope you'll examine yourself for anger and insecurity. Otherwise, you'll be unconsciously ruled by buried feelings that will keep you from achieving your cherished dreams or make you end up bitter, cynical, and empty.

Another indication of insecurity or anger is the attitude "Who cares what happens to others as long as I make it!" I'm not telling you to carry everyone you meet on your back. Do that, and you'll carry such a heavy load that you'll only get one-sixteenth of an inch progress a day or your back will just break! But being callous is not healthy competitiveness, nor does it actually have anything to do with success—it's just simple callousness. Being cold is not the equivalent of having the mind-set of a winner.

Strike a balance. Care about people, and help them succeed when you can. Never be so caught up in your goals that you don't notice if you're rude, thoughtless, or selfish. Care about people's grief and problems when they fail at a cherished undertaking. And enter into competition whether it is sports, business, or anything else, wishing your competitors well and really meaning it. But also do your best to win, using all your talents, creativity, determination, focus, and outer advantages. Feel entitled to succeed, knowing you deserve the best.

Balancing these two sides of the picture is not a onetime act. It's an ongoing matter of watching yourself for going to one extreme or the other, of making sure you listen when a friend points out your lack of balance, of discussing it with someone who'll talk straight and tell the truth when you're not sure which side of this perpetually up-and-down seesaw you need to sit on.

So, after giving a few minutes' thought to all the ideas and feelings about success that I've described, and all the advice I gave, get a glass of water and a saltshaker. Shake salt into the glass, then tell yourself, "I'll succeed, fair and square. It's healthy and good." Then, as you shake more salt into the glass, silently recite the following, adding more salt now and again. All in all, you needn't add much salt. Not even half a teaspoon is needed.

> *Each grain of salt, each flower bloom,*
> *every eye upon the moon,*
> *is part of one, when all is done.*
> *Each grain of salt, each flower bloom,*
> *every eye upon the moon,*
> *is part of one, so all is won.*
>
> *Every hair on every head,*
> *every dream in every bed,*

is part of one, when all is done.
Every hair on every head,
every dream in every bed,
is part of one, so all is won.

The game of life is of one part,
in which all players have one heart.
So let the heart within me sing
so that the game wins everything.

And as this salt melts in the glass,
just as a lad melts in a lass,
so shall my wins be in all things,
my victories with soft, strong wings.
Yes, I shall win the games of life,
with ease and strength, and confidence.
And have the victor's balanced view:
that you are me, and I am you.

Now repeat the entire chant. Then say out loud, emphatically, three times:

This is truth I have spoken, through and through.
So I shall win games old and new!

Then take one, single, tiny sip of the water. Then drink a whole glass of unsalted water. About a half hour later drink another. A half hour later, eat an apple.

The spell can kick in so much juice that it might go bonkers for a few hours before it settles down and won't backfire on you. Should the energy, while settling in, make you easily discouraged, resistant to teamwork, or unable to find your get-up-and-go, that's no time to take on the world and try to rule it! For the few hours after the spell, you might also find yourself tending toward workaholism, scattered thoughts, trying too hard, inertia, resistance to work, or other impediments to success. So do this spell only when you can kick back for at least an hour afterward, ideally three hours. Watch TV, visit an aquarium, do your nails, or otherwise participate in an easy-going activity. Also do what you can to avoid antisuccess thoughts ("I can't kick back! I've stuff to do! I at least have to use the next few hours to frantically *plan* my success." Or "I'll never succeed." Or "I don't care about the football game tomorrow anyway." Or "What's the point of trying?").

Even if the ritual makes you feel confident, sure, and ready to take on the world—and that's great should you be affected like that— still kick back after the spell. Otherwise, your newfound confidence might shatter, newfound direction might get you in over your head, newfound power might get you hot-headed and heedless of dire consequences.

I've only given you examples of how the energy might go awry, but as long as you get your kickback time, you're okay. An easy way to get that time is to do the spell so that you finish an hour before going to bed. Then you can have your second glass of water a half hour later, then your apple before calling it a night. And you also get some awake laid-back time, which is ideal.

You can do this spell a while before a particularly important or challenging event, or just for success overall. If you do the former, you'll likely get more success in other things anyway. In either case, the spell's the same. Feel free to repeat this spell when you feel the need as long as you're not doing it every day for months. That much repetition doesn't give the spell a chance to work.

Here are some times you might want to do this spell: before an exam (ax: study); for a sports match (ax: practice); before your first day on a new job (ax: be groomed, on time, and prepared with whatever knowledge and tools you need to start). And add any other needed axes (e.g., sleep well the night before a sports event).

A final note: perfectionism does not promote success, even in spellcrafting. So if, for example, you have to work at homework a bit, right after doing your spell, don't freak. Or if you didn't use your axes as much as you would have liked, ditto. As always, we do what we can in life, including our magic, and all will be well.

Mystical Tribalism

We all want a tribe—a community of supportive, like-minded friends,
relatives, acquaintances, and coworkers. It's fun and sometimes necessary to bounce your thoughts off someone who "gets" you. We all
need partners in crime when raiding the fridge. We all like the sheer
animal warmth of simply having people in the same room with us,
even if all we're doing is watching TV. Your tribe never thinks your
clothes are gross—unless they actually are! Then, out of love, a tribe
lets you know. Tribe puts in a good word for you when you're applying for a job. And we all need people who stick by us when everyone
else thinks we're bonkers—or worse.

Below are witchy community-building skills and magical ways to
create that tribe. I've mixed in some axes as well.

Finding your tribe can be hard, especially if you have unusual
beliefs, atypical tastes, or a different lifestyle. Interest in Wicca is only
one example. A teen who spends hours tucked away in a teeny box of
a practice room, repeating scales on a violin, might have a difficult
time coming by friends. Devotion to music, a branch of science, or
activism, to show a few examples, both create and supply tribe but
might not leave lots of free time for socializing. In addition, people
tend to misunderstand those with that sort of focus and dedication.

Add to the mix that any teen enraptured by the pursuit of an art form, a branch of science, activism . . . might not have a chance to develop the social skills required to meet the challenges of teenage-dom.

I can't name all the complications that can make it hard for a person to find a tribe. Shyness, self-defeating beliefs, on and on. Let's explore tribal life with a problem-solving approach.

Problem: Lack of social skills; feelings of awkwardness; open-mouth-stick-foot-in syndrome
Solution: Learn etiquette. Miss Manners is an absolute Goddess. Information about her books is in Guide to Axes. Her type of etiquette doesn't make you feel uptight; it helps you be comfortable in the company of others.

Problem: Can't find people you relate to
Solutions: See Wiccan Resources for other Wiccans. Search the phone book or Internet for local groups that focus on your hobby, or that do environmental work. You'll likely find tribe there. Also, look inside yourself and see if you need to be more open to other people's ideas and ways of life. It is really easy to feel rejected when you in fact are the one doing the rejecting. If you think this might be the case but are not sure pray, "Mother, please help me figure out what I need to do to have a tribe." This prayer is good in any case because it will help you overall in your attempts to build tribe. For example, you might get an idea about where or how to find friends. Also, remem-

ber that you can do "Spell to Remove Inner Problems" on the things inside you that make you push people away.

Problem: Shyness
Solution: See "Service, One of the Secrets of Happy People," chapter 6, as well as cleansing shyness away with the cleansing ritual.

Problem: Self-defeating beliefs such as "I'm too unusual for anyone to want to hang out with" or "I'm too serious for anyone to have fun with" or "I don't have what it takes to be really popular."
Solution: Don't buy into that stuff! Use the purification ritual.

Problem: The above doesn't give you what you need
Solutions: Look at "The Second Secret of Self-Confidence" and "Service, One of the Secrets of Happy People," both of which are in chapter 6. Using them helps you build tribe. Or thumb through the Table of Contents, the Table of Spells, and the book as a whole for other related material. Also, anything that helps you be more whole will improve your ability to build and keep a tribe. So keep using magic to become more internally clear and free as well as externally expressed. Other options: discuss the problem with a trusted relative, friend, or teacher; search for books that talk about the issue; if internal problems about tribe building are confusing, talk to a therapist.

A few last notes. If you lose friends, find new ones. If you get hurt, let yourself cry, shout, pout, sulk, withdraw, and be alone a bit. But then find new friends. A tribe sustains us in every part of our being, as well as getting us through hard times, and making the better times even better.

TRIBAL CHANT

This chant brings you the type of power and calm clarity needed to create tribe. It also helps protect and strengthen an existing tribe. Say it alone or with a tribe member or members, reciting it softly. Don't whisper, just a quiet way of speaking.

> *Ooh la la la, rah nee nah,*
> *now we are a part of one.*
> *Ooh la la la*
> *long-time*
> *old time*
> *new time*
> *done!*
>
> *Ooh la la la, rah nee nah,*
> *now we are a part of one.*
> *Ooh la la la, rah nee nah*
> *ooh la la la, la la la.*

Say the last two lines of the chant a total of six times.

4 Love! Love? Love!—The Wonders, Questions, and Complexities of Romance

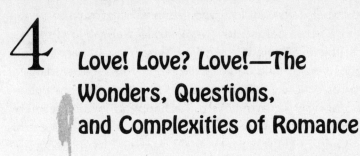

"Love is the magic . . . love gives life!"* The Goddess and God are in love. They bless all forms of romance: boy meets girl, girl meets girl, interracial, whatever the form, it makes the Old Gods smile big! If you choose to always be single, it is a healthy choice that the Gods will equally take delight in and bless, but most folks find romantic involvement crucial at some point.

And it's no simple thing! One minute you're flying and the next, you think, as did Rosalind in *As You Like It*, "Love is merely madness." So, check out the sections in this chapter: the Gods help out with this

*From the song "Love Is the Magic" on my album *Pick the Apple from the Tree*. See Wiccan Resources.

special part of life by giving us spells for *everything* to do with romance from a rite that helps you not lose yourself in a relationship to a ritual that reveals love's true nature, to several straight-ahead love spells.

And 'midst the love spells is one called "The Most Important Love Spell." It opens you to love and as such helps you avoid settling for poor substitutes or lousy relationships, and keeps you from unconsciously sabotaging your attempts to be happy in love. Therefore, doing that spell can help you with the issues in *any* section of this chapter. And *any* of the chapter's spells can work a million times better if you've first done "The Most Important Love Spell."

Read on, while the Gods carry you in their magic chariot of love.

Lotsa Love Spells!

Ooooh, love spells. I get more requests for them than for any other type of ritual. Everyone wants one. So this section gives you several to choose from. But, first, let me discuss love's madness. Romance is one of the areas in life where people, by and large, go, bluntly, bonkers! And nine times out of ten, as they stagger about in an emotional haze, making themselves and their romantic or prospective romantic partner confused, if not miserable, they think they're acting perfectly reasonably and to good effect. The madness seems to increase when they think about doing a love spell.

Perfectly reasonably. You would not believe the e-mails I receive. My website explains I do not respond to e-mail requests for spells. But everyone (a massive volume of "everyones") thinks I have to give a spell to *them* because of their particular romantic situation. The site also states one should never manipulate another person in the name of love, yet e-mail after e-mail explains why the correspondent has a good reason to manipulate. For example, the writer used to be with the person in question, so it's okay to magically make him or her come back. Oh, my, try that non-magically and it's called stalking! Doing something magically that would be wrong if done non-magically is still (guess what?) wrong! Or the person writes me "I just need her to notice me!" So wear a clown nose! It can be incredibly painful, even devastating, to be unnoticed, but manipulation is not the answer. Do not do a spell to "just" *force* them to notice you.

I also read "But I'll die without him." It can feel that way. But you won't, no matter how bad it feels. You can, honest to God, get through this, no matter how awful you feel right now. Search this book for tools that focus on feeling better or improving any particularly bad situation you're in; do one to three a week for a while and you'll shift! Hang in. Magic can work miracles.

If you are suicidal due to romantic tragedy or disappointment, I am committed to this book's ability to help you. Please, please use it to do so! I promise, if you accept help, and hang in, you can feel good about life and yourself. To employ magic for control of someone is not that help. It won't improve things. A love spell geared at the littlest, minutest bit of controlling another person—giving him thoughts of you, opening his heart to you—won't fix your problem. Manipulative magic backfires and things get even worse. (It can be subtle, so a big problem that appears may seem unrelated to your manipulation. But, to oversimplify magical science, any spell you do sends out psychic waves, usually unseen. Manipulative waves are unstable, and they circle back to the sender, reverberating problematic energy.) Instead, use "How to Deal with Troubling Feelings" (which is a subsection of the section "Removing Your Inner Blocks to Happiness"; read the whole section to avoid confusion) if you feel suicidal. You are a precious, lovable child of the Goddess and God, and you deserve a wonderful life. And you *can* do the love spells in this section to bring love into your life. You can have a love you want, and needn't be with the specific person you might have in mind, though that might seem impossible to you right now.

Another excuse for controlling someone: "But I love her!" That doesn't matter. No amount of control, no matter how small, is okay, no matter how large or dire your excuse. It simply doesn't work out for you. So don't use controlling love spells.

Now, having said all that, I'll add that, being human, we all make excuses for controlling or don't realize when we *are* being controlling. Therefore, before doing a love spell not in this book, have a friend read this material about control and love spells and then check the love spell for you. Love is one of those areas where we're all blind and need input from others.

So, none of the following love spells are done with a given person in mind. That would be controlling. They are not spells *on* someone, except those that are obviously on *yourself*. But they are all about finding the perfect, yummy, most fabulous love. Do one of these spells and love will find you. And if the person you're interested in is really right for you right now, the spell will work on them of its own accord. Love's like that.

Finally, love spells are powerful. A successful spell can initially cause disruption. So watch out for two things: a fight between you and your (prospective) beloved might easily occur. Be extra patient and noncombative until the spikiness ends and you'll be fine. Also, you might gain the attention of people you're not interested in. You're not in any way required to reciprocate. Just wait until the spell brings you someone *you* want, and be willing to fend off attention from wolves.

I know this is a lot of cautionary material. But there's nothing wrong with wanting romance. Love is beautiful and sacred to the Pagan deities. Enjoy the love spells in this section, have fun with them!

THE MOST IMPORTANT LOVE SPELL

If you are not open to love, no love spell can work. You may want to use this spell as preparation for any other love spell you do. In fact, this spell to open yourself to love is so crucial it might be the only love spell you will ever need. This is also a good spell if you're in a relationship and want it to be as happy and healthy as possible.

Look inside yourself: is there something in you that blocks love? For instance, do you feel you don't deserve love? Or perhaps you think that no one could ever love *you*? Or maybe you think you are too fat, or too thin? Maybe you are afraid to ask someone out on a date? Whatever the negative belief, fear, or other internal block is, get in touch with it.

Then use soap and water to "wash it away." Actually put your hands in water and wash them as a way to get rid of your block to love! Only wash away one or two blocks. Magic takes time and energy to work. If there's more you want to clear away, wait at least a few days before washing "off" more blocks.

But don't think you need to be perfect to be loved and have romance. Cleanse a bit, and get on with living—use your axes.

Everyone is different and has their own situation, so this section has many different *types* of love spells. If the above spell doesn't seem enough or quite right for you, use another!

A Spell for Beauty, Romance, and All 'Round Popularity: Adorning the Goddess You Are
(Guys, There's an Adaptation for You)

Be sure to think about doing "The Most Important Love Spell" before doing *this* love spell.

Self-healing plays an important part in romance. Here's an example. I am a shamanic counselor (psychic reader). One of my clients told me she was ugly, then asked for a spell to make her beautiful and popular. This is the spell I gave her.

Women, while putting on their makeup or otherwise preparing themselves to face the day, often think things like "How am I ever going to make myself look even half decent?" or "What am I gonna do with my awful eyes (eyebrows, skin, lips)?" Or "I'm ugly!" Instead, turn that around in a ritual: put on your lipstick chanting out loud or silently, "I adorn the beautiful Goddess I am; beautiful inside and out." When you believe this, others will too. If you prefer, chant as you put on body lotion or perfume or a dress or . . . You can repeat this rite often—if you want, do it whenever you put on makeup or lotion or . . . if it takes repetition to be effective. In fact, it's nice to do as much as you like, just because it can feel yummy.

An adaptation: **Adorning God.** A guy can do the above spell. Just adapt accordingly. Do the spell while shaving, combing your hair, or anything else that seems suitable. Say, "I groom the God I am." While washing your car, you can recite, "I polish a chariot for the God I am." (Do not then tell yourself what a lousy car you have! Bad magic.)

I told my worried client that when you think you are a wonderful God(dess), inside and out, everyone else will follow suit, and you will be popular. And maybe attract your dream mate! Also, when one realizes one is, well, absolutely divine, one captures the romantic worship of others. La! Another point: the female considered most gorgeous in any given group, and the male most attractive, would often be viewed by someone outside the group as rather plain or visually uninteresting. The reigning queen of beauty's assuredness of her desirability, the reigning king of the walk's assuredness, create their positions on the thrones.

This spell may not look like it works. Try it! If it seems like it may feel silly, try it anyway. Also, don't mistake this rite for just a bunch of affirmations. It is actual magic that can change you, so that instead of any little belief that you're not up to snuff, just the way you are, you see there's nothing to do, own, or change to be a God(dess). Guys, you particularly may feel you have to somehow prove yourself, thinking your worth is based on something *outside*—some action or possession. Don't "prove" your worth. Do the spell instead, you God you!

Beauty axes can be found in "A Witch Is Beautiful" (in chapter 2).

Next: Each of us is unique, so everyone needs a love spell that suits them best. The following love spell can be used instead of, or even with, the two spells already included. Again, if you do "The Most Important Love Spell" before the spell below, the latter may work better.

PROUD AS A PEACOCK: A SPELL TO DRAW ROMANTIC ATTENTION

I talk elsewhere about humility. But there's nothing wrong with receiving attention. Being humble doesn't mean wearing a bag over your head. Don't go to extremes.

Wear a peacock feather or some emblem of the peacock. For instance, cut off the decorative end of the peacock feather and pin it to your lapel, or wear earrings shaped like peacocks. Or don a T-shirt with a picture of a peacock on it. Earrings shaped like fans—you know, the things ladies used to wave to cool off in the heat, and coyly peek out from behind—will also do the trick, as will any piece of jewelry or clothing showing a fan. You can even take a very small piece of origami or other pretty paper, make the tiniest fan, and wear that on your lapel or elsewhere.

After donning your peacock or fan item, look in the mirror and say once—or repeat as many times as you want—"I am spreading my tail feathers." Leave the house and see what happens. The attention, however, may take a week or two to occur. You need not wander the streets until then! Just go for a walk, even if it's two minutes long. Wear the peacock items as often as you can until you receive attention, as well as when the attention is first happening.

When the spell is done, you can reuse the fan or peacock item again magically should the need arise, wear it solely for decoration, give it to a friend for either use, or throw it away. On the chance the spell doesn't work, the same instructions apply.

One last trick for the spell to work and work well: Since healthy, powerful spellcrafting is not about forcing other people to do something, getting attention magically needs to be done with special awareness of detail. This sort of awareness is what makes someone an effective magician, instead of a pretender. So take note: this is not a spell to make a person or people see you the way you want them to see you. In fact, this spell does not force anyone to even notice you at all. This ritual is like a peacock spreading his tail in courtship, but on a psychic level. Or like putting on a fabulous new dress or a warm, inviting smile. This spell causes you to exude a certain something that is very tempting.

In other words, if you were geared up in a great outfit because you wanted to appear attractive to a certain someone, you wouldn't grab that person's head and forcibly swivel it around so that he or she noticed how great you looked. He or she would think you were nuts and wouldn't want anything to do with you. To do the magical equivalent would have the same result: resistance from the person of your dreams.

Instead, this spell, "Proud As a Peacock," is a powerful courtship. And anyone with any good sense is going to sit up and take notice of you, even if they don't know what that mysterious something is that draws them.

So, while doing "Proud As a Peacock," think of it as how I've described it instead of how I've described it *not* to be. Hence the spell will work, and safely. There's no trick to what I'm asking here—just have your mind and intention clear about how I've described the spell.

Do not do this spell or the next with a particular person in mind. But through either spell he, she, or someone even better will be drawn to your special self.

The Path of True Love

This is a spell for your true love to find you. Get five red roses. Go about a block from your house and drop one rose. Drop three more on the way back home. Drop the fifth at your door. While you do all this, chant out loud or silently, "This is a path of love. My true love will find me." You have given your true love a path by which to find you! If you want to be more secretive and economical, use five rose petals, fresh or dried.

Someone asked me how long it takes before love finds you. My answer is relevant to any love spell and to love in general: it takes however long it takes. Patience is required for powerful magic, too, which, whether for love or for anything else, *also* takes however long it takes. Be patient regarding love. Otherwise you take the first thing that comes along. Ugh!

Thus ends our section on love spells. Read the next section if you want helpful hints about romantic intimacy.

Mother Earth's Bounty No. 1: The Natural Cycles of Feeling Close, Then Finding *Yourself*

Witches honor nature as one of our great teachers. Here is a lesson from Mother Earth. Trees reveal nature's cycles and these same patterns are in us. In spring, trees bud green, the color pale and hopeful. That time of year, the sap rises in us, too! Trees blossom, if all goes well. As do we. In fall, we might feel riotous and ready, matching some trees' brilliant orange foliage. Come winter, a tree looks dead. But it's quietly, invisibly, doing the work it needs in order to become lush in spring. This pattern of new growth, bloom, fruition, and seeming death does not just happen over a year's span. It also occurs in brief bits of time, even during the course of our day. We might feel amped and ready to go, and feel useless an hour later. But that useless winter, hour, day, month, year, is a necessary part of the cycle, without which none of the rest of the cycle can happen.

Romantic intimacy also has this pattern. By intimacy I am not talking about sex just now, but about feeling close emotionally, intellectually, or spiritually.

In the same way you might lose yourself in the headiness of spring, feeling buoyant and full, so might you lose yourself in the rich indulgence of romantic intimacy. Yum! Then, you realize you've lost yourself too much, so you back off a bit and focus on you, and you only. At which time, the relationship might seem like a winter tree—dead.

Once you feel full of yourself again, intimacy can recommence. Think of waves going in and out on a beach. Lose yourself, find yourself, lose yourself, find yourself, lose . . .

Now, my description of romantic intimacy sounds all well and good, but, often, it does not work out as smoothly and prettily as my description. For example, John panicked after a wonderfully warm date. He didn't realize he just needed to get a few hours to himself, shoot some basketball, and feel himself again. Instead, he felt smothered, and that he was not being a real guy. He became afraid that Louise, his new girlfriend, was going to take over his life and try to run it for him.

When he told Louise, "I need to cancel our date tonight. I just need some space," she panicked, in turn. She felt that they had been so close, what had gone wrong? Nothing! Think ocean waves again. After the wave pulls back, it returns again.

But Louise had lost *herself*, too. Caught up in all those warm feelings, she now did not feel *fully herself* without John. So she called him on the phone, crying. This made John panic more, which almost

caused him to break up with her. Fortunately, she came to me for a psychic reading, and I read what had happened. I explained what I've said thus far in this section. Then I added, "He's just finding himself. You need to do the same." (I don't usually do a reading for a teen, but I'm a friend of Louise and John and their parents.)

I created a ritual for her that would help. I also told her to apologize to John, in a way that would not demand intimacy from him at a time he couldn't give it. I said, "Don't be all emotional. Act as if you are happy, normal, cheerful. Make the conversation brief. Don't give a lot of explanations. A long talk, even about the weather, and any explanation of your apology may just overwhelm him further. Just say, in a bright tone, 'I'm sorry I went overboard the other day on the phone. I wasn't myself. I hope you'll forget I acted that way.'" I asked her to use my words verbatim in case she tripped herself up, and I instructed her absolutely "*not* to say them in a begging or tearful voice. Just be matter of fact, simple, to the point, as if it were all no big deal. Because the more you make of it, the more you're being unfair to him—you overwhelmed him once, don't do it again by the way you apologize for it!"

Since John also asked for my advice I helped him get clear about the cycles of intimacy and his reaction after their special date. Then I suggested he reassure Louise that he had panicked over nothing and all was well, he'd see her soon. He was smart enough to ask her to "Please support me having the time to regroup. I *really* need it."

Below is the ritual I gave Louise so that she could focus on finding herself. John ended up also using it. I suggest you do it whenever you lose *yourself* too much. Fill yourself up *with* yourself and the waves on the beach return.

NIGHT MAGIC: FINDING YOUR LOST SELF

Make your bed an appealing place to sleep. Ideas:

* fresh, clean sheets
* super comfy pillows
* perfume on the sheets
* gentle lighting
* scarves draped on the bed stand or headboard
* stuffed animals to cuddle with
* a glass of water by the bed if you tend to get thirsty in the middle of the night
* whatever appeals to *you*

Do not use candles for the gentle lighting. Too many witches have burned down their homes leaving a candle untended. Never sleep or leave the house with a candle burning. I have a tiny lamp that casts a cozy glow—perfect for this ritual. There are many little, little gorgeous lamps available right now.

Once everything is the way you want it, snuggle into bed, and recite:

> *Holy Mother, Holy Father,*
> *gently rock this boat as I travel into dream waters.*
> *In my night journey, and in the days and nights ahead,*
> *gently rock me, leading me to myself.*
> *Pour dream water over me, freeing me of fear or other*
>   *hindrances*
> *that prevent my personal fulfillment throughout the day.*
> *Come to me in dreams and in daylight,*
> *with the power I need to live the life I need.*

Then, go to sleep. You needn't make a big deal of it. For example, if you like to read a bit before falling off, feel free.

Over the next four days, focus on yourself, not your sweetie. What makes *you* feel happy? Do it. What inner blocks keep you from doing it? Cleanse them away. See "Removing Your Inner Blocks to Happiness," chapter 6. The prayer is for personal fulfillment. For many people, a romantic involvement is an important and legitimate part of that. But equally important is that they have a life of their own, without which personal fulfillment does not exist. In the case of this spell, the prayer must be for the latter, because only if you have *it*, can the former exist. (At another time, go ahead and use one of the love spells in the previous section.) And without that independence, intimacy in your relationship can't keep returning. Ocean waves. . . . So, in the couple of days right after the spell, focus on *your* pleasures, *your* responsibilities. Free time on your hands because you're without a date? Maybe use it to catch up on magical lessons, yard work, hangout time with your best bud.

If you remember your dreams over this time, they may be useful. Or not. But if you don't remember them, the God and Goddess are surely dream-visiting you anyway. After all, They are *always* by our side, taking care of us, whether it seems so or not.

If you suffer or have suffered a lot of rejection, or were abused, a focus on yourself instead of someone else might be really difficult. Whether or not you have faced rejection or abuse, when you *do* look inward, it may be too painful.

Use the ax! Therapy. Talking things over with friends or parents. Alateen. (Alateen is an organization for young adults who have suffered because of a family member's alcoholism. It helps you focus on your *own* life and improve it, instead of dwelling on the alcoholic and anyone else who walks by for two seconds.)

John and Louise represent only one way the natural ebb and flow of intimacy can get messed up. Brainstorm with friends for other examples and what to do about them. More axes!

Real Love

Real love cannot be avoided, but "falling in love," with all its intensity and perhaps even desperation, is not necessarily love. And you needn't act on your feelings no matter what you feel. Real love is kind; if you love someone you wouldn't hurt them, which means you won't get involved with them if it is inappropriate.

Do the following spell to better understand the nature of love and/or to know your feelings in a given situation (e.g., Is it love or do you just want someone in your life to distract you so you can avoid your frightening problems or boring responsibilities?).

SPELL TO FIND OUT IF IT'S LOVE

Put a dab of water on your forehead. Then pray, "Please show me both the true nature of love and my real feelings." Sit for a few minutes and see if any thoughts come to you. Or the answer may come later, over the next few weeks. It might come in a dream, or through the advice of a friend, or maybe even through a song on the radio. Or via any of endless other possibilities.

When it comes to love, we all want the answers *now*. But it may or may not work that way. Magic, like the rest of life, can take time.

If there is a pressing reason for immediate solutions other than terrible longing and an aching heart, take steps on *that* reason right away, while you wait for the spell to work. For example, if you're debating leaving a boyfriend who hits you, hitting is the issue, not love. So learn about violence in relationships; see the following section, "What to Do When Romance Sours." Or, if your pressing problem is something else, and you don't know what to do, either thumb through the book or get help elsewhere.

After you get the info you need, if you have to make a hard decision, do this spell:

POWER OF CHOICE

This charm will help you have the courage to do whatever it is you need to. Draw the following symbol.

You needn't draw it well. Rip the paper you've drawn it on into five parts. Keep one on you or in your special witch place (see below), and throw each of the others away in a different place. The courage to do the hard thing will more likely come now.

This spell can be used to gain the courage for any number of things, such as asking someone for a date, breaking up with a wonderful person who's not "it," leaving a bad relationship, refusing to go out with only one person, as well as activities that have nothing to do with this chapter-section or love: to apply for a job, try a new hobby, break the glass ceiling, tell someone about abuse that's happening, refuse to participate in a peer's bad behavior.

This charm also helps with courage overall.

Your Special Place

Occasionally this book refers to "your special place." Some witches like having a special place where they keep their Wiccan books and supplies. Having Wiccan stuff there—whether a lucky charm or book of spells—gives you magical power.

This place might be a handsomely decorated shelf, but could be anything and anywhere—under the bed, on top of your bureau, up a tree. The Goddess is in everything! The special place gives you power, just because you consider it your special place. In fact, you can have as many special places as you want. Sometimes, the entire planet is mine, mine, mine. The Goddess is in *everything*!

If you have no access to or privacy in which to have a special place, and I tell you elsewhere to put something liquid in your special place, recite, "This drain is sacred, and belongs to the Goddess," and pour the liquid down it. No reason the plumbing can't be your special place for that moment! A witch is resourceful. If it's not liquid you can bury it somewhere, or use your imagination as to where the best place—or even just a possible place—is for you to put the magical item. If throwing it away is the only solution, again, the Goddess is everywhere! When tossing, simply think "This is going to my special place, where the Goddess keeps it for me."

What to Do When Romance Sours

Romance seems to reduce strong, confident, and serene women to frantic, worried, and insecure neurotics. A carefree, sweet, and competent man becomes tongue-tied, fumbling, and boorish when he meets *l'amour*.

Love shakes us up. While it can get us high, it also brings out our insecurities, fears, and other negative traits. And that's only on the first date! So when things go sour we're often not at our best in trying to deal with them.

Therefore, "What to Do When Romance Sours" is a section that looks at the various ways love can go bad, and which other part of this book you should go to to cope with each one. The magical solutions needed are not specific to romance. It may *seem* special magic is needed, but, really, life has its ups and downs in all arenas.

While reading "What to Do When Romance Sours" please keep

in mind that one of the almost inevitable insanities of romance (and the lack thereof) is to think that all advice is irrelevant. This is because we all, every last one of us, will want to find a reason *our* particular predicament is different. We "hurt so much" or, "He hurt me so bad." Or "But this is *real* love" or "But you've never felt like this" or "But *she* would never hurt me" or . . . or . . .

I beg you to put all that aside, because otherwise you could blind yourself to the oncoming traffic of heartbreak—at the least—and far worse. I'm not saying exceptions don't happen, but most people insist that *their* situation is an exception. Instead of doing that, read on, and also dialogue with others who won't let you be in na-na-denial-land.

The most common way romance sours is a lack of feeling close, or a sense of being smothered. If this is the case, go to "Mother Earth's Bounty No. 1: The Natural Cycles of Feeling Close Then Finding *Yourself*," this chapter.

If your relationship is usually good but right now you're fighting or not communicating well, steep a little tiny pinch—not even a tea-spoon—of basil from your kitchen in a cup of water. Anoint your ears with the "tea" to better understand what your partner is trying to convey. Your partner can do likewise, but he or she needn't even know you're doing your part.

Understand that discussing romance, any part of it, even some-times the good stuff, can be difficult with one's partner, and most teens are just starting to learn how to do so. Axes for communication: Ask parents and older siblings for advice. Read Miss Manners (see Guide to Axes). Read *Men Are from Mars, Women Are from Venus* (if you're heterosexual). If your communication skills are horrendous, ask a school counselor or librarian for books that might help. Therapy may be a solution, too. With that:

If the relationship seems like it might be ending, refer back to the section "Real Love." But don't leave it at that. Also discuss the situation with someone—ax.

If romance has turned into physical or verbal violence or sexual assault, the prayer "I am a Pagan, a Child of the Earth" can help you totally change your life. You may want "Spell for Getting Out of a Bad Situation." "Power of Choice" is also good. (See Table of Spells for easy access to page numbers.)

Don't delude yourself about abuse from your partner, telling yourself it isn't happening or won't get worse. Statistics show that violence in dating or relationships is common, including sexual violation. Same-sex situations are not free of these problems, either. The number of deaths from violence in intimate relationships is *huge*. If there's violence in your relationship, then you can't afford to pretend it isn't happening. Not if you want to avoid the serious injuries, severe emotional problems, and death that are a common result of battering relationships. And if there's any violence, it could escalate into these things—it *often* does. Value yourself enough to get away from an abuser!

 See Guide to Axes for, well, axes. If it's a problem in your life become educated about violence in relationships. There's a lot you need to learn that this book can't cover.

 Romantic problems range from small to horrendous, annoying to ridiculous. Take control of your life to have the romance *you* want, and the peace of mind and freedom to enjoy it. You deserve the best!

5 No Shame About It: Sexuality

When you are underage, your parents have the legal, and moral, right to dictate what you do. So writing about sex for you is very tricky. Who am I to tell you what I think is right? All that aside, it is *still* tricky because I don't know where I stand on the issue of whether it's okay for a teen to be sexually active or not. It's not that I am afraid to take a stand on the issue. I honestly don't know *where* I stand.

It is absolutely imperative for spiritual teachers to admit it when they haven't yet figured something out. Try as I can, I can't decide. And since we learn more by example than through lecture, spiritual leaders do enormous harm pretending to be perfect, because that's a lousy role model for you. If you pretend to be perfect, as I've said elsewhere herein, it destroys not only your spirit but your life.

However, I can definitely help when it comes to sexual issues. So, let's go.

This chapter addresses pivotal and crucial aspects of sexuality not addressed elsewhere in this text. We'll hit them head-on. One of them will be whether to engage in sexual activity or not.

A whole book about sexuality wouldn't be enough to help an individual navigate his or her way through the veritable land mines of sex. Argh! But wait! There's always a solution! Ta da! Talk with an adult about what you read here or other sexual issues that arise. And see Guide to Axes so that you get the sex education we *all* need.

Whoo Hoo! Sexuality Is a Blessing: Fun, Passion, Guilt, and Morality

Sex is a blessing from the Goddess. We needn't be ashamed of our passion nor for wanting the fun of sex as long as we are responsible.

Many mistake passion for lack of control or abuse. Passion is the zest for life, whether we're talking sex or math. Sexual passion can be an enormous joy, sweeping one up and into life's currents, to great ecstasy. But what you see in the movies—people throwing away their lives and goodness because of so-called passion—is *not* passion. It's just throwing away your life and goodness because you haven't learned self-control, or because you lack self-esteem or are fueled by insecurity or for any other number of reasons. If any of these pertain to you, then cleanse such inner blocks with "Spell to Remove Inner Problems," and talk it over with a trusted adult or perhaps even a therapist.

As to guilt, witches know there's nothing to feel guilty about unless you hurt someone or act against your own morals. If you feel shame about wanting sex, or about the intensity of your sexual feelings, or about sexual desires for someone the same sex as you, use the cleansing ritual. (Did you know there are gay Gods?)

Forget the foolish preachers who insist that sexual passion and morals are opposing forces. Our Pagan God is the embodiment of passion coupled with integrity. He sexually desires the Goddess, yet also respects her. Not only are sexual ethics a part of Wicca, but we can't enjoy sex as much as we might without them. Unless you're careful about hurting someone's feelings, taking advantage of someone, causing a pregnancy, and the like, some part of you, even if unconscious, is not free, and therefore passion cannot run its full course. I want the best sex possible, and have learned to have a great time in bed. I've also learned that moral behavior is one of the things that has allowed me to enjoy myself so much. Trust me on this.

Fun and being uninhibited is not the same as careless acts and no restraint.

The fact is, I'm monogamous. Fun is very important to me—I'm a *Pagan*. It's a *lot* more fun for me to be sexual with only one person. The wild abandonment that is so dear—and necessary—to my Pagan spirit can happen full tilt only if I'm with one person. And I wait until I find that one special person. For one thing, monogamy allows one to build a deep relationship, which in turn deepens the sheer physical pleasure of sex. Also, one builds trust so that one is more likely to feel unembarrassed and relaxed doing, or asking for, what one wants in bed. Finally, practice makes perfect, and monogamy gives me the chance to practice and practice with someone until, ahem, we've really got it down. And then we can practice some more.

Feeling relaxed and comfortable enough to fully enjoy sex also means not doing anything in the process that hurts you (e.g., your feelings, morals, physical safety).

If you want sexual joy and power, read the next section in this chapter. Also "Your Limitless Power as a God(dess), Your Tremendous Human Limits, And How This Relates to Sex, Drugs, and Personal Achievement," chapter 7, addresses some of the sanity, caution, and common sense needed to really enjoy your sexuality, without paying dearly. If we have a high cost hanging over our heads, sex is not going to be as much fun nor is it worth it.

And don't forget: Some people masturbate, some don't. It's a choice, healthy either way. There's nothing sick or ugly in either choice. Making love to yourself can be very pleasurable, and even beautiful and holy. One creation myth states the cosmos was created when the Goddess made love to herself!

Be confident that sexual feelings are healthy and sacred. And if you choose sexual abstinence—whether it's because you want to wait until you're older, you need to feel closer to your partner, you need your attention focused on getting into college, or any other of the many sound reasons that exist—don't be ashamed of your sexuality. In fact, shame makes it harder to abstain, adding pressure when one already may feel overloaded and ready to burst. (Note: just as sexual feelings and urges are normal, so is sexual frustration. Learning to cope with frustration regarding sex, jobs, sports, friends, and so forth is part of maturing and part of adult life.) Whether you choose to be sexually active or not, remember that your sexual *feelings* are holy. They echo God's beauty, power, and mystery.

Sexual Power: Do I or Don't I?

There are so many issues when it comes to sex. And you may feel helplessly spun into dizzying circles by strong, puzzling, and chaotic sexual feelings. Therefore, this section of the chapter is about taking control of one's sexuality.

Taking control is a necessary step to having sexual power; a woman or man is sexual even when they say "no." Sex is part of who we are whether we are actively engaged or not. It just exists as part of us. And taking control is also needed to have sensual joy should we choose to make love. Sex with another person is a choice.

Witches know that celibacy is a legitimate expression of sexuality, either as a lifestyle or temporary state.

Let me be clear about power and control: I'm not talking about controlling other people or power over them. I'm talking about having control over one's *own* life and the inner power to do what one wants. Sexual power and control are not the same as manipulating or coercing a partner. Ever!

Nor are they simply about saying "no." So also look at "Your Limitless Power as a God(dess), Your Tremendous Human Limits, And How This Relates to Sex, Drugs, and Personal Achievement" because it shows other parts of taking control, such as safe sex and avoiding pregnancy. Back to "no":

Any woman or man who cannot say it does not have sexual power. And, as repeated elsewhere, witches celebrate sexual power.

I'm not saying you have to refuse, but a woman or man has a right to a satisfying sexual life, when (s)he's ready for it and on her or his own terms. Unless (s)he has the ability and support to say "No" (s)he is not having sex as (s)he sees fit.

Sexual freedom is too often defined as always saying "yes." Ugh. Many women in the freewheeling '60s suffered a great loss of self-esteem and sexual pleasure because of that. Freedom means choice.

And saying "yes" to one thing, for example kissing, is not a "yes" to other things. Again, sexual power = your own terms.

Freedom is the right to say "no."

If you can't because you don't think you have the right to or are ashamed of your need for control—a need that witches learn is healthy and part of self-respect—or have any other negative belief, fear, or other inner block keeping you bound by *other* people's sexual choices, cleanse them away in "Spell to Remove Inner Problems" and talk with a trusted adult or counselor about such blocks. And don't believe anyone who says, "Everyone is having sex." That is so not true!

And there is no need to hurry out of worry: you *will* find someone with whom you have a mutual sexual attraction and the right relationship.

If lack of self-esteem (self-respect) keeps you from saying "no" though you want to—"I'll lose him if I say 'No'" or "No one will want me unless I put out" or "I'm not a real man if I don't do it" or "I have to have sex with him just to make him like me"—cleanse such beliefs away and also use one of the book's tools for building self-esteem. Again, talk it over as well.

COURAGE POTION

This potion gives one the bravery to not only say "no" but also, if one wants, to go after true love instead of settling for a poor substitute. One brews a cup of basil tea—yes, basil, the stuff that goes into spaghetti sauce. Take a wee pinch—not even half a teaspoon—of the dried herb, let it soak for five minutes in hot water, then drink. Do no more than once a week. Other than that, repeat as often as you want.

Courage is easier to drum up if you have friends or family stand behind you egging you on to do what you believe in. Ask them to help support your self-respect and boundaries. You can feel sexy without having to put out.

Abstinence from sex is not easy, by any longshot. And it's called sexual *drive* for a reason: it's so intense it can *drive* you, unless you get a handle on it. Well, we need ways *to* abstain. We looked at some good aids already, such as the courage potion and using magic to develop self-esteem. Here is more: check out "What to Do If You Have More or Wilder Energy Than You Know How to Handle," chapter 9. Also, many people find celibacy easier if they find a creative outlet or stay busy. And don't forget: plain old self-control's part of it. You can also brainstorm with a trusted adult about what to do with all that sexual drive. If they can't help—unfortunately, it's not something people in this culture give enough thought to—pray, "Mother, Father, help me" and keep trying to find out what to do. Prayer combined with persistence works wonders in life and can triumph over anything.

This section talked about saying "no" but not about saying "yes." There are plenty of repressive people preaching "no," so I wanted to add a new perspective. Also, "yes" is preached plenty, too. But if you want to see ways that "yes" can be healthy and joyful rather than the thoughtless sex that often happens, look at the section "Whoo Hoo! Sexuality Is a Blessing," earlier in this chapter.

6 Magic Is an Inside Job: The Mystical Art of Inner Transformation

Because they are on a spiritual path, witches try to be the best people they can be. This effort includes self-improvement. But some religions teach self-improvement within a belief system that says

* Humans are inherently bad.
* Life is black and white with no gray areas.
* Contradictions are not compatible with spiritual truths.

None of these beliefs are Wiccan. Let's deal with these erroneous beliefs and look at the Wiccan alternatives a bit:

People are *not*, I repeat *not*, bad, bad, bad, bad, bad, and therefore needing to hate themselves or be ashamed for everything they say, do, feel, and think.

Sure, we're far from perfect. In fact, we all do terrible things to each other. (We're in the gray area here!) Every human being is a mixed bag of goodness and failure, the latter in each of us constantly ranging from great to small.

And though it is healthy to feel guilty when you do something wrong, because guilt prompts you to make reparation and try to change your behavior (about to enter more gray area), our Divine Parents do not demand we grovel in *unhealthy* guilt. Self-debasement, in fact, keeps one from picking up the pieces when one has messed up. It also impedes change, perhaps even making personal growth impossible.

Our Divine Parents love us. Period! This love from Them is echoed by our self-love. We can love ourselves just the way we are. In addition, what with all this love, we can feel safe and strong enough to change what's needed.

None of this implies that we are not responsible for what we do, do not need to repair damage we cause, or do not need to try hard to grow and change. (Wiccans are okay with contradictions!)

Look at my books, *Be a Goddess!* and *Goddess Initiation*, if you want more info on the issues thus far discussed. Though written for an older age group, a lot of the material is relevant to any age. But for now I've covered enough to proceed to the matter at hand: this chapter focuses on spells to improve your inner being so that you can feel *great*, not because you're "bad" and need to hate yourself. You're fine the way you are, in fact, fab. Though spirituality is about growth and change, it is also about loving yourself just as you are now. And love means not telling yourself things that make you feel crummy.

Now let's look at negative thoughts that are not based, or only partially based, in oppressive religious nonsense. Everyone seems to have them to some degree. The following remarks are typical examples: "My hair always sucks!" "I am too weird." "I am ashamed and confused because my feelings and desires are so intense." "I'm stupid a lot." "I must be crazy to act (or feel or think) the way I do."

Again, you're fine the way you are, in fact, you're fabulous. You just may not know it. Learn to see how incredibly beautiful your hair, other physical attributes, personality, skills, and soul already are. It's a painful thing to be blind to your good points or not see their full extent or be judgmental about the things in you that need change.

Try to change, however slowly: practice thinking well of yourself, even if it feels like lies or seems pretentious or arrogant or stilted.

Don't say things to yourself that hurt your self-esteem. Forgo perfectionism. Self-deprecating thoughts have strong magical power; the more you say them, in ritual or not, the more you believe them. And dwelling on them during ritual makes them *even* stronger. Especially when you use spells for inner change, try to refrain from such thoughts. I mean, it's okay to be *aware* of them during the spell if doing so helps you let go of such negativity. But if you cling to them while doing magic, you might believe them more than ever. At least pretend they're not true.

Now don't get all paranoid and worry that you must be perfectly Pollyanna during your rites! The Old Gods no more demand perfection during ritual than They do any other time. Just try, and the attempt is enough.

After a ritual for inner change you may find your negative thoughts or emotions stronger for a bit. That can be a good thing—it is sort of the way they fight back before they give up. Don't worry. Just do your best to trust your spell and try to replace the negativity with positive thoughts and deeds. For example, hug a sibling or tell yourself "I'm fab!" Replacement is important—when you get rid of something bad, it leaves an empty space and you want to choose something good to fill that space so the negativity does not return or be replaced with something else negative.

The following section has a spell that can help with all this. So can "The Second Secret of Self-Confidence," also in this chapter.

Onward!

You're the Best Thing Since Sliced Bread

No matter how much you love yourself, you can always strengthen and reinforce that. Enjoy the following spell!

No matter how *little* you love yourself, you can change that until you think you are just great! Enjoy the following spell!

Wow, I'm Fabulous! A Charm for Self-Love and Self-Esteem

This magic helps you better appreciate your strengths, love yourself more—shortcomings and all—and be good to yourself in thought and deed. The charm can be simple or fancy, and I will show the range for each ingredient needed. It is *your* choice. A simple ingredient is no worse—or better—than a complex one.

While making the charm and doing the rest of the spell, try your best to refrain from criticizing how you do any part. Don't say, "Hmm, I could've made a better bag" or "That's not the ideal ingredient to have chosen from Francesca's list."

1. The container can be a scrap of fabric or paper. On the other end of the spectrum it can be a beautifully crafted bag you make or purchase. Pink is an excellent self-love color, so I used that for my self-love bag and suggest it to you. (Guys, pink doesn't bite!)

2. Place inside the bag an amulet that has the magic power of self-love. This can be any one of the following:

   * a rose quartz crystal. This and the tourmaline below can be just a little tiny chunk or wee bead, which I prefer to a

larger piece since the bundle ideally is carried on your person for a while. Rose quartz and tourmaline are found in metaphysical, bead, and jewelry stores.

* green or pink tourmaline, another crystal
* a pink rose (you can take the stem off a fresh one, or use a dried bud)
* a single strand of your hair
* a heart drawn with lipstick on a piece of paper
* a fresh, soft-green leaf
* or the merest drop of your own saliva on a tissue.

3. Take a sheet of paper, tiny scrap of old newspaper, lovely parchment, ripped paper towel—or whatever else—and write your name on it three times.

4. Put this in your container and close it up.

5. Add your personal power to the charm. This is easy: simply
   * Spray a favorite perfume or cologne on the container.
   * Or hold it over burning incense, the smell of which you enjoy.
   * Or sprinkle the container with fairy dust—cornmeal, glitter, dirt, cookie crumbs, cracker crumbs, baby powder, or any other finely granulated substance. If you prefer, put the dust, crumbs, dirt . . . in the container before you close it.

6. Carry this bundle with you for a week. If you can't, put it in your special place (see "Your Special Place," chapter 4).

During this week, try to love yourself up. Go hog wild and totally indulge if you want! On the other hand, if you're not used to being really good to yourself it can be best to start small: You may be able to make a list of self-love activities as long as your arm, but, in the spirit of self-love, you might want to start gently and choose just a few things and then practice them. However, you're great, so *you* decide. Do a lot, a little, or in between for whatever reason you choose.

When I did this spell, I made a list of only three things for my week: (1) don't automatically tell myself that what I just thought (did, felt) was wrong; instead, tell myself that what I'm doing is great; (2) stop and remind myself that my Divine Parents love me; (3) eat one fab yummy thing a day! Other ideas: Practice thinking nice thoughts about yourself. Give yourself nonfood treats like clothing, gadgets, or activities. Indulge in fun daydreams. Avoid situations that don't support your self-worth.

If you do a bad job at this, love and respect yourself by saying, "I'll get the hang of it eventually."

If you don't see results from the spell, don't give up, criticize yourself, or otherwise invalidate your attempt. Sometimes, change is slow. Results from a spell may come bit by bit and so slowly you think they're nonexistent. Besides, most of the time we're changing, but can't see it until long after. If you can refrain from negative thoughts about not seeing improvement, then that's self-respect and self-love right there! Ha!

Whatever your case, praise yourself for any little teeny-weeny improvement. The congratulations build self esteem (ax!) and the mini-changes are stepping stones for large change.

After this week, if you need or choose to, continue adding to your list of self-loving activities and trying to execute them. Even if you're already good at something, it can take small steps to get better at it. So you may want to add only one to three items at a time—often little goals are best. Keep this up for as long as you choose.

The First Secret of Self-Confidence

The first Wiccan secret of self-confidence is feeling good about yourself because you've done the right thing. Many try to feel better about themselves by acquiring things. They buy, buy, buy, trying to purchase self-respect. Save your money. The right clothes, car, and crowd are nothing compared to the self-confidence you gain by taking care of Mother Earth. And that overall confidence is one more step toward staying relaxed and assured in all areas of your life, including the social realm. Confidence also attracts people to you.

Wiccans honor Mother Earth as a Goddess. Instead of wasting her resources, feeling insecure and frenzied while buying far more than could ever make an individual feel good, Wiccans take care of her.

Here are ways to feel good about yourself from having done the right thing by Mother Earth: recycle. Buy bulk food instead of pre-packaged food. Eat organically grown instead of buying food the production of which pollutes the Earth. Give a donation to an environmental group. Join an environmental group (see Guide to Axes). Use organic skin care and hair products, again because it reduces pollution. Walk instead of drive whenever you can, thereby also reducing pollution. Research more ways to help the planet by doing a Web search, going to the library, or looking in the Yellow Pages for a local environmental group.

I've given lots of examples. Don't feel you have to do all of them now—or ever. If all you did was recycle, it might take some time to plan and get used to. Just do what little thing or things you can. It can take years to feel environmentally sound. And even then you'll be far from perfect. There's no way out in this culture. For example, I don't know a single person, myself included, who eats organically grown food 100 percent; we do what we can and often that means nonorganic. But those little attempts give you quiet confidence while others are subject, even if it's unconscious, to the lack of self-confidence caused by overconsumption.

Taking care of Mom Earth is only one of the many ways you can gain confidence by doing the right thing. A few ways you can check them out: "Service, One of the Secrets of Happy People," later in this chapter, and "The Vision Quest and Rites of Passage," chapter 9.

The Second Secret of Self-Confidence

Self-love is the second secret of self-confidence.

It hurts when I see a woman blind to her beauty. A parade of models, actresses, and others telling me "I look at the mirror every day. I am so ugly. I look all day at the mirror—I almost always am ugly." Each of these women is a stunning, loving beauty. Teenagers are particularly prone to not appreciating their own fabulous looks. Truly blind!

Teen males can be the same. "I'm ugly, I'm klutzy, I've no charm, nothing suave about me, I'm like an ape around girls." I feel so bad!

It hurts the same way when I see a person doubt their innate goodness. Each cell of your body if given the chance (and you are giving them the chance by using this book) reaches toward God, usefulness, and loving deeds, like a seed sprouts up toward topsoil. Like a sprout that has pushed *through* topsoil, you turn toward the fresh air of loving companions. Like the plant growing from that sprout, you turn your body so as to drink in the maximum light of God's sunny reflection, who is yourself. Darling, a plant is made of sunlight. So you are made, your very substance, of God.

Maybe you doubt this—I have doubted these things about myself. But we are both divine, and our innate godliness, goodness, will express itself in fulfillment and service. Or it will shine when we have fun for no reason other than the fun. Dancing is God.

Society often insists that men's worth resides in having the right car, right job, right home, right hobbies, right woman. Yet God, our good father, resides in each of us. He loves *himself* simply because He exists. Our values are of the same ilk—we're innately worthwhile and worthy of love and respect for ourselves and from others. We needn't *do* something to be worthy.

Although one cannot feel much self-love (self-respect), if one's always being a creep, or never pursuing goals, that is a different issue altogether. We certainly have to behave decently to *feel* decently about ourselves. Nevertheless, there is a certain type and degree of self-love that we deserve regardless of any other circumstance. No matter what, we have the right to it from ourselves and others. And feeling good about yourself is more likely to help you improve your behavior than is not valuing your innate worth as a child of the Gods.

Women may feel these same issues as men. But nothing—others' opinions of you, academic failure, sports defeats—can destroy your worth because ultimately your worth is intrinsic—it just is! When you doubt your physical beauty or innate worth, reread "The Second Secret of Self-Confidence." We all need a pep talk now and then. And try this self-love chant. Maybe memorize it to repeat (in your mind or out loud) when you're needing confidence.

Ra, Ra, Ra Chant

I will find a better way to see things, to recognize that every fiber of my being shouts "Life!" I will recognize myself as God, fully express-ing Herself, walking as the Muse and as the poet.

The Muse is God Herself. She creates a world most joyous. Blessed Be!

Guys, it may seem odd to think of yourself as a female deity. There's a purpose to this gender-bend. Try it.

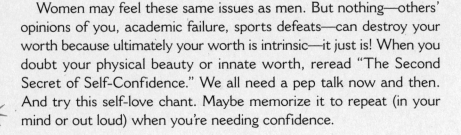

Mother Earth's Bounty No. 2: How Nature's Patterns Help Us Live Fully, Change for the Better, and Overcome Challenges

Wicca is a nature religion, another term for which is *earth-based spir-ituality*. Let's touch on some of the things this means. First of all, Wiccans believe the material world is sacred. Don't get me wrong, we're not greedy, oversexed, emotionally rampant, or irresponsible. Um, at least not more so than people of other religions! But neither are we taught to be: ashamed of wanting nice things, guilty about having a sex drive, suppressed about our feelings, or *so* "responsible" we never do anything for ourselves.

The earth is a gift to us from our Divine Parents, who want us to enjoy it and to take care of it so that there's enough to go around for generations to come. Furthermore, the Goddess and God are *in* the earth—the trees, the bees, and you and I. They're also in my cell phone and refrigerator. Because They are in everything! Every last molecule. So of course it's all sacred to me!

The cell phone, refrigerator, and all the atoms therefore are my Gods helping me to have fun and be happy and healthy. This could come in the form of the crickets that I'm hearing right now—every minute my Gods are with me, on this earth! The crickets are soothing me, helping me not worry about a romantic problem I'm having, quieting my mind and heart, so I can just enjoy focusing on writing.

Of course, since *everything* is the God and Goddess, the examples are as many as there are atoms! I decided to make a coffee mug with the following lettering on it: "This cup is the Goddess." (See Wiccan Resources for information.) This is a little fun reminder that everything is the God and Goddess and therefore, in one way or another, taking care of me.

Other more *general* ways the Gods manifest in the material world:

* This planet *feels* good to be on. Think the sound of the ocean (*my* favorite rock band), the feel of warm sand under your feet, chocolate.

* Trees, animals, and the rest of nature have patterns that are role models for us. This helps us find better ways to heal our spirits, live fully, and overcome challenges. (See "Mother Earth's Bounty No. 3: Divination—A Personal Vision," chapter 9, for more.)

* We have those same patterns in ourselves, so by studying nature we gain self-knowledge.

* We can draw on nature not only as role models and teachers, but use nature itself to empower us. A balmy breeze sweetly warming your face as you watch a gorgeous sunrise can wake up your deepest essence, inspiring you to really claim personal power and go for what you want.

* In the same vein, nature can *heal* your spirit. Think of the crickets.

The Goddess and God, as I said, are also in each and every person. We have that power in us: when we call on Their help, we might find it right inside ourselves—guidance from our inner voice, the discipline needed to ace the next exam, the courage to stand up for what we believe are just three examples.

Here is a Pagan prayer to help you draw on the divine in all you encounter.

I Am a Pagan, a Child of the Earth

> *I am a Pagan, a child of the Earth.*
> *Help me understand and draw on the patterns of nature*
> *in and around me with all their power, healing, and divinity.*
> *May the sun and the moon heal me,*
> *may ocean tides heal me,*
> *may my body heal me,*
> *may my spirit heal me,*
> *may all beings, from plant to person,*
> *plastic fork to stone, heal me.*

[Yes, it's okay to laugh at the plastic fork line. We're Pagans! We don't have to be dour in our spirituality. In fact, jokes *help* our spirituality. Humor heals, uplifts, empowers. It also helps us persevere and not become pompous.]

> *May the sun and the moon empower me,*
> *may ocean tides empower me,*

may my body empower me,
may my spirit empower me,
may all beings, from plant to person,
plastic fork to stone, empower me.
May the sun and the moon shower me with divinity,
may ocean tides shower me with divinity,
may my body shower me with divinity,
may my spirit shower me with divinity,
may all beings, from plant to person,
plastic fork to stone, shower me with divinity.
This is the truth I have spoken,
and has always been, and shall ever be. Aché.

Nature religions, like all spirituality, can be confusing. Here's one issue: Since the waxing and wanings, ups and downs, chaos and stillness, and all other natural patterns are sacred and from the Goddess, it's easy to think one has to be a doormat to whatever is going on. Or to believe it's okay to get swept up in life's mad currents, instead of being responsible for one's decisions and emotional state. Or to make any number of other mistakes.

Here's a Pagan prayer to help with that. You may want to always say it with the above prayer, so that you don't go overboard.

PRAYER: WHO AM I TODAY?

Water might be a brook, shaping itself to its surroundings.
   Water might be a torrent, shaping surroundings to itself.
   Water might mist, gently touching the surface of things. Or
   dry up, and away. Which am I, today? Tell me, am I even
   water?

When the universe created itself, it was in an explosion
   of chaos.
Life's constant chaos is part of life's constant re-creation.
Midst this chaos of atoms, feelings, and events,
help me accept this turmoil as natural.
Help me also know when this acceptance
means finding relaxed stillness midst the storm,
or being part of the storm, or staunchly resisting it,
or any endless number of other possibilities. Thank you.

Taoism is an ancient Chinese religion that, using the natural world as a role model, was an early "go with the flow" way of life. Yet it did not make one a doormat. The basic Taoist text is the *Tao Te Ching*, which is spelled different ways. A good translation is by Stephen Mitchell and published by HarperSanFrancisco.

Taoism is *very* Pagan. It teaches us to use the patterns of nature to find those same patterns in ourselves, and use them to be happy. We learn to honor, instead of condemn, our human instincts. This is all exactly what a witch does.

So if you like this section, maybe explore Taoism. It's an excellent way for a witch to tune into nature. Some people might think a young teen is too immature to understand Taoism. Taoism's hard for almost *everyone* to understand. That's why one *studies* it. You take a few lines and try to figure them out and then apply them. Spiritual development is a lifelong process. So it doesn't hurt to start young. And if your attempts are total fumbles, or you can't figure out even how to try, that's part of the journey.

Service, One of the Secrets of Happy People

As a Wiccan teacher and spiritual counselor, I've learned that many people who are trying to improve their lives or heal themselves of inner pain work very hard yet never take the last steps needed to be happy. They don't know what those steps are!

One of them is service. I don't fully understand why this is true but know it in the depths of my being, because of how serving others has helped me and because I've watched person after person not being fulfilled because they did not serve. After long years of rites to cleanse your inner blocks to happiness (see "Removing Your Inner Blocks to

Happiness," later in this chapter) spells for empowerment, rituals to gain fun, success, and romance, you can still be quite miserable unless you serve. Then you can get snared, looking for fulfillment, self-respect, and contentment in ways that hurt you and the people around you.

Somehow, being there for others brings one serenity, fulfillment, happiness, and confidence in a way nothing else does. It can heal the otherwise unhealable wounds, as well.

If you find you cannot serve others, ask Goddess, "Help me to be of service," every day. You can also cleanse inner blocks to service. (Again, see "Removing Your Inner Blocks to Happiness"). Here are examples of blocks.

Many of my students, upon hearing me talk about the necessity of service, immediately respond, "But I already help others. In fact, I do it too much, and that's the *real* problem: I need to learn to do it less."

Good point! In their case, though, they sometimes serve for the wrong reasons. They too often are afraid to say "no" or use service like a drug, to run from their problems. Or they help someone to control or manipulate that person. Or they have another reason. Perhaps they have low self-esteem so are trying to prove themselves. If you're like them, find your inner reason(s), then cleanse away. And though I often say, "Cleanse one inner block at a time," in this case, you can do it all at once. After that, pray, "Mother, Father, help me serve for the right reasons."

Other people might not serve because they fear looking foolish, or not having enough time for their own needs, or not being good enough, or that their little bit won't make a difference.

If that's you, or you've yet another block or blocks, you can cleanse that. And one of the most important things to learn about service is: *your little bit counts!* Even if all evidence is to the contrary, do what you can, even if it's minuscule.

I cannot tell you how many times I've worked on a project that could have helped a lot of people but it lacked vital support because community members either didn't think their little, tiny bit would make a difference or didn't brainstorm about what one individual could do *to* help.

Serve small, if you must, but serve. Serve your elderly grandmother with garden work once a month, or serve a stranger every day by being cheerful to everyone you meet (okay, no one could become anywhere near *that* cheerful, but it's an ideal to work toward), but serve.

And though you *can't* be perfectly cheerful every time you interact with someone, you can and should *strive* to be of service to everyone, whether family, friend, teacher, or stranger, in all your interactions.

Trying to do this really embodies, remember, one of those ultimate steps toward happiness mentioned when we began this section.

When I say "strive" I mean you can only do your best. It's an ideal to work toward, not a measuring stick you beat yourself up with.

(Repeat the following sentence three times: "This is true when it comes to all one's efforts and ideals.") That said, how *does* one strive toward this? Try to think of others, not just yourself, as much as you can. For example, fifteen-year-old Alice is really shy. So at parties she learned to seek out someone who looked uncomfortable or who had no one to talk to. Being friendly with them, her shyness instantly vanished. She's not so shy anymore.

Another example: Babs, age seventeen, says, "When I'm really nervous about what I need to say to someone, I try to focus on what I can do during our conversation to be of service to them. Maybe that means making jokes—service can simply mean helping someone have a good time; after all, service is, again, basically thinking about others' well-being. Another time, I might serve by trying to listen to their problems. In any case, the focus on that person's well-being makes my fear vanish."

These examples are not only stories of serving, they also happen to show how serving helped someone become happy! You may feel fine in the first place—but no matter how good you feel, you won't stay that way unless you think of others *a lot*.

Service also means being courteous. Thanking a store clerk is service. But empty formal politeness is not enough. The courtesy that is service is a warmth, graciousness, and consideration that make the clerk's job easy.

There are many ways to serve and to each his or her own. Doing your chores. Babysitting for sibs. Filling in when a friend can't babysit. Recycling. Playing sports, performing, or anything else that helps spectators enjoy themselves. Throwing a party, or otherwise providing pleasure. Pouring someone a glass of OJ so that she or he doesn't have to get up and get it. Helping with a fund-raiser. You'll find *your* ways.

"Celebrate an Initiation and Wiccan Secrets (Avoid Harmful Teachers and Damaging Cults)," chapter 7, explains that being a priest(ess) basically means being of service. Being a priest(ess) is hard. Being unhappy is harder. I choose happy.

Your Secret Identity—The Hero: How to Step Up to the Plate

Being a hero—aka, being of service—is great. (I use *hero* as a gender-neutral term.) You feel good about yourself when you do the right thing. You might get to make a difference in someone's life. You feel powerful.

Being a hero is also hard. It may mean sacrifice. Or the bad guy not only wins a battle but hurts you in the process. Or people might slander you or at least misunderstand. Heroism can also be searingly lonely.

But witches understand that we all need to be heroes—the world requires that of us. Here's why. Witches believe the cosmos is all interwoven, in an intricate pattern. Each part affects all other parts. I sneeze and atoms move in China—literally! Because this weave is so thorough, when any of us fail to fulfill our obligations it affects the whole. Each of us is required to be the hero, it can't be left up to just a few.

Also, Wicca is not a religion in which a priest tells us what to think and do. If we are not to be mindless followers who let others create our world, every last one of us must take the responsibility to shape the world ourselves. It is our Wiccan duty. Some religions say it is your duty to obey. I think it is our religious duty to be a hero.

Furthermore, we each need to be heroic to fulfill ourselves and have self-respect. When we live according to our convictions, we can be happy. Otherwise, at least on an unconscious level, we'll feel guilty and fake. We also only feel fulfilled when living truly. Finally, when you're a hero, you get to wear a big hero-symbol on your chest.

Although we've said that service and heroism are synonymous, whichever you call it, let's define it further. My friend, Phoebe Wray, always says, "You have to do what's appropriate." I think that sums up heroism and leaves a wide range of acts that one could call heroic from the obvious ones—demonstrating at a peace rally if you're a pacifist, going to war if you believe in it—to the less obvious ones, such as emptying the garbage. Do what's appropriate, whether it's large or small, and you're a hero.

When it comes to the large acts, not everyone is meant to deal with all types of them. But life will sooner or later present chances to "do what's appropriate" in a large way. Here are some examples:

* saying "no" to drugs, cigarettes and/or alcohol when to do so makes you feel uneasy or even badly uncomfortable
* refusing to participate in vandalism despite pressure from friends
* ditto hurtful behavior
* standing up for a friend who's picked on
* expressing an unpopular opinion or an idea that's not typical in your circles
* listening to a friend's problems all evening because that friend really needs you, and you rejected a great date to do so
* giving up a big treat you wanted to purchase, in order to donate to an important cause

Then there are the small acts of heroism. These are just as important as the large ones, because, again, it's all about doing what's appropriate. And if you don't think your emptying the garbage is important, then look at it this way. Unless everyone pitches in, someone gets stuck with all those little chores that, when added up, leave that someone overworked and exhausted. Yes, it might be a drag to haul out the garbage bags, but it's just as much a drag for everyone else, too. This is another example of thinking of everyone's well-being.

Being a hero out in the world but not in your home is only part of heroism. It's just as bad as being a hero to your dear ones and not caring about anyone else. Heroes do the right things, large and small, near and far.

Other small acts of heroism:

* thinking of others, even when you're upset or in a hurry
* refraining from gossip (and respecting confidences)
* sharing a treasured possession with a sibling
* doing an extra chore when a parent is exceptionally busy
* owning up to your folks that you did something wrong
* apologizing when you've hurt someone

You get the idea. (Though any of that list might qualify as a large heroism depending on the situation or person.)

Please don't think that all acts of heroism are yours to take on. One person helps with environmental issues by being on a crew that cleans up a beach. Another contributes by writing an article in the school newspaper about saving the rain forests. And yet another person doesn't work on environmental issues at all, because that person is swamped with household chores and it's all they can do to get passing grades—their heroism might be getting so much work done! Another person's heroism might mean being good to others in small and ordinary day-to-day ways.

"Appropriate" doesn't mean rushing in headstrong either. This section causes me to worry, because I don't want you running out and getting in over your head. Don't let unhealthy guilt or impetuousness drive you into half-baked heroic acts that get you really hurt. If something's really threatening to you or someone else, discuss it with an adult. They can help you strategize, choose your battles, and stay safe. If there are really large battles confronting you, don't go it alone. Heroes don't, despite the movies' portrayal of them. Real heroes rally their troops for support. And teens need adult input; that's part of troop support.

Of course, sometimes there's no time for discussion. If you come upon a friend who is being physically hurt, what might you do? If you don't know, discuss this with parents, teachers, and peers. Take a poll in your school—ask everyone their thoughts about the issue—to get clearer yourself, then publish the poll in the school newspaper to help others become clearer as well. And don't give yourself a mindless answer, saying automatically "I'd help" or "No way." First, think about risk, the fact that you'd want someone to intervene if *you*

were attacked, your ability to fight, how bullies become more and more bullying over time, hurting more and more people if unchallenged, the possibility of weapons, how many assailants might be involved, and so forth. This will better prepare you to make a sane decision should an actual situation occur. Run through possible scenarios, as a way to thoughtfully pursue your answers.

Myself? Quite honestly, I don't know what I would do. So I better go discuss it. Practice what I preach. I do know this: I am seriously disabled physically, so would be of no help in a fight. I would have to factor that in. Being appropriate means looking at all the facts.

It also means assessing risks—I mentioned only a few above—as well as understanding the difference between healthy and unhealthy sacrifice. I could hardly sum all that up here, but will say the following.

It's easy to sacrifice more, or less, than is appropriate. It's easy to sacrifice the wrong things. Think about this. Pray "Goddess and God, help me sacrifice as much as is appropriate. Help me sacrifice only the right things." Dialogue with friends, family, teachers. Chat online about it. Ask people what they think is appropriate sacrifice.

As to risk assessment, that is not a strong point of youth. Get adult input. And any political strategist will tell you—sometimes if there's no support, just wait. So if your parents, teachers, or other adults cannot give you advice and other help, back off from the heroic act.

Heroism is a complex issue that I've only just touched on here. It's too complex to be dealt with without ongoing dialogue with adults (this is true even *for* adults). Yet its complexities must be dealt with because there *is* possible risk. So don't be a hero alone. Be careful, go slow, talk with adults, pray for guidance.

If you don't feel like a hero yet, then start small, until you understand what being a hero is, and how to lessen risks. You're young, and the time you are in is your training ground—go slow, so you survive to perform many heroic acts once you're fully adult. And then? Real heroes still assess risks, dialogue with folks more experienced, choose their battles, and keep cool.

For now, start with taking out the garbage.

Finally, be aware that taking care of yourself in ways both large and small is a service to others. We need you! Take care of your spirit, too, with fun and sun. That's also a service. We need you happy!

The Witch Who Is a Bitch

This section's for the gals.

Francesca's dictionary for bad-girl witches says, "*Bitch:* a free spirit. This woman answers to *herself*. She's not afraid of raising a ruckus, let alone a few eyebrows."

The word "bitch" has been used to keep women in place. If you stand up for yourself, you're called a bitch. If you express your opinion, especially in a way that is confident and unapologetic, you're a "bitch." Take care of yourself, instead of always putting others first—someone might define you as a "bitch."

So in more recent years, women have claimed the word proudly. The word "bitch" means a woman who lives the life *she* believes in. She is feisty. A bitch may demonstrate mischievousness, a deep, throaty laugh, and regal cockiness. You get the picture. If you want to try it on for size, do the ritual below. Or use the rite to celebrate, or expand, your already existing impish grin.

SPELL TO BECOME A BITCH

Use the following steps in the order given. The first three steps may take a few days, weeks, or longer. Or you may do them all in one single hour!

1. Think of all the stupid, stupid things you've heard that keep women meek, timid, bound, or unconfident. Write them down.

2. Bury it! Or rip it up into pieces so tiny they won't plug up the toilet, and flush. Of course, some plumbing's so old *anything* plugs it up. Plugged toilets are not good magic—you want this list *gone*!

3. Choose a famous bitch for a role model. Maybe you like the gutsy, no-holds-barred vocals of a certain singer. Or the sultry confidence of an old-time movie star. Maybe there's a proud, sure political activist who stands her ground in the face of bullying corporations. Maybe there's an activist who's not contemporary but whom you learned about in a history class. If you don't have a role model already, search for one.

4. Write her name on a piece of paper.

5. Do this and the rest of the steps one right after the other. Don't for example wait an hour between steps. On the floor, lay the paper on which you've written the name.

6. Take five minutes during which you recite the role model's name over and over, like a mantra. This can be out loud or silently. As you do so, prance about like a crazy lady, moving in a circle around the paper with the name. This might mean you make faces, stick your tongue out, jump up and down, pretend you're a dancer in a chorus-girl kick-line, play air guitar, act like a gorilla, or imitate a macho guy's walk. Or how about falling down on the floor like a puppet whose strings have just been cut, and doing it again and again. Whoo!

   Those are, of course, just some ideas. Just act crazy, however you choose. (*Real* magic can be terribly dumb!)

If you don't feel capable of being really silly, just do what you can. If you can do nothing, then instead use "Spell to Remove Inner Problems" to cleanse away whatever is inside you that keeps you from doing this step. After all, I'm asking only that you *act* crazy. Do the cleansing after doing steps 1 and 2 of *this* spell. Then proceed with this spell only if you feel able to act at least a *little* nutty in step 6. Otherwise, this is not your spell (yet). But steps 1 and 2 plus the cleansing might bit-by-bit kick in and after a few weeks or months—*voilà*—a dancing fool.

The inner blocks you cleanse in "Spell to Remove Inner Problems" may coincide with negative beliefs listed in *this* spell. No problem. If they get addressed in one spell, you needn't deal with them in the other.

7. Do something fun or challenging. Have this activity planned before you start the ritual because otherwise you might not be in a state to choose something, or might choose something inappropriate.

   Do not choose a challenge that involves talking with someone who is problematic. The spell *will* help you have the chutzpah (nerve) needed to stand up for yourself, but right now, during step 7, the power will still be too fresh, and not have settled in properly yet.

   You might get carried away and embarrass yourself, or lose

control and make a mess of whatever you're attempting. Worse, you're likely to go too far, lose your cool, and do something serious you'll regret.

And choose a small challenge. Maybe you're a *little* afraid of trying to write a song. Write the song. Or you've written a story and *almost* have the nerve to submit it to a magazine. Submit the story. Maybe wearing less dowdy clothes is a big challenge. But perhaps window-shopping for them is less intimidating though still a bit of a challenge. Window-shop.

You instead could do something fun. But nothing high risk. In other words, you may be a champion skier, but now's not the time to ski. Neither challenge nor fun should involve much risk during step 7. And do not choose a challenge or fun activity that could end up putting you in a volatile or especially vulnerable situation.

8. Lie down, rest for five minutes. If you fall asleep, and take a long nap or are out for the night, that's fine.

   During the five-minute rest, try to not plan, meditate, or do anything else but rest. Operative word: try. If you feel fidgety, don't worry, no matter how fidgety.

9. As soon as the rest or sleep is over, rip up the paper that has the bitch name on it and scatter the pieces wherever you want.

Wait three days, ideally, before trying out your newfound "bitch wings." They need time to grow properly and beautifully feathered, powerful enough to carry you in your flights as a "wickedly" free spirit. And if you try to fly with them too soon, you might crash. For example, you might take on more than you can handle in a confrontation, or cause a situation to blow up on yourself. (If you were healthily a bitch when you started this spell still do the waiting or the same problems could happen. You've affirmed your power. It needs a chance to establish itself correctly before you can safely use your new level of strength.)

After three days, you're a witch-bitch (or more of one than ever). The spell is done!

Celebrating Menses and Other Passages

Many bodily events mark a person's passages through life—for example, the onset of menstruation, the onset of menopause, childbirth, and the acquisition of hair in the genital area. These moments in time earmark coming to power! Each represents wonderful new powers in a person's life. Unfortunately, our culture tends to embarrass us about most of these bodily events. Society tends to view them oddly, and so avoids these topics.

Okay, these are very private issues, so I don't go along with people who go to the other extreme, ignoring one's tender feelings about life's changes. Change can be frightening, puzzling, and upsetting. So you have a right to privacy about such things. But this society's fostering of unnecessary shame and mortification regarding issues that we may already feel awkward about makes it worse.

Witches claim and celebrate new powers through ritual. Witches appreciate their power! And such rites can be an antidote to shame.

RITUAL TO CELEBRATE FIRST MENSES AND OTHER PASSAGES: A POWER BUNDLE

This ritual can be done any time after one's first menstruation. It would be nice to do it right when you have your first period, but if you do not have that opportunity—perhaps you bought this book after three years of menstruating—do it when you choose.

You can instead, or in addition, use the spell to celebrate the appearance of genital or facial hair.

If you are a woman who grows more facial hair than others your age, celebrate it in the rite! Mind you, I don't sport a mustache! I wax. But facial hair on women is not freakish. And some women are comfortable keeping lots of hair on their face. Whether you "wear" your facial hair or not, honoring it ritually can bring you power. (By the way, ladies, don't get rid of a bit of fluff on your face. No one notices it!)

Read through the following rite to see what supplies you need. Have them all at hand when you start the ritual. You want to focus as much as possible during the spell, undistracted by the collection of your supplies.

Step 1. Depending on what you're celebrating, snip off one pubic hair (one!) or dab a bit of menstrual blood on some tissue. If facial hair is the celebrated item, men, wait until you can shave. Then put a nominal amount of the shaving on a tissue. Women, don't cut off facial hair—tweeze a single hair and use that. Neat option: fold your hair or shavings between pieces of scotch tape so that you don't lose it. Add both facial and genital hair if you choose.

If you're a gal, you can collect both hair and blood.

Step 2. Put a pinch of the culinary herb, thyme, and a pinch of salt into a small red pouch. Small pouches of red flannel are traditional for making power bundles (which is what we're making here). Another color or fabric will work, as will a flat piece of fabric that you bunch up and wrap a string around to secure. You can buy the red flannel pouches in occult shops or make them yourself. They're just simple drawstring bags. In a pinch, use an envelope. It'll work fine.

Step 3. Recite silently or out loud as you hold the hair, blood, or both, "I gain power." Say this three times. Then add, "Mother, Father, show me the beauties, meanings, mysteries, and purposes of my new powers. Teach me to wield my power well, both effectively and ethically."

Step 4. When we gain a new power, we also gain responsibility. For example, with the sexuality of adolescence comes the need for sexual accountability, morals, boundaries, prudence, and restraint. Part of this is thinking things through instead of causing a pregnancy, for example. Say three times: "I honor my new powers by acknowledging the responsibilities they carry." Power without responsibility hurts you.

Step 5. Put the hair and/or blood with the thyme and salt. Close the bag (wrap the bundle, seal the envelope).

Step 6. Sit for five minutes and breathe in and out through your nostrils as slowly as possible (unless, of course, you have a physical condition that does not allow this). See if any thoughts come to you. You might receive a divinely inspired message. If not, it might come later. But if something does, you're lucky. However, if something frightening pops into your head, it may not be the truth. It's very easy to mishear the Goddess and God, whether you're a novice or longtime expert-magician. And if nothing comes, not to worry. You've opened yourself to guidance, and it'll come when you need it.

Step 7. Say, "Thank you, Divine Mother and Father, for my new powers."

The power bundle you've made is very precious. Kept in your special place (see "Your Special Place," chapter 4), it feeds magical power to all your spells. Kept on your person during an important or challenging event it might quietly, invisibly help you stay calm and give you whatever else it takes to succeed.

As you mature, your power bundle will acquire more magical power. You will never outgrow it, and more uses for it might be revealed as time passes.

If, however, you decide you don't want it (I don't know why you might make that choice, but I'll tell you just in case):

Say out loud or in the silence of your mind: "To the four directions, to all directions, to the Mother and Father, my power goes, but it is always mine. No harm can come. My will be done as my strength spreads touching all things, and all things feed my strength back to me."

Bury the bundle. If no place exists for this, or if it might become unearthed within a year after it's buried, or if you simply prefer another method of disposal, tear or cut the container into small pieces, and throw it away. Then throw away the rest of the power bundle in another receptacle.

When you dispose of the bundle you do not lose its power. Rather, the bundle weaves with the cosmos and your power remains. However, it's a different energy than if you kept the bundle, and you can't use it the same way. These different usages are outside the scope of this book, but I gave disposal instructions in case you need them, sigh, because of a nosey sibling or other problem.

Should you ever lose your bundle, here is how to see no harm could possibly come to you, for example, an enemy using the bundle to control or hurt you. Take a pair of scissors, or use your index and middle finger as if they were scissors, and while you make a cutting motion say silently, "My bundle is not my bundle. My power is mine alone" or something similar. Then put on a shirt, blouse, or T-shirt inside out or backward. Next, walk away from where you put the shirt on without looking back. Walk away for at least thirty seconds. Then, use Glinda's bubble every morning for a week or so or use "Spell of the Thin Red Line: Trust and Protection." You're safe.

There are many types of power bundles, with varying degrees of strength. This one is very strong and, as I said, can become stronger and stronger as time passes. While making this bundle is by no means obligatory, it's good to claim any power within your reach. It's fun! And we need all the power we can get!

Removing Your Inner Blocks to Happiness

There are often blocks inside a person that keep them from being happy. Feelings or thoughts can give us terrible trouble. For instance, Beth believed that no one could enjoy her company, so she never said a word when in the company of others, and it was a self-fulfilled prophecy. Or look at Ariel, who stayed angry at her best bud for *months*, so that they finally parted ways. How about George's jealousy making him miserable, or Bruce's fear of failure keeping him from trying out for sports? Or Mary's belief that she could *never* learn how to dress prettily so she didn't realize she had a good eye for clothes? They all used the following spell to help them overcome the problem.

SPELL TO REMOVE INNER PROBLEMS

Do each step before moving on to the next, rather than trying to do several at once.

1. Choose one thing inside you that you want gone—examples: a troublesome thought, stifling feeling, self-defeating belief, pressing fear, nagging resentment. We often have to do magic in little chunks, so that it gets the chance to really work. Therefore, it is usually best to choose just one thing that you want to get rid of. Here are more ideas of things to choose: shyness, confusion, guilt, the belief "I shouldn't care about material things," fear of looking dumb or being laughed at if you do what you want. As you see, this spell has a lot going for it.

2. Then, hold a pinch of salt in your hand while you get really in touch with the thought, feeling, whatever. Or at least get as in touch with it as you are able. If that's not at all, you can continue on with the spell anyway.

3. Throw the salt over your left shoulder.

4. Say out loud or silently, "Mother Goddess, take my problem. Cleanse me of it. Or, if you think I need it, exactly as it is or in a different form, do what you will, and show me how to live accordingly. Thank you."

5. Don't worry if the problem doesn't seem gone. Give the magic a month or even more to work. Which is not to say the block won't leave immediately. It often does!

At the end of the month, you may not realize you've changed. One's terribly blind when it comes to one's own self-improvement. It often takes us months if not years to see we've made progress. If you only make a little, that's great, too. Fact is, that's how huge changes are done—step by incremental step. For example, athletes have to train very hard to make just a little improvement. Perseverance is everything.

In fact, after you've cleansed one inner block, please don't feel you have to stop there. Using this ritual twice a week, on a different block each time, is a great way to bit by bit overcome your major inner challenges. Or, if you prefer, only use the cleansing when a block becomes apparent.

And what's wonderful is that when you cleanse one inner block, even if you see no improvement, other blocks often disappear or are more easily removed. Also, after you've worked on a few, a cleansing you did months ago may now have effect.

Don't go crazy and do this spell constantly. By and large two blocks per week is *plenty*, and that *only* now and then. As I said earlier, you are not damaged goods; don't do constant cleansings as if you are. You'll just feel worse. Do spells for other things or you become one-sided in your view of yourself.

If you don't see change, feel free to repeat the spell on the same block after a month or two passes, or give it more time before repeating. Or maybe you should trust that the spell is done, and the Goddess has Her own plan: note the ritual's prayer. The Goddess may bless your magic by removing the block or bless your spell by doing something else. Here's where we learn a secret of the adept (advanced practitioner): go with the flow. The Goddess knows best. And if you think that means you need to be miserable, no, no, no. Using this book will teach you something different!

This spell is one of the most all-purpose I know. You'll see it suggested throughout the book because it can help you in *any* area of your life. Applying it a few times will show you why.

How to Deal with Troubling Feelings

Wiccans understand that our emotions are blessings. It might be tempting to wish to be free of them. To never have your feelings hurt, to be free of fear and embarrassment, to always somehow rise above an otherwise extraordinarily painful situation—this is tempting. But we're hard-wired to feel. And because of it, we experience love, hope, joy, healing, and fulfillment.

And we are not capable of experiencing only the pleasant feelings. Suppress the difficult ones, you suppress them all. We *can*, however, learn to deal with unpleasant feelings better. This can be a lifelong study, but here are a few Wiccan ideas.

First of all, use the cleansing spell to get rid of inner turmoil that *can* leave. No point in dealing with *unnecessary* inner turmoil. Plus the prayer opens us to better coping with the problematic feelings that are inescapable. We've asked for guidance about how to do that, and it will come.

Moving on, let's be clear about the wild ride our feelings might take us on. Some of us experience widely disparate feelings from one moment to the next. We love someone, then hate them, then are indifferent, then hate *ourselves* for feeling fickle, and only two hours have passed! *Do not judge this as wrong!* Wiccans understand that feelings are just that—feelings. If you are a person who is passionate about life, the Goddess has blessed you with emotional abundance. Likely, every single feeling in the said two-hour span is valid, despite how contradictory they may be.

In addition to not condemning yourself as sick, unstable, silly, or otherwise wrong for your Goddess-given intensity, it is also important to not make your decisions change with the speed your feelings do. No matter how strong you hate, love, fear . . . , no matter how valid that hate, love, fear . . . , don't make spur-of-the-moment decisions or take spur-of-the-moment action.

Sure, our emotions help inform our decisions. But if we always let our outer life follow the route of our ever-shifting feelings, we constantly destroy whatever we build and never achieve our goals.

What of feelings of terror or suicide? These can be caused by any number of things. For one, if you have been, or are being, abused physically, sexually, or emotionally, or have been or are presently in another traumatic situation, you may have these feelings. Again, do not judge them! And realize your range of feelings may be all over the chart, and extraordinarily intense. This is a situation that requires special attention and probably special help.

Do the cleansing, but remember the ax. If you're in an awful situation, take the concrete measures needed. See Guide to Axes! Also read "Reject Physical, Emotional, or Sexual Abuse—You Are a Sacred Child of the Earth," chapter 7, because there's more you need to know. Unless you use the axes to improve your circumstances, they just keep causing you more awful nightmarish feelings and thoughts.

Sometimes, in addition, we need counseling to help us be free of our inner turmoil, confusion, or pain. Resources in the back of the book can refer you to counselors. Don't use magic *instead* of a counselor.

Suicide is the third biggest cause of death for people from ages fifteen to twenty-four.* If you want to kill yourself, you're not a freak! But it is very important not to act on these feelings! Don't be ashamed and don't stay mum out of fear. Speak out and get the help you need. The epidemic of suicide among teens is known, so the help is there. Even if the reasons *you* feel suicidal seem unique, don't give into them! The help is still there. See Guide to Axes! Get your axes!— even if you don't think you need them, don't think they will help, don't want them to help.

If you have terror or suicidal feelings, and can find no reason for it, still get help. You can also call a friend. There are people who want to help.

And, if you don't get the help you need, keep trying, no matter how many or how painful or how discouraging the roadblocks. As they say in the alcoholism recovery community, "Don't quit before the miracle."

Some people want to kill themselves because they want to feel nothing. Or they think it's the only way out. Wiccans, however, believe in reincarnation. This means that you live again and again. Which also means you don't have the choice of escape; instead, you have to solve your problems, or they just follow you into the next lifetime.

I think though that there's hope in this, and I say this despite the fact that I have had suicidal thoughts in the past. (Important: lots of

*www.cdc.gov

people feel this way, they just don't talk about it. Suicidal feelings don't make you a freak! Despair is part of the human journey. Which brings me to my point.) The reality of reincarnation forces us to, here and now, get out from under our despair and triumph into hope and joy. This means taking action, concrete action, to get the help you need to change your life and yourself. And if you don't do it now, you'll just have to, guess what, do it now anyway, because life, according to Wiccans, doesn't stop.

Great artists and movers of social change all have hit despair. If you are an innovative thinker or take a hard look at our crazy world, despair might come. But God, *no matter how much it seems otherwise, doesn't desert us. Instead She will help us replace despair with hope, tragedy with victory*. We can overcome despair and make good lives, as well as help others do the same, and change the world. I realize this doesn't make logical sense, and all I can say is: give it a try. Then try again and a zillion times again. I know this myself because I've got stories in my background that most people don't survive let alone become happy after. And I'm nothing special. So if I can do it, you can. But persistence is everything, never stopping, no matter what, even if you have temporary periods when you give up. Just pray, "Goddess, give me your power!" as often as you need.

Moving on to depression: A friend once said to me that when you're depressed, you don't think, "I'm depressed." You think, "The world's a terrible place." Often, we don't realize we're depressed.

Once we're over that state, though, we may no longer view our outer circumstances as bad as we originally did. Or, if we're in a terrible situation, when we change our emotional state, we're able to see a way to change our outward circumstance. Now, all this is very oversimplified. I'm leaving the overall topic of depression to therapists—the experts. What I *do* want to do is tell you to use the cleansing spell, in conjunction with, not instead of, the experts, should you need one. Also, I'm trying to make the points that depression can convince us we're utterly and forever defeated, living in an unsolvable nightmare; and we can change that belief. In addition, if our circumstances *are* a nightmare, then of course we're very likely to feel hopeless and depressed, but we need to fight our way out of the situation despite our feelings.

Take action! Even if it's tiny, do it. That's how all big things are done—with many tiny, tiny steps. Take action on your inner landscape, take action on your outer landscape.

Even if the ax in question seems like it won't work, you should maybe try it anyway. Example: My seventeen-year-old friend Frances was angry with her boyfriend who had hurt her feelings. She said, "I couldn't let go of it, was just *obsessed*, so remained miserable. I did a spell to focus on myself and my own happiness. And there I was, still *obsessed*. Then, as I was cooking dinner, a song popped into my head—an old tune about getting your heart broke, but then the brute loses his heart to someone else who in turn breaks *it*. The refrain is 'Goody, goody!' and all this is sung in a gleeful little melody. It's a perfect little revenge song.

"And I thought, 'I should sing this while cooking; it'll cheer me up a little.' My next thought was, 'Yeah, but it won't cheer me up very *much*.' Then the spell I had done kicked in: I said to myself, 'Every little bit helps. If I wait for something that makes me feel *totally* better, I may wait forever. Don't be all or nothing.'

"Well, I sang and sang, gleeful and merrily. And sang. And sang. And got happier. And happier. And got to feeling just fine—which I had not thought would happen—I felt great! For one thing, my feelings of revenge got vented right out of me because I let myself feel it in a fun, harmless way. I felt normal, relaxed, easygoing."

Moral: When upset, a solution might be to do *something* to get out of that mood. The activity needn't seem ideal. Something's better than nothing, every little bit helps, and your actions may work better than you think. All this is true for the most intense miseries, far worse that Frances's. The same goes for changing the situation if that caused the inner problems.

I also suggest you refrain, while taking action, from repeating to yourself, "This won't work!" or "This is stupid" or any other defeating comment. They are very effective magical chants, causing negative results!

And don't forget therapists as a vital ax for depression!

7 Spiritual Concerns of the Up and Coming: Witchcraft as a Religion

Wicca is growing at maximum speed because it offers searing relevance to a lot of people. The sections in this chapter focus on religious questions that haven't been dealt with elsewhere in the text.

Some people can't see witchcraft as a *real* religion because they become confused at magic being any *part* of a religion. Fact is, nary a religion is without it. They may call it something else—faith healing instead of healing magic, positive affirmation instead of chant, the Holy Spirit speaking through one instead of psychic reading—but it's there.

And we Wiccans celebrate that magic.

With that, on to the sections about our oh-so-magical religion.

Goddess and God: Not Your Typical Parents

Rather than going on about the Wiccan God and Goddess, let's go right into a ritual. Experience conveys Their love, beauty, and mystery better than mere words.

We'll start with just the Goddess. Later, if you want, adapt the spell for the God instead. In any case, She is the source for Wiccans so we focus more on Her to stay in touch with the source within and without. Yes, as I said earlier, the Great Mom and the Big Dad are so in love that, if She's there, He's there anyway. Never leaves Her side. But if you *focus* more on Him, you have a harder time being in touch with Her. The opposite is not true. Thus I more often do this ritual with *Her*. And, again, experiencing Them gives you a better sense of why this does not denigrate men than all my words.

THE GREAT MOTHER

Do each step *before* moving on to the next. Don't worry about how well you do any parts, how focused you are, or anything else. Simply *trying* is all that counts when it comes to the Pagan deities. And in the attempt, we improve our spirituality.

1. Think of the best mother you know or can conceive of. Perhaps she's pretty, soft-spoken, gentle, kind, nurturing. Or maybe she's

vivacious, fun, accepting, and easygoing. Maybe she's fiercely protective, competent, devoted, and endlessly loyal. Or whatever—it's up to you. It might help to write her qualities down.

2. If you can, think of another great mom. (If you're writing, continue to do so.)

3. Then another. (Write it out if you're writing.)

4. Now, the Goddess is all of the above, and more. She's *everything*. After all, She's God! (The same goes if you've adapted this rite for our Good Father.) So add to your mental or written description that She's everything above, but *perfectly* so. You can simply write down or state to yourself the last six words of the sentence before this one.

5. She is also Pagan. Thus, She is not a mean-spirited, jealous, vindictive God. She accepts us for who we are, loves and celebrates us, warts and all, and nurtures us when we're blue instead of shaming us for not being saints. When we screw up, She helps us become better people, instead of threatening us with endless punishment. She—again, remember, She's Pagan—wants us to have fun, loving companionship, yummy food, and safety in all we do. And of course, everything in step 5 is true of our male God.

6. Now, talk to Her. You can tell her about some cool event, complain about your problems, or share your plans for the next few days.

I just want you to get a feel for Her, so don't make requests. That would get in the way of what I want you to experience— how well She listens, with love, acceptance, and warmth.

As you talk to Her, use your own words—She loves *you*— and keep reminding yourself of the various things you imagined Her to be as well as my description.

7. Take a moment and be quiet, just in case anything nice happens.
8. Thank Her for listening.

I hope this ritual gave you at least a tiny glimmer of what She is like. On the other hand, perhaps you actually felt Her with you. Whatever occurred, it's a start. And starting can be the hardest part.

This is a good ritual to do in the morning if you wake up on the wrong side of the bed. Or any time you're upset. If you feel really bad, cry "on Her shoulder." Rant and rave. Wave your arms up and down in anger, explaining the injustices done you. And now that you've done steps 1 to 4, you needn't create the lists of motherly attributes again. Just reread them, as well as step 5, which is the description I added, to get back in touch with how great the Great Mom is, before you do step 6—the talking portion of the rite.

If you've done this writing in your magical journal, you'll know just where it is when you want it.

As to not asking Her for anything—there's nothing wrong with that. But sometimes it's important just to feel Her with us or, if this rite doesn't do that for you (yet?), to be reminded we are not alone. Illogical as it may seem, praying *for* something might get in the way of that. In fact, a request of Her might get in the way of the even better gifts She wants to bestow.

Let's move on to how *to* ask for stuff from our Divine Parents. They are all-giving.

A Spell to Get the Goodies

Say the following chant once:

> *Good golly, ivy, holly, God's in love with sacred Mom.*
> *He's in the earth, the trees, the leaves, the toys, our clothes,*
>   *and everything.*
> *Car or book or DVD, he lives inside it all for me.*
> *Holy Mom through Father's love, bring my heart's desire*
>   *to me.*

Then write down one concrete item that you want such as a new outfit, car, record album.

Kiss the paper. Then put it in your special place. (See "Your Special Place," chapter 4.)

Now be patient. While your desired object may come to you immediately, the Gods have Their own timetable. It can sometimes be slower—much, much slower—than our own. In addition, be open in case the object comes to you in another form from what you expected. For example, if you asked for a new dress, someone may offer to make it for you. Or if you wanted tickets to a show, a job might manifest through which you can earn money for the tickets.

If you don't get what you want, it doesn't mean the spell didn't work. You're asking for your heart's desire. That may be different from what you consciously understand.

If you don't get what you want the Gods are not punishing you or being mean. I once went through two years of hell during which I had to literally fight for my life—I was quite ill. Sometimes I could stay happy and trust that the Gods loved me and had not deserted me. Other times I was depressed and full of despair. There was so much work needed to become healthy it was almost overwhelmingly difficult. But those couple of years caused a shift in my psyche, which allowed me to make an enormous change in my life that I had wanted since childhood. This change had seemed impossible and gave me a level of happiness that I had so deeply, ardently desired. So I am not mouthing platitudes when I tell you to trust the Gods despite hard times. And, in fact, the story of the illness is nothing compared to other nightmarish times that I went through and later could see the benefit of.

If there is something you want that is not a concrete object—for example, to get out of a bad situation or to win at a basketball game—look through the book. The Gods give us many tools through which they can love us.

Read on, to get the big picture.

Glittery Gods

The Goddess and the God can be or give anything we need. They both have many aspects. Each aspect shows us one of the innumerable facets of Their power and love. But mostly I draw on the God and Goddess in Their *entirety*. That way, all bases are covered. A simple prayer—"Mom, Dad, help!"—that does it!

Being a witch, I not only get to have that trusting, fearless relationship with my deities, I also can enjoy Their glittery, magical aspects. Sometimes, She appears as the White Lady, the Muse who inspires the creative thinker. Other times She is the Dark Mother: the quiet ocean sea bed that offers us pearls and watery mysteries; the Fairy Queen who sends us visions that make us chase our truest destiny; and She whom I call either Mother Made of Emptiness or Mother Made of Blackness, the living void, Her womb the dark universe out of which all things are created. The first invocation that follows asks these aspects of the Goddess to visit you. The second invites the aspect of the male God who is magical, earthy, and filled with passion for life. I don't mean just sexual passion but the way you can have passion for a political cause, or just for living. His passion is in every green leaf, mote of dust, breath of air. He also brings us visions of a better life as well as the drive to achieve it. And he protects us, every second of the day.

These invocations can be said, or thought, to start any ritual or party, while waiting for a date, washing dishes, before doing one's divination, or during a walk on the beach. . . .

INVOCATIONS

Lady without beginning and end, come. Be in me.
White Lady, come. Be in me. Mother Made of Blackness,
   come. Be in me.
Be in us, weaving through us, and weaving each to the other,
with power, passion, joy, and healing.
Welcome, Lady.

Lord, who is the fruit of Her body, come. Be in me.
God, who is the stars in Her womb, come. Be in me.
Father who is the safety of all Your children, come. Be in me.
Be in us, weaving through us and weaving each to the other,
with power, passion, fire, and vision.
*Welcome, Lord.**

*These invocations are set to music on my album *Pick the Apple from the Tree*. See Wiccan Resources.

When you ask Them to be in you, you are asking for Their powers, love, and joy to fill you. Though you say, "Be in us, weaving through us, and weaving each to the other," you can use these invocations when alone. At such times, the "us" can be the cosmos.

When one invokes it is important to devoke. After your party, ritual, beach walk . . . say both good-bye and thank you:

Thank you Goddess and God for all your gifts. Farewell.

More on the topic of the Pagan Gods:

The Bottom Line of the Old Ways

Here's the bottom line. No matter what else you are doing spiritually, the most important thing is to *try* to both understand and do what your Divine Parents want. Of course, my obedience is to *Pagan* Gods, who want me to enjoy life in the material sense and, being Gods, know better than me how to accomplish that. For one thing, if we are all on our own, we do things that make us unhappy, without realizing it. For another, we never become as fully comfortable in our own skins as we could be, without a strong, constant connection to God and Her plan. I find this obedience an enormous struggle, and not only believe it is a goal toward which one makes a lifelong journey, but also that we'll do it far from perfectly, *every minute of the day*. Let me repeat, enormous struggle!

So don't beat yourself up. Can't get yourself to stop and consider what the God and Goddess want for you? Or you don't care? Join the human race. If the best you can do is, well, to not even try, *that's the best you can do*. I am not letting you off the hook, mind you. You are responsible for your actions and part of that is trying to do what the Cosmic Mom and Dad want. I'm just saying, we're *far* from perfect.

Anyway, whatever else you are trying to do magically or spiritually, ideally the first priority is what They want for us. I mean, believe me, it is *so* easy for me to think "Well, but They want me to be happy, so *of course* I have to go to this movie (do this spell, use this particular meditation) because it will make me happy."

But although the spiritual precept "God wants me to be happy" is vital, more important than all other spiritual tenets is "I must *try* to know and do what my Divine Parents want." For one thing, it is the ultimate way *to* your happiness.

So if, for example, you're doing a spell for success, remember that the Goddess and God's success for you may be different from what you had in mind, but it'll be even better. Even if you don't understand why.

And, if you're looking at a grassy lawn, and watching a butterfly, hoping that the greenery and butterfly might impart wisdom to you regarding a dilemma you have—all of which is great, and *so* Pagan—remember that you should ask Goddess for guidance, to help you correctly interpret the butterfly's message.

Or, if life seems to present several options, one of which you really want, remember that there may be yet another which our Cosmic Mom and Dad prefer for you right this minute. For example, if a prayer or lecture in this book suggests a few ways to deal with something, there's a million other ways not mentioned. And only divine guidance can know all these options and hence reveal which one is right for you at any given moment.

Here's the prayer for all this.

PRAYER FOR POWER ANYTIME, ANYPLACE

> *Each moment is unique.*
> *Reveal and bestow upon me its*
> *unique wisdom, unique gift, or unique solution.*
> *Help me open to the joy, solution, wisdom, and gifts you offer.*
> *Guide and empower me every moment of the day so that I*
>   *come to be fully happy. Thank you.*

Say this whenever you want. Such a prayer often helps us to fill that bottom line. Suggestions: say it when you need a boost because of a challenge ahead, resist doing what you think the Goddess wants of you, are confused, feel despair, or are fine but just want to feel *great*.

If anyone thinks, "Obey my Divine Parents? Francesca's talking down to me, telling me to mind Mommy and Daddy as if I can't think for myself. She wouldn't have said the same things to adult readers!" that frightens me. The more I teach, and the longer I live, the more I see how urgent obedience to my Goddess and God is. And that is what I have in mind, rather than the age of this book's reader. I am constantly trying to live according to the will of my parental Gods! And I see how unhappy we are when we don't. No matter my age, I will always be Their child both in the sense of Their love and care of me as well as my need to obey.

Speaking of being connected to God and Her plan:

Kind Divine Parents Hold You in Their Care (No Matter *How* Much It Seems Otherwise)

There's an old trick of tying a string around your finger to remind yourself of something. I am not talking about magic. Many people, instead of putting a note on the refrigerator or in their datebook, use the string to help them remember to mail a letter, take out the trash, or return a phone call. All this dates back to an ancient Pagan practice. The spell below works big time.

SPELL OF THE THIN RED LINE: TRUST AND PROTECTION

In ancient times, one would tie a red thread around one's wrist to remind oneself that the Goddess was there for one, totally kind and loving, no matter *how* much it seemed otherwise.

When things are good it might be easy to trust this way. But other times, or even when things *are* going well, it can be next to impossible. In fact it often *is* impossible. Strive for this trust but don't expect anything near perfection. Our busy schedules, the violence we see, the greed, cruelty, and callousness of others, our legitimate worries, fears, and perhaps even terror knock all thoughts and feelings of trust right out of us constantly. One minute we trust, the next three hours we don't. It's hard.

But do what you can to trust even though trust comes and goes with more regularity than TV commercials. Here's why:

* We need that trust or the attempt to have it to open to the guidance, protection, and strength that help us achieve our deepest desires.

* Without at least the attempt to trust, we are more likely to thoughtlessly or angrily rebel against or ignore Gods whom we mistakenly think are mean, irrelevant, or useless. Then we end up miserable despite our external fortune, or, as I said, not even have life's goodies, because we didn't let God give us what's needed within and without for happiness.

* If something awful happens, that trust or the attempt to have it helps us turn to God for whatever it takes to not give up, as well as to do everything needed to change the situation.

* Finally, trying to trust opens you to feeling cared for and embraced by the whole planet! This happens because you have opened to God's care. It is horrible to feel cosmically orphaned instead of finding the flow of goodness that is in everything and takes care of us. You might not see it because horrible events or terrible people or even life's ups and downs, busyness and dizziness hide it, but you can find it. Don't quit until you do. If it becomes hidden again as it will, find it again, and don't quit!

Wearing the red thread has another effect: it's a very deep protection. We're connected to our Parents. This safety is not separate from the trust discussed thus far. Trying to trust opens you to protection.

I know that sometimes people pray, trust, and try to live as God wants but still are in nightmare situations. Eventually persistence will prevail—I said *eventually*, so don't quit using your axes until you triumph!—and trust helps our Gods keep us safe enough to at least try again and again until we win out. Slim though the red thread is, slim or even nonexistent though God's protection might seem, the protection of the red thread is strong and will lead you to victory and happiness.

If your thread breaks, that means it's time, if you so desire, to renew the reminder of trust and the magical protection by tying a new string on.

If you've no red thread, use red ribbon or cloth, or another color thread.

Guys, now that you've been introduced to the Goddess and God— "Hi, how do you do? So, you're a God, huh?"—we're in a position to discuss your relationship with the Gods as a man:

The Goddess and Guys

This one's for the men.

The Goddess loves guys! Why else would She have made them? Why else would She have a boyfriend? It's soooo easy to think that Wicca's emphasis on the Goddess is gender biased. Goddess-focused spirituality is not the exact polar opposite of God-focused religion. Nor does it fall into the stupid trap of saying men and women are the exact opposite but equal. We're equal but not opposites! Just different, in complex, wonderful (sometimes confusing) ways. Wicca honors that complexity, embraces the male principle, and celebrates it.

Elsewhere this book talks about how the Goddess and God are in everything that exists—you, me, the trees, the TV. There are many reasons They choose to be on earth with us. But one is that He incarnated here as a caretaker to protect life and uphold those who need defending. As such, the male force in every atom of the universe has a deep desire to fulfill this job. A man who is a witch has also been given this responsibility—to protect the earth and its children.

At the time of creation the Goddess knew that Her beloved was to be caretaker of all things, an observation that She could only make of an equal, for She, Herself, is also and just as much that caretaker. They just each have their own ways of stewardship, though there's a great deal of overlap.

As you explore Wicca in this book and elsewhere, you'll see the ways the religion revels in and creates gender equality. Since gut understanding is how we come to know what Wicca is, don't try to understand too much with your head. Instead, experience. Don't read the book and judge. Try the rituals and see how it *feels* and what those feelings teach you. Then you'll experience the complexities of Wicca as a religion that loves *you*.

As to being a steward, don't run out and get in over your head, or beat yourself up for only doing what little you can. Just use this book, as it's written, and you'll see ways to, for example, take care of the earth, and do so in a sane way.

Witches whose words or deeds do not honor men are falling down on the job. Shame on them.

If you want to learn more about the gender equality of the particular Wiccan tradition I teach, enjoy an in-depth read about the complex differences that make us who we are as men and women, discover how Wicca works with that complexity to honor both, and read more Wiccan material specifically for men, check out my books *Be a Goddess!* and *Goddess Initiation*. (Don't be put off by the titles *Be a Goddess!* and *Be a Teen Goddess!* That's marketing. The content of my books isn't and to the best of my ability I wrote for both guys and gals.)

The Goddess said to God "You are my beloved, my self, and my other half." A Wiccan teacher taught me that a man needs pride. (Not that women don't, but we're not discussing them here.) Take pride in being a male witch and as you strive to do so you will be blessed beyond your wildest imaginings.

Here's a prayer to help with that. Say it when you will.

A MAN HAS PRIDE

> *Our Sweet Lord, I know you are with us on this earth, and, as a man, I reflect you. You who were born worthy of her love, just as She is worthy of yours,* Good God, as a man, I reflect you. You who walk by her as her equal, you who never leaves her side because of love—as a man, I reflect you. Good God, you whom we need not fear, as a man, I reflect you.*

---

*A gay man can use this prayer. The love can be platonic.

YOU who lead the spiral dance of ecstacy
YOU who lead the spiral dance of ecstasy
YOU who lead the spiral dance of ecstasy, as a man, I reflect
*   you.*
You whose dominion is like that of the sun over the land,
*   as a man, I reflect you.*
You whose green sap drives spring budding
You who are the willow dancing and the willow dancer,
*   as a man, I reflect you.*
For I am your child come to you in love. Bring me your
*   pleasure, and share my joy.*

Divine Discussion

Having a healthy relationship means dialogue. When you dialogue with anyone, of course you both talk, you both listen. Let's look at dialogue with deity, starting with prayer. Prayer is simply talking to God.

How Pagans Pray

How Pagans pray: laugh, sing, dance, or tell God "I'm really mad at You." Or, *while* praying, Pagans might sit still, play football, wash dishes, or . . .

When you use the prayers in this book, you needn't be afraid of the Gods, cower before them in body or spirit, kneel, press your hands together like in church, or be in a designated area. All you have to do when you use the book's prayers is *use* them: just say them—out loud or silently—unless I give special instructions. That's it. If you prefer though, and I don't give instructions to the contrary, you can sing them, or dance while saying them.

You can also hurry to school while saying them, quickly recite one in a moment of crisis, run to the bathroom to get a moment's peace and pray on the toilet, or do anything else in order to either fit them or any other prayer into your life—Pagan spirituality is practical—or to enjoy the prayer.

Unless you sense otherwise, there's no need for a protective bubble when using the short simple prayers in this book, or some of the longer more complex ones. Do use the bubble for most of the latter, though, using your intuition and logic to determine if something's an exception. Prayer shouldn't ideally need protected space, but teens are psychically quite vulnerable; some of the prayers in this book move a lot of energy—they're intense! Intensity on the energetic plane can leave you too open without your sphere.

As to praying without a script, prayer needn't be formal. Our Cosmic Mom and Dad don't need fancy words. Sure, that can help, if it's *your* way of doing things. Then create poetic prayers, or use ones you find. But if your way is plain speech, be yourself with the Gods. They love *you* not an actor playing your part. ("Hi, I'm *not* a person loved by the Gods. I'm just playing one on TV.")

Feel free to say no more than "Halp!" to them. Or "Tell me what you think, *please*." Or to talk at length, the way you would to a sympathetic listener. Tell Them whatever you need to. Ramble on forever, if your thoughts are unclear. If you're angry with Them, it's okay to say so. If you're frustrated with school, it's fine to let Them know.

Prayer can also be an action, if you think of prayer as communicating to the Gods. Putting a flower in a vase as a thank you to Them is a prayer that communicates thanks, the way you thank a friend with gifts. A dance portraying love communicates love. Communicate what you will, how you will. Your Divine Parents love you, love you, love you.

Listening to the Old Gods

Guidance from the Old Gods can come in a myriad of ways.

Breathe slowly in and out through your nostrils, slowly as you can yet still feel relaxed and comfortable. This calms you down and you might receive a message about something that is going on with you. For example, a great decor for a current party you're planning or the perfect solution for a pressing problem might pop into your head.

Divination is another way the Goddess talks to us. See "Mother Earth's Bounty No. 3: Divination—A Personal Vision," chapter 9.

The Goddess also often guides us via "coincidence": song lyrics that seem relevant; unsolicited—or solicited—advice from friends, teachers, and parents; words on the side of a passing bus . . . Or, you can flip through the book and see if something leaps out at you. In other words, guidance is everywhere. You might ask, "Mom, Dad, guide me," then be open. They'll talk to you, even if it takes a week or far longer before you hear.

And don't forget, your hunches and own common sense are God speaking loud and clear.

Guidance from the Gods is not free from misinterpretation. Whether you're Christian, Wiccan, or anything else, proclaiming "It's what God(dess) told me" as a way to prove you're right when someone challenges your decision proves nothing except your pomposity.

The most spiritually advanced person knows that when you're alone with God, delusion can feel like "But I'm sure, deep in my bones" or "I have that feeling I get when I just *know* I'm right." Those feelings of sureness are wonderful guides. You're blessed if you have them. But, even when you do, they're not foolproof—input from a person is needed as a check and balance. No matter *how* sure it feels, you can still be wrong. Don't be a pompous person who's a danger to self and others.

Listen to God, trust your intuition, but then check out what you get by bouncing it off someone just to make sure.

Spiritual Maturity and Rebellion

Rebellion is a normal part of life. When a person, situation, or other influence has dominion over you, to an oppressive extent, you might rebel, and that's healthy.

In other situations, rebellion can be part of finding your own way of life. In other words, to use parents and their offspring as a relevant example—duh!—the parents may be perfectly nice, and their way of life all well and good. But perhaps it does not totally suit the offspring, who then find their own way. Often, the first steps of said offspring is rebellion: defiance, revolt. "My parents are idiots."

Oddly enough, the parents may *not* be overbearing, their ethics *not* that unfair or ridiculous. But it seems part of the human psyche that sometimes one must blame the parent, think more poorly of them than is the actual truth, then rebel against this unfair vision of the parent. Who knows why we're made this way.

So it happens.

But from there, comes the real test.

Is one going to *live* in rebellion or truly according to one's own beliefs? In other words, rebellion, as I use the word here, is a *reaction* against something. It is not an action *toward* something that is

actually one's own truth. So one might, for example, go to the opposite extreme of that which one rebels against. And two extremes are
just flip sides of the same coin! (Reread that last line! Uh huh!)

So with the two types of rebellion I've mentioned, where do you
go *after* the rebellion? Here are some ideas:

If, after the initial period of rebellion, your lips are pinched together
and the lower one is stuck out, you are still reacting not acting.

If, after time has passed, you're still seething, you are still reacting
not acting.

If you continue to blame circumstance, parents, God, or anything
else for your problems, you are still reacting . . .

Mind you, people and events *can* cause us all sorts of problems.
I'm not telling you to be in la-la land, pretending everything's pink and
dandy!

But no matter what is going on outside you, only you can do what's
needed to get your life together. Also, if one has rebelled, down the
line being open to that is part of getting it together.

Here's a rite for spiritual maturity.

THE POWER OF THREE

Find three stones, pennies, or other objects that seem suitable for this
spell.

Say the following chant.

The first power is to look back. I contemplate my past.
Who hurt me?* How? Who did I hurt? How?
What could I have done better?
No matter the fault of others, great or small,
I look back on my own, name them, and leave them behind.
I leave blame, my pain, and all my shame.

Now throw *one* rock, penny, whatever, in the direction you face. Later, you can pick it up and keep it, leave it there forever, or whatever else you choose. But for now, turn to face the opposite direction and say:

The second power is to look and move forward.
If I look behind I stumble, trip over old rage, blame, regrets,
    and shame.
So I refrain.
And in front of me I see
the person that I hope to be.

Imagine what you want to be like. If you can't, or don't know, just try to feel positive, hopeful, and dignified as you walk forward. If you do a bad job of that attitude, so what! It's trying that makes the spell!

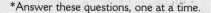

*Answer these questions, one at a time.

Then, throw a stone (penny . . .) forward, to be left there, or retrieved later, as you choose. Next recite,

> *The third power is to look within,*
> *and see the God(dess) inside of me.*

As you hold the penny (stone, rose, ice cream cone) close your eyes, and breathe slowly in and out through your nostrils. After a minute of that, leave your eyes closed, and see what happens. Maybe you'll feel great power, or perhaps an important image will pop into your head. Or you'll feel at peace. Or you'll trust that all is well. Or any number of other possibilities. If you feel nothing but antsy, that's fine, too. Magic works in mysterious ways.

Now, the grounding: talk or sing loudly. Sounds crazy but is needed, psychically. Do this for a full minute. The song or poem or whatever can be anything at all.

Then, and this is vital: lie down for five minutes and rest. Even if it makes you totally restless, do it. Otherwise, the spell can tie you into a psychic/emotional knot! This five minutes is not to meditate, think, or plan. It is a nap. Much good work happens when we rest and a deeper part of ourselves takes over.

This ritual can be used again if you face another time when you need to "grow up" and move from rebellion to spiritual maturity. This means that you, I, and anyone who is honest with themselves will need to resort to this spell occasionally until they're 106! We're never done growing! Ever.

Your Limitless Power as a God(dess), Your Tremendous Human Limits, and How This Relates to Sex, Drugs, and Personal Achievement

I am blessed to be a person who doesn't acknowledge limits—I believe I can achieve anything I pursue, and overcome all obstacles. I am also *unlucky* to be a person who *doesn't* acknowledge limits. I always think I will be the exception to the rule, and so make foolish choices, for which I pay dearly. I regret so many actions!

How is this relevant to Wicca?

Wicca teaches me that I'm a God(dess). This belief nurtures my Goddess-given feeling that nothing can stop me. All my Divine Parents' powers are within, and I can draw on them. They, like any loving parents, give me all They are able, and since They are *Gods* They are able to give a lot! This includes conferring Their powers onto me.

When others tell you your dreams are unrealistic and impossible, know you've divine power in you. If an awful situation seems to own you, heart and soul, keep telling yourself you can overcome it with your divine power. In other words, don't ever quit. Keep going after your dream life.

On the other hand—this is one of those places where accepting a contradiction is vital—Wicca teaches me I'm only human and I needn't be ashamed of my human limits and in fact have to acknowledge them and act accordingly. When people are taught by parents, shame-based religion, or culture at large that their inevitable flaws are part and parcel of some overall evil inherent in us—ick!—who's ever gonna admit to making mistakes, needing help, or being unable to do something that is really needed or desired? These individuals obtain a false pride instead, which helps them pretend to themselves and others that there's nothing they can't handle on their own, and they're never wrong, thank you very much!

Let's apply all this practically now, to sex. It's such an enormous, driving force that it can seem overwhelming. This is the power that since ancient times witches have believed spins the world on its axis. And, with the vigor and assuredness of youth, it's easy to be swept along life's sexual currents feeling invulnerable, the exception, and not needing adult input.

Fact is, *adults* need adult input. At least *mature* adults acknowledge this need, especially when it comes to sex. Sex is an enormous blessing, joy, and force for goodness and healing. With all that power, the flip side of sex is that there is little in life more confusing, compelling, and capable of harm. Even those who choose celibacy still might get bumped about, for example, by the intensity of their feelings or those of their partners. No one, adult or teen, can figure out their sex life without input from others. And teens need adult input. The same goes for drug issues.

Fact is, no one can live their life well without input from others. Important decisions cannot be made and we cannot navigate life's mazes. When it comes to teenagers, this means *adult* help. This doesn't take away your inner wisdom. But do not trust that it is absolutely right. Don't go too far. It is simply a matter of balance. Elsewhere this book explains the dangers of trusting your own wisdom so completely that you make a mess of things.

One of the strengths of Wicca is that you learn to trust the quiet sure voice within you—it reflects the deity you are. I've made sure this book helps you do that! Just as important a strength of Wicca is that you learn that other people's ideas are *equally* the voice of Goddess speaking to us. The most advanced spiritual practitioner knows when to simply bow to the wisdom of someone else; even if that practitioner is not sure the other person is right, they know there's a time to act as if the other person is right. (That is, if the other person is really trustworthy—you might try following their advice and see if it works.) This is not being a sheep and may not make sense. It is not a matter of logic. Evidence proves such humility leads to people becoming happy on the material and spiritual plane. If you have not seen such evidence, then I hope you'll trust me on this long enough to see for yourself.

Another Wiccan power is elder respect: we listen to our elders and often do what they tell us, trusting that they know better than us. I'm an elder but have elders myself whose wisdom I bow to. Not all elders are smart; some are even abusive in what they say. Find the smart elders and let them help you.

Next point: if you're going to have sex, educate yourself. If you plow ahead into sex instead of becoming educated about it first it's the equivalent of saying you're the invulnerable exception to the inevitable human consequences of uninformed sexuality. Don't put blinders on that way, and act as if by pseudo-magic there can't be consequences for sexual activity. (Ditto drugs. Educate yourself about drugs.) Pregnancy and heterosexual sex go hand in hand. In addition to pregnancy, there's a myriad of other possible problems. Sexually transmitted diseases (STDs) for one. STDs are far more prevalent than most people realize. The amount of misinformation that leads to transmission is huge. For example, it's a misconception that HIV (the AIDS virus) is basically an issue that concerns gay men. AIDS is a major problem in the heterosexual community, and an enormous percentage of infected heterosexuals are quite young and not drug users.

What few bits of misinformation (and information) about sex, sexually transmitted diseases, and drugs that I point out above and below are drops in the bucket. I mention them to make two points: there's a huge amount of misinformation *and* an enormous amount of information that you need to stay healthy, both in terms of drugs and sexual activity, and to avoid an unintended pregnancy. Get informed. Then get informed some more. See Guide to Axes.

Being informed is not enough. Discuss what you learn with an adult. Wiccans acknowledge their limits instead of hiding them in shame, embarrassment, or arrogance. Why teens need adult input regarding sex or drugs is discussed later in this section.

Here are two samplings of the enormous amount of misinformation about birth control that people will tell you are the absolute truth. "Oh, but I won't get pregnant. He'll pull out" (one of the most ineffective modes of birth control around), or "I'm on my period" (during which it *is* possible to become pregnant).

As to STDs, many teens don't know that oral sex can spread STDs. Learn the facts. (See Guide to Axes.)

Why is there so much misinformation circulating these days? Often, without intending to be mean, people spread misinformation or lie about themselves. This is not just a teenage thing. People want to feel important or bolster up their low self-esteem—"Yeah, I've had sex, sure," "Nope, marijuana won't hurt you. I know, I've tried it"—or perhaps someone thinks it helps to tell you something *wrong* rather than to tell you nothing at all. I don't get it but you'd be shocked how often people do that. Other times, people are embarrassed to say they don't know. Additionally, both adults and teens try to control others by lying.

You need to know many things to stay healthy if you choose to engage in sex. I want to *touch* on just one: use condoms and learn to use them *effectively*. I can't teach you. You need to educate yourself if your folks or school don't. Again, please refer to Guide to Axes.

Here are a *few* reasons to use condoms and seek out education for condom use:

* Properly used, condoms help prevent STDs.
* Condoms are needed during oral sex to prevent STDs; don't let anyone tell you differently.
* Most people—including adults—use condoms ineffectively, for example, breaking them in the middle of sexual intercourse. This is not necessary if you learn proper usage. You can go ten years and not break a condom.
* Condoms are only effective when used correctly.
* Instructions on condom packages may be incomplete, insufficient, or misleading. And as I write this, legislation is pending that may make labels more confusing.
* Sex with a condom can feel fabulous.
* Heterosexual ladies and gay men, don't leave proper condom use up to your partner. Make sure your partner knows how to use the condom and that they are willing to do so.
* It's too risky not to have "safe sex." You are not the exception, and one exposure to HIV can give you the virus.

Clearly, if there's any reason you cannot convince yourself to have "safe sex," change that. For example, if you are afraid of losing your beloved's affection by saying something, talk with a counselor. Or if you need more self-esteem and assuredness to take care of yourself, you can pray for it. Or use "Power of Choice" for the courage to ask for what you need from your sweetie, or look through the book for spells or axes that might feel more to the point for *you*. If sex topics make you too uncomfortable, consider waiting on sex until you're comfortable enough with your partner to talk about things that matter so much to you.

With that, let's refute a few lies about drugs. Alcohol *is* a drug: it is addictive and destroys people's minds, and both deadly violence and car crashes often involve alcohol. Drugs are *not* a way to handle family, academic, social, and other pressures. Fact is, they make you less able to cope. Look through this book for other ways. Witches have them!

When I was a kid (Oh, no, not the "when I was a kid" rap—but you knew it had to happen eventually) we laughed behind the teacher's back at the film showing marijuana to be a serious, dangerous drug. Now that I've been around the block, I know that marijuana does lead to what many people consider more serious drugs and is incredibly dangerous in itself. For example, it causes horrible paranoia and auto accidents. Marijuana also evaporates common sense so people have unsafe sex, which can lead to STDs. And marijuana is addictive: people often can't quit using it on their own. These are only examples of the many potential problems. Educate yourself.

Don't use drugs. Sure, you're at an age when experimentation is important, you may want people who use drugs to like you, and relatives may use drugs (remember: alcohol is a drug). Don't use drugs.

Drugs and magic combined can turn you into psychic toast. There's some chance that won't happen. Not much. Being doped does not a God(dess) make.

In ancient cultures, drugs were used magically; folks had ways to do it safely. People were trained for years so that their psyche would not be damaged by the limited—note the word *limited*—magical drug use that happened. This training, along with a mind-set that had been drummed into them since birth, and which cannot almost ever be duplicated in today's culture, is the reason the drug did not cause psychosis. In addition, there were rituals and social structures in place so that after the limited drug use a person had what was needed to, again, stay sane. Respect the limits humans have.

Magic aside, drugs *might* open you up to mysticism but almost always you will not stay open. Mysticism is not something you get by taking a pill, no matter what some old hippie says (and I'm an old hippie, so I know what I'm talking about). The ancients did not use drugs alone, but with training before and after so that the mysticism was authentic and practically useful. Drugs do not give you mysticism—

end of sentence. If you want to find or increase your mysticism, use this book—including the spells for personal transformation—instead of drugs, even if the book seems irrelevant to mysticism. Wiccan training is a subtle, complex weave.

In my tradition, some of the adult students pursue a lengthy, vigorous training, which, among other things, tremendously increases and refines their psychic perception. Many of them say that drugs or alcohol actually decrease what they've gained. That is the case with me. I can't take so much as a sip of alcohol without all my psychic pores shutting down. I am enormously psychic otherwise.

For more about developing your mysticism, drug-free, see Wiccan Resources.

You need to discuss with an adult the info you learn about sex and drugs. Information about STDs, pregnancy, drug problems, etc., is not enough. Many a person well past the teen years has ignored the facts they knew because he or she couldn't say "no" or refrain from acting on impulse or sexual desires, and thought, "Maybe it'll be okay." That thought however has caused a large number of serious problems, including AIDS cases and drug deaths. Acting in self-love and self-respect when it comes to sex can be almost overwhelmingly difficult *at any age*. Maybe drugs, too. But it is possible if you don't do it alone. So though you need to be armed with the facts, that's not enough. Discuss your facts, dilemmas, and particular situations with a parent, a trusted relative, or another reasonable adult.

Summary of this chapter-section: you can live your dreams; if you know your limits; you are not the exception to the harm done drug users or the consequences of sexual activity; don't go it alone; get informed from a professional source; listen to adults; run your info about sex and drugs by them; and drugs suck.

One of a spiritual seeker's challenges is to be teachable. You can simply ask, "make me teachable." It is a great prayer to use as often as needed. Even a God(dess) needs to learn and grow.

Celebrate an Initiation and Wiccan Secrets
(Avoid Harmful Teachers and Damaging Cults)

This section teaches you how to do a self-initiation. An initiation is a powerful ritual, so there is a lot of background to read before doing the actual rite: A witch's first initiation is a *dedication*, the act of

* Committing oneself to the spiritual principles of the Wiccan religion

* Putting oneself into the care of the God and Goddess as Their child, for Them to empower, guide, protect, and in all ways care for

* Pledging to be a priest(ess). This means one commits to the service of others; this is the true meaning of priest(ess)—to serve humbly as opposed to lording it over others. The service can take different forms. "Service, One of the Secrets of

Happy People," in chapter 6, says exactly how people can be of service. A Wiccan needn't lead rituals, tell fortunes, or perform magic for anyone in order to be a priest(ess). Just be good to people, whether that means doing your part of the household chores, driving Mom to the doctor when she's sick, or getting good grades because that will enable you to be of service in your future.

Finally, a dedication entails a few other things that will be discussed.

Though one doesn't need to do an initiation to practice Wicca, if one *commits* to the path, or at least wants to try it out at a deeper level, initiation is one of the steps for many witches. Other witches attain the same ends through different means.

Don't get into an ego trip about your initiation or anyone else's. Ego trips are one sign of cults or Wiccan groups that do more harm than good. Like any segment of society, Wiccans have their share of both the good and the bad. Initiation is one keystone of how to distinguish one from the other.

Initiation and the secrets of the Wiccan world that I will get to soon are also pivotal doors either into power or into the clutches of a bad practitioner, cult, or other damaging occult group. Then there are the lesser harms that seem to gather around the issues of secrets and initiations. Therefore I will try to address some of what can come up, along the whole spectrum, from the disastrously harmful to lesser problems. (Note that lesser problems can often lead to the larger ones.) Having said all that:

Initiation does not make anyone superior. Nor is one initiation better than another.

If someone acts better than you and declares him or herself privy to Wiccan secrets that make them superior, better-equipped, or deeper; whether said high-muckety-muck offers to share said secrets or not, run! You will always feel you're not up to snuff around them. And that's the *best*-case scenario. At worst, they could be an immoral psychopath.

Secrets may come as part of your self-initiation. They may also come by sitting at a pond, or by cleaning the house for someone too ill to do it.

Wiccan secrets (defined below) come to open hearts and discerning minds. Secrets come to the ardent seeker. Secrets also come from teachers.

But no matter how good the teacher, the student may or may not hear the secret. Because if the secret is not in your heart anyway, or you're not ready yet, the teacher cannot reveal it to you. And perhaps a given teacher is not the one to teach you *your* secrets. Everyone has their *own* secrets.

Which brings me to: what *is* a Wiccan secret?

Many things.

It might be magical—a certain powerful spell that is not taught until one has studied the psychic techniques needed in order to do the spell safely and effectively. Or the secret might be mystical—a wonderful experience that you discover on your own or a teacher leads you to.

Secrets often come in or after initiations. The initiation rite, for example, might be a profound experience. In which case, the experience might be the secret, or prepare you for a secret or secrets taught you by universe or teacher. This experience in the initiation is a gift from the Goddess for ultimately it is She who initiates anyone.

And the self-same secret might come to you without the initiation! I cannot emphasize this enough! Read this paragraph three times. The Goddess gives her gifts where and as She will.

The secret also could be something other than magical or mystical.

I'll tell you this—if it is represented in a snotty way, then someone's desecrating it, so don't study with the person(s) involved. You may encounter peer pressure and want to be accepted. But sometimes, if you want to dedicate in a real way, you have to refuse to fall into line. Secrets, as we've defined them, are often of a nature that they should only be spoken of humbly and *rarely*. Otherwise the ego gets in there and destroys their immense value. And your prospective Wiccan pal is at best an egomaniac. He or she could even be quite damaging.

And if someone starts to divulge secrets that make you ashamed, don't hang with that person. Leave immediately. Shameful secrets are signs of cults, misguided practitioners, and evildoers. Should someone tell you a secret they want you to lie about, watch out. Lying is wrong, not part of Wicca. Anyone asking you to lie could be anything from evil to foolish. You might end up just as hurt going along with the latter.

There's also the spiritual secret. It is your time alone with the Gods, or the service you do that people don't know about. (This time alone with deity might be at the dinner table while your parents are fighting and you're praying for patience. It's an *inner* solitude.)

A spiritual secret just means that you don't brag. Of course, one's relationship with a God is so wonderful and precious. It can be like water to a person struggling in the desert. It can get us through the hardest times and be sheer joy during good times. But as soon as we boast of it, we lose our way and we lose that secret. Because this relationship is a gift given, and one is ungracious to brag of gifts.

Therefore, we keep the gift a "secret." Mind you, we *can* talk of it. But it depends how. Here's what I mean: First of all, it's OK to take pride in your good acts. That's self-respect, a Wiccan trait. But don't go too far. The ability to do good is also a gift given. Be grateful for it, and speak of it *that* way rather than brag about it.

In the same vein, it's really good to let someone know you love your relationship with the God and Goddess, and how it helps you. Perhaps this will motivate your listener to grow spiritually.

But as soon as you brag about your spiritual secret, you lose it. And people who boast of their special relationship with God are cult-minded fundies: "I'm so special, the rest of the world is lost." Ugh!

Keeping mum can be really hard. If, for example, other witches slander you, saying you do bad things, you may want to fight back, and state all the good things you do.

But fact is, good do-ers are often slandered. People attack greatness. And to address their hurtful claims only feeds the fire. (See "Gossip," in chapter 8, for more info on how to deal with it.) And this is what separates the successful people, successful witches, from the wannabe: you just go about your business, having special times with the Gods, being of service, enjoying life, and being responsible.

This advice is difficult to follow, no question. You might find yourself sobbing repeatedly, alone or on a friend's shoulder. You might temporarily lose faith in humankind or in some segment of it or in Wicca. You may not be able to *completely* refrain from trying to impress the gossiper or others with your goodness.

But, fact is, as soon as the relationship with deities or good acts become badges, emblems of our worthiness, we've lost our spiritual way. And as such, we've lost a "secret" that we need to regain. We're also approaching cult mentality, and this is true whether we're Wiccan, Christian, or anything else.

I watched a major Pagan leader go down the spiritual toilet. It was terrifying to observe. He had sacrificed much to serve the Old Gods. What goodness! Then he became impressed with that. He thought his sacrifices and the enormous amount of help he had given others made him better than other people. He did not understand that since the ability to serve selflessly is a gift *he could not take credit for it. Others simply had not been given that gift.* (Yes, again, be proud of your good works. I'm talking about having a balanced way of looking at things.) His feelings of superiority eventually caused his demise, big time.

As soon as you feel superior, you start to cut yourself off from the Goddess and God. Because you are no longer connecting to Them within Their human children, you no longer love and honor Them within other people by respecting those people.

We will address all this in the following initiation. To dedicate as the child of the Goddess means to be humble.

THE INITIATION OF THE COPPER ROSE: A SELF-INITIATION RITUAL

The Initiation of the Copper Rose is used, among other things, as the Third Road's (my tradition's) teen initiation.

Step 1. Read the section "Service, One of the Secrets of Happy People," in chapter 6. If you've read it already, reread it.

Step 2. Read "The Second Secret of Self-Confidence," chapter 6, within a week, maybe two, of executing step 1.

Step 3. Within a few days of finishing step 2, find an hour's time for all the rest of the ritual. In that hour, start out, of course, with your Glinda-like bubble.

Step 4. Say out loud or in your mind: "I will try to learn, live, and grow the Wiccan Way. I put myself into your, my Mother and Father's, care so that you may give me your love, power, and protection. I pray you always give me the humility to be like a child so that I stay open to your help. I pray for the pride of the Old Ways—to know I deserve joy, know I am a unique shining star in the heavens, know I am beloved of the Old Gods. To know that I am a God(dess) with the power to accomplish whatever I want in life. I pray for the discernment of the Old Ways—to know when to be humble or when to be proud."

Step 5. This step is broken into pieces. Do each before going on to the next.

* Picture in your mind's eye a rose.
* See its stem.
* See a few leaves and a thorn on it.

* This is a magical rose, so imagine its petals are copper colored like a penny, and shine like polished metal. If you've not been able to visualize *any* of the rose, the attempt is all that matters.
* Say, "Holy Mother, Gentle Father, I give you this rose. It is myself: In giving myself—this rose—to you, I honor my beauty, power, and godhood. I am a copper rose."

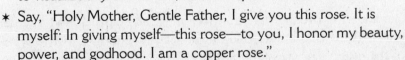

If you don't believe you are beautiful, powerful, or a God(dess), say the above anyway. At least *I* know it's not a lie! It's true the moment you're born. You are a God(dess!)

Step 6. If there is a piece of jewelry you wish to wear—whether occasionally or all the time—use this step. The jewelry can be any material or shape. Its job is to remind you of and tune you into the power of Wicca. Hold the item and say, simply, "Mother, Father, use this to help me."

Step 7. Sit, lie, or stand, but as you do so, use the nostril breathing in "Charmed Jewelry," chapter 2. As you do that, see if any thoughts about service, humility, power, healthy pride, or anything else come to you. Write them down even if you think you'll remember them.

Step 8. Read "What to Do If You Have More or Wilder Energy Than You Know How to Handle," chapter 9, and use it if you think you need to.

Step 9. Do the ritual "Grounding" (see Table of Spells).

Step 10. Eat a solid meal, one low in, or without, sugar.

The initiation ritual gives you more magical, spiritual, and mundane power. But ritual alone, once again, is not enough. In the weeks, maybe even year, after your initiation, face life's challenges and your power will be great! We also learn, get magical power, and grow spiritually by facing the challenges life presents us on the mundane plane.

These challenges are also the very axes that are the mundane coun-
terpart to the rite.

Examples of challenges/axes: humbly and cheerfully serving your
family; learning to treat yourself better; giving up drugs; taking environmental action; studying harder; refusing to gossip; standing up for
what you believe in; letting yourself take a break to have some fun;
listening to advice from adults as well as following it; humbly helping
others without being noticed for it; letting others praise you for your
good works; learning to trust the Gods; and respecting your own skills.

If you wrote anything down in step 5, look at it in the weeks after
the ritual. It may be important. (It may also be gibberish, misleading,
or untrue. See "Mother Earth's Bounty No. 3: Divination—A Personal Vision," chapter 9, and "Listening to the Old Gods," chapter 7,
for thoughts about that.) It may also be important for years to come.

I recommend that you do this rite only after you've explored Wicca
for at least a few months. That way, your pledges have real meaning
for you. But I leave it up to you.

Reject Physical, Emotional, or Sexual Abuse—You Are a Sacred Child of the Earth

You are a sacred child of the Earth! Wicca is a nature religion, teaching us we are sacred and can love ourselves. This book helps you love
yourself up in many ways.

This section of the chapter focuses on a specific aspect of that: the Wiccan view of abuse and how witches overcome it. I am neither a therapist nor an expert on issues of child abuse, so I offer a *layperson's* opinion, touching on a limited number of things. If you have been or are being abused, you need more info and expertise than I have. I beg you to find it. Look at Guide to Axes. I also offer a Wiccan perspective.

Wicca is a nature religion and honors the material world. One needn't feel guilty about wanting to enjoy life in the most mundane sense of what that means. The Goddess wants us to be happy!

If you are ridden with guilt or confusion for wanting to be free of abuse and happy, use "Spell to Remove Inner Problems" to cleanse that guilt or confusion away. (In fact, witches use the same rite to cleanse away guilt and confusion about wanting other aspects of material happiness: nice clothes, social success, academic achievement.)

Moving on, people who are suffering physical, sexual, or emotional abuse are often told it's their own fault. Or they see some little thing they themselves did that seemed to have caused the problem, not realizing it was in no way their fault and the incident would have happened anyway. And perpetrators of abuse often tell their victims "You caused it" or "If you didn't act this way, I wouldn't need to hurt you" or "You want this violence (sexual abuse, etc.)." *No matter what*, no one deserves to be hurt, the *abuser* is solely responsible for the abuse, and sex between adults and children is abuse on the part of the adult. No caring adult has any sort of sexual contact with a child. I don't care if, despite your age of fifteen, you look twenty-one, dress like a sex siren, and act like Marilyn Monroe. If an adult is having sexual contact with a fifteen-year-old, there is absolutely no reason the fifteen-year-old is the cause. Again, the responsibility rests solely on the adult. And you, as a sacred child of the Earth and beloved child of Divine Parents, have a right to a better life!

Abusers often tell their victims that they are worthless. That might be part of emotional abuse that's perpetrated. And being hit or molested can destroy one's sense of worth, making one feel one doesn't deserve better.

If you are in an abusive situation, and anyone—*anyone*—tells you that you deserve it, or *you* feel you don't deserve better, or you feel worthless, listen here to these witch-words:

You're the beloved, precious child of the Earth. These is no one like you; the Goddess gave each of us unique selves, which are blessings, and whether you know yours or not yet, they're gifts that the world needs and that only you can give. If you've been abused you may find that impossible to believe. Pray, "Goddess, help me see my worth, my beauty, my holy spirit." And whether you believe you've worth or not, pretend you do by trying to escaping abuse. The self-worth will come eventually.

Also, if needed, use "Spell to Remove Inner Problems" to clear away your feeling you don't deserve better. Use the ritual to be free of *any* belief that makes you think you must accept sexual, emotional, or physical abuse, whether from teacher, relative, romantic partner, school bully, minister, or *anyone* else. Wicca is a religion of love for others *and self*.

If you're not clear whether the emotional, physical, or sexual situation you are in is abusive, understand that often victims are told that what's going on is not abuse, or the victims talk themselves out of it just to bear it all. People in the proximity of the abuse often pretend nothing's wrong, further confusing the victim. A young male may be confused because we don't hear as much about sexual abuse of males as we do of females. In a bit, I'll show you who can help you figure out whether you are being abused or not.

In any case, a vital ax if you *are* being abused is to tell an adult: parents are ideal, but if they are the abuser, cannot grasp the seriousness of the problem, or are otherwise unsuitable, you must tell someone else. I don't care if you're an honor student, a whiz with magic, *and* the best hockey player in the state, all rolled into one. No one, adult or child, can deal with trauma alone. And teens are not old enough yet to overcome abuse solely with peer support.

So, other options are a school counselor, your doctor, or a trusted relative. Look in Guide to Axes for more options of who to tell. Once you tell someone, they can help you find other axes. That is often how God works!

Any of the people I've mentioned can also help if you do not know whether you are in an abusive situation. Discuss it with one of them, who will either help you determine what's going on or refer you to someone who can.

One more ax right now: if you don't get the help you need, keep trying until you do. And if you have to try a million times, keep trying. It's hard, I know. We live in a nightmare of a world. (Yes, we also live in a wonderful world!) Terrible things go on, and the resources to change conditions are often not what they should be because of funding, politics, and just plain old uncaring. Agencies whose job it is to help often don't! But, despite all this, I also believe that each of us has to think, "Anything is possible," then do our best to make decent lives for ourselves. Please, please, please, do so!

So, if the first person you talk to doesn't help, try again. If the second is the same, try again. Keep trying until you're free no matter how long it takes or how many roadblocks you meet or how hellish it is. And keep trusting something will work. I've dug myself out of holes so deep and black, no one even thought they had a bottom! And one tool I used was persistence.

I fed that persistence by trying to believe the climb out was possible even when *all* evidence was to the contrary. And when I lost faith, I acted as if I believed anyway. Mind you, I would often despair and just plain old give up. That's to be expected. But I would also try again. I also was willing to take little steps. It's easy to think that tiny bits of progress are worthless in the face of really bad situations. I fall prey to that a lot. But it's not true at all. I've seen from my own life.

There are other relevant resources in this book if you need them. There are rituals and spirituality to boost you if you fall into despair, ways to cope with suicidal feelings, and tools to help you better understand and deep-down feel that you deserve the best life. In addi- tion, chapter 8, "Keeping Things Good, and Changing Bad *to* Good," offers more solutions.

8 Keeping Things Good, and Changing Bad *to* Good: The Troubleshooting Witch

Witches are blessed; we get to use magic to create a good life, keep things going as well as possible, and take care of problems when they arise. This chapter offers additional ways Wiccans can accomplish everything I just mentioned—ways that may not fit in elsewhere or that are specifically about problem solving. Onward!

When Someone Has Been a Jerk

This song might make you feel better—perhaps even great!—when someone's done you wrong.

How to Cheer Up When Someone Has Been a Jerk

Use the following words to the tune of "Way Down Upon the Swannee River." Don't worry about getting the lyrics and melody to line up well—you don't want to take the fun out of it. Just be easygoing. If you don't know the melody too well, that's fine. If you don't know it at *all*, use another tune, and don't worry if the result is disastrous, lyrics and tune not matching up at *all*. This spell's a thoroughly modern magic, done for fun.

Chorus

> *You're not fulfilling yo-ur karma,*
> *you're gonna get screwed.*
> *You're not fulfilling yo-ur karma,*
> *And it'll come back to you.*

Verse

> *All your days will circle ro-und,*
> *right back to this place,*
> *so you'll just have to deal with ev'ry*
> *last thing that you didn't face.*

(*Repeat* **Chorus**)

Everyone!

The lyrics are dumb but I wasn't going for a Grammy Award. I was furious because someone had been a jerk and I started improvising this ditty, almost unconsciously. My mood immediately brightened. So I want to share the tune.

If you're in truly dire straights, you may be asking too much of yourself to have a sense of humor about it all. And, sometimes the worst situation demands you laugh about it or go nuts.

This is a spell on yourself—it helps you laugh at things for a second, and lifts your spirits. Some modern Wiccans may not consider that magic. But the witch of ancient times was clever: if an action changed a situation, it was defined as a ritual. I do not mean that external or internal additions are needed. Just the simple singing of this song, for example, without doing, feeling, or thinking anything additional is a spell! Oh, for that old-fashioned magic to be back in style!

This song also embodies Wiccan spirituality. Wiccans *play*, as a way to heal their spirits. Also, the song is about karma. Some people believe that wrongs you do, unless rectified, eventually come back to *you* until you learn better! This is a simplified version of karma. Many Wiccans believe in karma, but they also poke fun at their own beliefs, as is shown by light-heartedly singing about them in this song.

However, it's a whole other thing to take glee in the fact that someone's falling down on the job so that their karma will get them.

But, it's a harmless glee. Everyone!

. . . please do not sing this in front of said jerk.

"I Really Messed Up": What to Do When You've Done Wrong Big Time

Here's what to do when you've done wrong. Admit it to yourself. If need be, figure out why you did what you did. Learn a better way. If something in you needs to change for your behavior to be different, take care of it. Own up to what you've done. Repair the damage. And as much as possible throughout all this, be compassionate to yourself.

The above order should be used, but not rigidly. To a great extent, each step can be too hard to do without having done the ones before it, but you sometimes need to jump around in order to do a step at all.

With that, let's explore each of the actions listed above. Admit it to yourself:

Acknowledging to yourself that you've done something wrong, even without the pressure of letting anyone else know, can be almost impossible. Many religions teach us to be ashamed of our mistakes, explaining that they're a sign of how despicable humans are; and that once a person admits error, he or she must beat themselves up, groveling in self-debasing guilt. We are all far from perfect, and we all make mistakes both minor and horrendous. But while *healthy* guilt motivates us to admit our errors, unhealthy guilt stands in the way of it.

When you think you might have done something wrong, be open to the idea. Ask for input if necessary because, without checking in with another person, it is just as easy to blame oneself when one is not at fault as it is to let oneself off the hook. When we admit our wrongs, we are free to live our own lives. Otherwise, we are hampered by the guilt, self-deception, and evasiveness with others that can tie us up in knots and leave no internal space for the Old Gods to fill us with the power to magically and mundanely achieve our dreams. For example, Mike was filled with guilt for stealing money at his job. He kept his mind busy with worry about his next history exam so he wouldn't have to admit to himself how badly he felt. And he couldn't look his dad in the eye. With all this going on, there was no room inside him for the Gods to fill with the courage to enter into the prestigious chess tournament he dearly wanted to win.

Onto the next step: you may have to figure out why you did whatever you did. One of my teachers taught me that we hurt people because of some injury we ourselves have sustained. On the one hand, this makes it easy for us to say, "Well of course I hurt them. I was depressed about my grades" or "She was so mean to me, I had to be mean back." That's all very well and good and with some real truth to it. Sometimes, you're backed into a corner and the other person is the *real* troublemaker or the situation is a train wreck waiting to happen. But then, we still have to admit our own mistakes, because, the fact is, there's always a good reason to hurt someone: we're tired, we're upset, they hurt us, or whatever. Just admit it so you can move on. And then, whatever your reason was for hurting somebody, see if you can learn a better way, which was the next step in the list of things to do. For spells and axes that are those better ways, there are many herein. As there are means to fulfill the next step—if something in you needs to change for your behavior to be different, take care of it. So whether you need a spell, therapist, or anything else, go to it!

You may find you can't change yet. Or ever. Some inner problems don't leave, but you'll never be left forever with any inner or outer problem that is unbearable. The Gods aren't like that.

Also, none of the process I've outlined can be done 100 percent correctly. I do some of it quite poorly. Just do what you can. It's a lifelong lesson.

The next step—owning up to what you've done—can be quite hard. Witches are practical. They borrow anything that can be helpful. The methods of Alcoholic Anonymous (A.A.) can help more than alcoholics. A.A. advises owning up to your mistakes to the person(s) you have harmed "except when to do so would injure them or others." They explain that figuring out whether further harm would be done is not easy and requires not only other people's help but that anyone else who might be hurt by your admission should have a say in the matter. Additionally, don't own up if to do so is insanely hurtful to *yourself*; any of the things you should do when you've messed up are not done in order to punish or hurt you; determine if owning up in a given situation is too hurtful to you by talking it over with an adult.

So, the next step is repairing the damage: if you steal something you give it back; if you break something, you fix it; if you hurt someone's feelings, you try to help them feel better again. As is the case with breaking something, apologizing *in words* for hurting someone's feelings may or may not be enough. For example, if you take down a friend's self-esteem, is there any *action* you can take to help build it back up, such as helping him or her develop an athletic skill that will bolster self-confidence?

Finally, as much as possible throughout all this remember to be compassionate with yourself. I've addressed this already but here are some last items: in making admission to others and repairing the damage, you needn't grovel or accept cruelty. Sure, you may have to listen to something difficult, but you're entitled to self-respect and respect from others. They may not be able to give this to you if you have done them grave wrong. Be honest with yourself about that; they may need time and healing before they can forgive or even act decently to you. And I suggest you be patient to *anyone* you've hurt regardless of the degree, if they're a little put off or not all sunshine and flowers when you make your admission. They're only being human. But don't feel you deserve it if they are over the top about it.

Love, not hatred, heals us. I've already talked about not beating yourself up. Sometimes self-love does mean being hard on yourself: admitting to having really caused someone a lot of trouble by being a terrible gossip or by taking sexual advantage of them is a difficult act of self-love that allows you to move on and make a happy life.

This has been a beginning look at what to do when you've done wrong. You'll often need far more information, in which case pray for it and don't forget your ax: The best material on the subject is in the literature of A.A., which can be obtained through the contact info in Guide to Axes. What little else that's been published mostly supports people making excuses for themselves or leaves out the vital necessity of admission and reparation, which people need to move past their errors and be able to grow not only in ways related to their immediate problem but in their life overall.

I Want Out of Here!

This section's ritual will help you get out of bad situations, great and small. Here are examples:

* not enough time to finish a big homework assignment
* lack of support from friends or family
* loneliness
* any sort of abuse that is happening to you
* being blamed for something you didn't do
* lack of money that is vitally needed
* violence at school

* negative beings or energy on the psychic plane
* lack of ideas or insights when you need to figure something out

Ax ideas: asking a teacher if you can turn in a paper late sometimes works; Guide to Axes has places you can turn if you are being abused; if you're lonely there's axes in "Mystical Tribalism," chapter 3. Also, keep trying to see situations and possibilities that present themselves as stepping-stones to a solution—important!

Spell for Getting Out of a Bad Situation

Gather up any of the following:

* plastic snakes
* plastic bugs
* plastic spiders
* dead spiders
* other dead insects
* gummy worms
* photos or drawings from magazines or other sources of bugs, worms, snakes, frightening animals, or monsters
* thumbtacks
* nails (not the ones on the human body but the ones you hammer)

You need only one item. You can do the entire spell with one plastic spider. If you want more, combine the items listed anyway you choose. For example, use seven gummy worms or three items from each category.

Drop the items on the floor. (Henceforth, I will use plurals like *items* or *objects*, just to make things simpler but, again, all you need is one item.) Sweep everything out the door. In the process bat the objects about a bit so that they move about the floor instead of in a straight line out the door—think of a hockey player's or cat's movements. If you want, tie a fresh sprig of rosemary to the broom or take a tea-spoon of dried rosemary from the kitchen spice rack and put it in a little piece of paper or cloth that you tie to the broom. *Then* do the sweeping.

Instead of sweeping, you can use your feet to nudge, kick, and/or shove the objects out the door. You can attach rosemary to one or both of your ankles first, if you so desire. Again, don't move the stuff out in one straight line—bat them about a bit.

Okay, once the icky stuff is out, pick it up without touching it. No, I don't expect you to levitate things. Before you start the ritual, find a paper towel, old sock, rag, or anything else you can put over the objects so that you touch the paper towel, rag, whatever, instead of what you've swept out the door. A glove is great, but whatever you use must be either thrown away or washed in soap and water when the spell is complete.

If you mess up and accidentally touch the objects, the spell still works, but try really hard. The attempt is important.

Once you're holding the objects, go to the nearest public trash bin and throw them in, along with the towel, rag, whatever, unless you're going to wash it.

If there are no public trash bins nearby—I don't expect you to travel for more than a few blocks—bury the stuff, throw it in a lake or ocean, or leave the house and walk away for ballpark one minute, come back, and throw this stuff away at home.

Wherever you go to make your disposal, do not run or otherwise rush there. I would prefer you not drive to the disposal site, but if there is some reason you absolutely must, be extra careful, as if there were ice on the road; the magic of this spell moves a lot of energy that we often won't notice. This makes it easy for the most mature person and advanced magician to not even realize that their concentration has dangerously faltered behind the wheel. Furthermore, since this is a spell to get out of bad situations, some of the energy will be extra unstable for a few hours after you bat the stuff out the door. That is part of why I do not want you rushing or running; you need to be extra careful for a few hours after the ritual until the energy works itself out and stabilizes for you to get your wish. By *careful* I mean not engaging in athletics or rough-housing. It also means avoiding tricky people, paying extra attention if using scissors, and so forth.

This also means that for a few hours after the spell is finished, do what you can to avoid any bad situations. This may not be possible, but do your best. Don't freak at this suggestion; magic is a science, so the instructions I give you in a spell are in keeping with that science. However, whether we're talking applying science or applying makeup, everyone, I repeat *everyone*, falls one million miles short of the ideal application. And whether it's with magic or anything else in life, they still succeed at their goal.

Finally, after you've done the disposal, do the following ritual, "Grounding."

If for some reason you cannot or prefer not to do "Spell for Getting Out of a Bad Situation", but still want to apply magic, look elsewhere in the book for a spell specific to the bad situation you're having. Or, brainstorm for a way a ritual that might seem unrelated can be applied. For example "Academic Success," chapter 9, shows how magically eating an orange can help you focus. With the improved concentration, you're better equipped to figure out a way to resolve your problem. And remember, prayer is the most powerful magic of all. The prayer "Help"—one single word—never fails.

GROUNDING

You probably won't need this spell except after "Spell for Getting Out of a Bad Situation" and a few other rites, the texts of which refer you back to here. I teach it to my adult students and it's one of our staples because the style of magic I give adults is different and often requires this grounding. In any case, everyone is different, so if you're the teen exception and need it other than for the above spell, here it is:

1. Gently slap yourself all over, from head to toe. Don't skip any part of yourself. When you get to your face and head, don't slap. Use your fingertips to gently tap your face and skull. Otherwise, ouch!

2. Stretch each part of your body just a tiny bit. Though these two steps are important it needn't be a big time-consuming deal: you only take a second or so to slap each place; all the stretching need only add up to about two minutes because although you need to stretch everyplace a tiny bit, it *is* only a *tiny* bit.

3. Tune into your body and see what it needs. For example, are you thirsty? Do you need to put on a sweater to be warm? Do you need to go to the bathroom? Take care of whatever is needed.

4. While and after you do step 3, tune in to the mundane plane in a, bluntly, moronic manner. It is very easy when doing "Spell for Getting Out of a Bad Situation" to become spaced out and not even realize it. You feel alert and do not realize that you're alert to, for example, your thoughts, but not to oncoming traffic when you're behind the wheel. The four steps of this grounding take care of this. So, in order to make sure you're on this plane, pay extra attention to

it: drive as if you had just learned your lessons, giving extra special attention to driving laws and safety rules as if you were still learning them. If you're cutting vegetables cut them extra carefully. If you're out at night, keep your street smarts about you. All this not only keeps you safe, but it grounds you back into the mundane world. It also, believe it or not, might help the spell work: although it is tempting for me to stay in a magical headspace when I'm done with a ritual, unless I instead pay attention to my mundane obligations and pleasures, the magic is just a nice daydream and won't work. I am not talking about the practical need for axes; the actual magical power of the spell won't have a chance to work.

Continue paying simple-minded attention to the mundane plane until your focus is securely and safely there.

In my grounding instructions I discuss driving, and, fact is, this grounding does make one able to drive safely after spells that require this specific type of grounding. So now you understand the grounding in its application to spells in general. But there are always exceptions: after "Spell for Getting Out of a Bad Situation" you may want to refrain from driving for a few hours.

As I said, I don't think you'll need this grounding elsewhere but it *can* be used after any spell when you're feeling spaced or if you want to make sure you're not spaced without knowing it. Or as an extra step to ensure your spell works well.

Gossip

Gossip is evil. It is not a bit mischievous, or just a little bitchy. It is not a pastime, simple fun chat, or harmless way to fill up silence when you feel awkward. It is not a minor, okay fault.

When a world of gossip is created about someone, that person can really suffer. Or worse, gossip can destroy lives. That is a dramatic sentence but it is not rhetoric. Widely spread lies or misinformation, or inappropriately shared private information that should never be passed on can leave a person seriously crumbled, or a lifetime's work ruined. Gossip is defined for our purposes as: spreading lies; sharing confidences that should be kept private; spreading confidences—or facts—that will embarrass, humiliate, or otherwise needlessly hurt someone; and *repeating anything you heard secondhand*. About the last item: even if your best friend said something, it is only her or his opinion, so do not repeat it. That's difficult, but crucial.

There *is* some info that should not be held in confidence. If someone feels suicidal or is otherwise in serious trouble; if you think someone might be heading for trouble or possibly about to hurt someone else, blow the whistle. Tell a trusted adult. Witches try to be responsible; sometimes it's okay to rat.

Also, it's not gossip when you discuss what you see going on with schoolmates, family, or others to become clear about life and yourself. That's important talk. It's needed to develop and strengthen your insights, empathy, and people skills. Do it bunches! And realize we often might start this sort of a chat with the intention of light-hearted fun, not even realizing we have the more serious agenda of personal growth—that's great, too.

We also need to be able to discuss situations we're in—both problematic and not—without the person or people involved present, for all sorts of reasons. Perhaps you need to talk out your feelings to figure out if you're in love, or to vent frustration without taking it out on someone. Or maybe you need to talk about the best way to handle a situation's opportunities, problems, or complexities before directly dealing with those involved. You may have yet other reasons. Go for it!

And sometimes we have to break confidences or share sensitive info because it's the only way we can talk about something that affects or worries us.

It's a simple fact that while doing any of the stuff I've just defined as *not* gossip, you may find yourself *getting* gossipy, for a variety of reasons. For example, you're upset and not doing your best. It is important to be able to talk about life, both its problems and joys, and you won't ever be perfect in the process.

If you are the subject of gossip, here's what to do.

The ax: do not gossip. This includes defending yourself against it. As soon as you say, for example, "But it's not true," or "No, here's what really happened . . ." you're hooked into the gossip. You're pretty soon spouting, "Here's the real story. They were really bad to me . . ." and it becomes a no-win game because you'll not only sound spiteful, and feel spiteful, but you'll also be gossiping yourself, in a way. Or, in trying to show your side of it all, you just dig yourself in deeper and deeper because, guess what?—you're trying to *prove* yourself to someone, which never works. There are two ways this might happen.

First, the person to whom you're defending yourself has a certain view of you. In responding to that view, you are buying into it, instead of speaking on your own terms. So you can't win. In other words, gossip has a language and as soon as you respond to it, you must respond in that language. And according to that language, you've already been condemned. Second, you can't prove yourself because in and of itself talk can't do that. Only action can.

You *can* give people a chance to learn gossip is not true by letting them hang out with you and see you in action. But this will not work if they're committed to believing the gossip and just want to see you upset and squirming, and you're totally on the hot seat. Therefore, use this option only if you think the person in question is truly open.

You should also know that gossips attack anyone doing anything worthwhile. It's awful, but true. It is not easy trying to do something important. Yet one also has to deal with the pain and damage caused by gossips.

All this means it's really difficult to not respond to gossip. But you can't win if you do.

Moving on, if someone shares gossip with you about a third party, don't join in. You probably shouldn't tell the speaker he or she is gossiping because it's likely to make the person defensive, which helps nothing. But you can say and do what *you* want. So change the topic

as soon as possible. Say, "You know, that's hearsay. Let's talk about something else," then plow into another topic without pausing for breath. The only way this will work is if it is said and done pleasantly, calmly, and courteously. Or try "I know someone you really love and trust told you that, but it's still hearsay." Ditto say it nicely.

If someone asks, "Have you heard about . . .?" and you know where it's going, respond, "Naw. I don't want to talk about it." Again, say it pleasantly, in an off-hand way as if it's no big deal. (Once I hear a little bit of someone's gossip I might get hooked in and listen to it all and get all wound up. So I like to nip it in the bud.)

In some cases, you may want to stand up for a friend who is being gossiped about. We need our friends during such times. But, again, don't try to *prove* anything to the gossipers or anyone who believed them. You may just fuel the fire. The best route might be to just refute the gossip in simple terms without going into explanations, details, complexities, stories, or private matters. A straightforward sentence like "My friend would never do something like that" or

"That story's not true; my bud's a good egg," may be all that's needed. And people will see that the subject of the gossip is not alone! Reread my instructions for dealing with gossip about yourself—you might get more ideas about how to best defend a friend.

If someone brings you gossip about yourself, say: "The next time someone says something about me that is not nice, please don't tell me." Or "That's hearsay." If someone says, "So and so says such and such about you. I'd like to give you a chance and listen to your side of the story," I respond, "I do not participate in gossip. That includes defending myself against it."

The ways I am offering you can be incredibly difficult if the gossip about you is really bad. But, fact is, there's no choice about whether to defend or not. Defending oneself against gossip is impossible. (See exceptions later in this section.)

What you *can* do is stay true to yourself. Take the time you would have lost if embroiled in trying to refute gossip to live your life to the hilt. Be yourself, help others, pursue greatness! (And that'll disprove the gossip to a lot of folks!) And don't despair! Though you might feel *really* bad, if you become overcome, they've won! Do what it takes to stay strong! Look through the Table of Contents and Table of Spells for ideas.

And, now that you've read all those axes, what you can *also* do is defend yourself magically, with the following spell.

SPELL TO STOP GOSSIP

Do the following steps in the order given.

1. Look inside and see what in *you* might make you gossip. Do not skip this step! Whether you would actually gossip or not, the impulses, at least, are in you. Whether you find them or not, continue:

2. Pray, "Help me not gossip."

3. Sprinkle a bit of salt into a small box or paper bag. If box, choose one that can be closed.

4. Put something in the box that is roughly the shape of a tongue (almond, leaf, false fingernail, jalapeño pepper, piece of paper cut in the shape of a tongue).

5. Add something approximately mouth shaped (wax candy lips, shelled pecan half, rough sketch of a mouth, two leaves, seeds, or sea shells glued together).

6. Add something somewhat ear shaped (seashell, seed, leaf, photo of ear cut out of a magazine, false ear from a Halloween costume, dried apricot).

7. Close the box or bag, as you say, "Gossip, be weakened."

8. Tie up the package with some string, thread, rope, tape, or anything else. A rubber band or two is fine. When you finish this say, "Gossip, be bound!"

9. Jump up and down on the package—or hit it with your hand—ten times. Then say, "Gossip, be crushed."

10. If the package falls apart, get a new box or bag, stuff everything into it, and re-wrap with string or whatever (it needn't be the same thing you secured the package with the first time).

11. Dump the package in the trash. Gossip is trash and should be treated as such. (Conversely, gossips are not trash. They have a problem and need to be loved into health.)

12. Brush the palms of your hands back and forth against each other several times as if brushing the last traces of gossip off them.

13. Say three positive things: one about yourself, one about life, and one about someone you dislike. If you dislike no one then someone who's not a favorite. You needn't believe anything you say as long as you sound like you do.

Don't forget all the axes. If you gossip now, the spell won't work. And telling someone, "So-and-so gossiped about me" is still being plugged into the language, headset, and lifestyle of gossip. You would just be keeping it, and the bad energy, going. Bad energy both in the sense of the sort of nasty feelings that end up in gossip, and in the sense that the spell may not work. Also, talking about gossip is—guess what?—gossip!

If you slip up and gossip, forgive yourself. If you're at least trying, the spell should still work. Spell or no spell, if you gossip a bit now and then, forgive yourself, and keep trying. If you gossip a lot, forgive yourself, and try to stop. Get whatever help you need (ax!), because you are likely causing horrible pain in someone's life, and no one, I repeat no one, no matter what you think of them, deserves that.

Talk about your tendency to gossip with your folks or a therapist (ax). Use the spell to stop your own gossip—it will help. When you perform the ritual, be self-loving instead of thinking bad thoughts about yourself and telling yourself how awful you are—if you are trying to change that's great; try to have compassion for yourself. Don't hate yourself—you are not evil, for crying out loud. We all make mistakes, really bad ones sometimes. Part of maturity is facing up and admitting to our grievous errors. Unless we admit them we can't change them. Read the section "'I Really Messed Up'—What to Do When You've Done Wrong Big Time." If you've been a bad gossip, you may need it in order to change.

You'll learn to stop gossiping bit by bit, perhaps even really quickly. When tempted, use the prayer in step 2 of "Spell to Stop Gossip."

A last word: if the damage of gossip has hurt you, get support from friends and family. The loneliness, pain, or despair you're going through might be too much to deal with alone. And you may also need help dealing with the problems the gossip might have caused at school, with an employer, or in another situation. Don't go it alone.

Of course, in such circumstances, you *do* need to say "So-and-so gossiped about me," tell your side of the story, and so on, and maybe find a wholesome way to defend yourself and clear your name.

How a Wiccan Seeks Justice

Okay, the last section discussed gossip. *This* section is about justice—and offers a magical antidote when life is unfair. So, actually, you could use it when dealing with gossip, in addition to or instead of the last section's anti-gossip spell. Other times when you might want to apply a justice ritual include: you've been blamed for something you didn't do; someone is cheating so you keep losing at sports; an adult is abusive; you are involved in a court case.

Don't forget your ax. A court case requires lawyers, preparation, items relevant to the case at hand, and so forth. Abuse should be reported and necessitates other steps as well. (See "Reject Physical, Emotional, or Sexual Abuse—You Are a Sacred Child of the Earth," chapter 7, and Guide to Axes.)

JUSTICE SPELL

Read through the spell to see what ingredients you need. Gather them before starting the spell. Have all your ingredients at hand, ready to go, or you will have to keep interrupting the ritual to go get something, and in this particular spell that can stop the flow of magic.

Sprinkle a teaspoon or so of rosemary on the floor or ground. Cupping a penny in your hands, say silently or out loud:

May the money go where it belongs.
May right triumph over wrong.

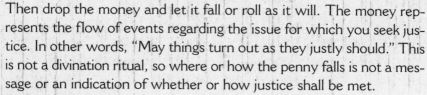

Then drop the money and let it fall or roll as it will. The money represents the flow of events regarding the issue for which you seek justice. In other words, "May things turn out as they justly should." This is not a divination ritual, so where or how the penny falls is not a message or an indication of whether or how justice shall be met.

Next, sprinkle the penny and rosemary with water. It can be a nominal sprinkle.

Clean up the rosemary and toss it. Leave the penny where it is. If your kid sister, for example, scoops the penny up, no problem. If your mom sweeps it away, so what? If you accidentally kick it aside, ditto. It's going where it belongs, and that's part of the magic. If after three days, it is still there, you can spend it, either then or whenever, or keep it as a lucky penny.

Understand that this is not a spell asking to win whether you're right or wrong. Justice, as they say, is blind and will choose whoever is in the right. However, in every situation, both parties are at least somewhat at fault. You needn't have been perfect for justice to decide in your favor. The overall picture is what's important. Before deciding to do this spell you may want to examine yourself to make sure that, by and large, you are the one in the right so that if justice is served, it will be in your favor.

This is not a revenge spell. When life is unfair, revenge calls to us like sirens call to sailors. This is not the correct way to seek justice. The dangers of using magic for revenge are many. Revenge magic always backfires. Plus the bitterness in your heart caused by revenge sours your magic and whole life. Furthermore, there is no justice in revenge.

Anything you do magically or on the mundane plane comes back to you threefold. It's not Pollyanna talk but a basic magical principle called "the law of threefold return." Ask any witch about it. Plan revenge and it will be planned against you three times as much. Be unkind and unkindness will come your way all the more. Be loving and three times the love will come to you. Be generous and the universe will be generous in kind, more than you could ever manage to be kind in the first place. It can be almost overwhelmingly difficult, even completely impossible at times, to believe that your goodness and restraint from bad-doing will ultimately come back to you. But it does. I've seen it happen, for example, to people who had so little going for them in the way of material advantages, yet their kind acts came back to them not only in warmth and love, but in material gains such as receiving a free trip to Europe or living in beautiful homes. It's a struggle, but do what you can to believe in the power of goodness to triumph over all. That's a kind of justice in itself!

Do not take anything above to mean that if bad things happen to you they are necessarily your fault! Oh, my Goddess, don't. You would have taken what I said way too far. Bad things can and will happen to the best, and most innocent, people. (And, again, goodness *will* triumph in the end—three times over.)

Protection

I give several magical protections in this book—not all in this section—so you have your choice. Everyone is different. The following simple charm may appeal to some people more than an elaborate spell.

A CHARM FOR PROTECTION

When you want to be safe on the mundane and/or spiritual plane, take a clove of garlic and just a pinch of rosemary from the kitchen. Wrap them, along with a penny, in a piece of paper, and keep that under your mattress, in one of your dresser drawers, or on your person. If you want, renew this spell in a month by tossing out the garlic and rosemary, and starting again with the same or another penny. If not, toss anyway—do what you will with the penny.

You *must* use concrete measures to keep yourself safe. They are needed not only for you to practice safe, powerful magic, but also to really have protection. If you don't know what to do, and none of the axes I point out in *Be a Teen Goddess!* are right for you, ask a trusted adult relative, clergy, teacher, or school counselor for ideas. Keep asking people until you figure something out. Different axes are needed, depending on the situation. For example, a physically abusive boyfriend has to be dealt with differently than an abusive parent.

If all is basically well in your life, so you're using this spell just as a preventive measure, your ax is to act safely when you drive, play, and otherwise live. If you're in any serious danger you may need to use the ax before you do this spell—be sensible, instead of running away from the reality of the situation by doing a spell first, and getting hurt. On the other hand, maybe the spell done first in a dire situation will help you somehow do your ax.

Here's an alternative to "A Charm for Protection."

ARACHNE'S WEB

Witches put protection on themselves and what they care about. They might do this only in threatening times or all the time as a safety measure, the same way we lock doors or install alarms to prevent thievery. Some Wiccans use protection "insurance" on an ongoing basis once they've been practicing magic for quite a while and magic's become a real part of their lifestyle. You choose.

This spell protects not only you but also your home, nearest and dearest, possessions, and projects from both mundane and psychic harm. Thread a needle with black thread. Don't forget to knot the end. Take any piece of paper large enough to use as follows.

Make stitches in the paper delineating the shape of a circle. Then sew lines repeatedly dissecting the circle through its center. Then stitch a few smaller circles within the original one. The result should look something like the drawing on the next page.

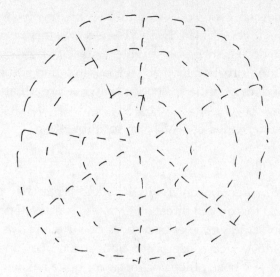

Arachne's Web

The illustration is merely a guideline: don't worry if you create something totally different, thoroughly messy, really rough, or terribly "bad." For the thread to be manageable during the sewing, keep rethreading the needle. Otherwise the thread is so long it tangles. What you're doing here is of course called embroidery—using thread to create a picture. You are not "sewing" in the sense of sewing pieces of fabric together. Just make a design with stitches. The paper will likely become quite wrinkled in order for you to sew it. That's fine. In fact, if the paper accidentally rips, consider that part of the spell's "weave" and additional strength to the protection. You needn't knot the thread when you finish making stitches with it.

As you sew, say the following chant repeatedly until done stitching. If possible, use the chant also while rethreading the needle. Fact is, it only took saying it twice for me to finish my piece.

> *Arachne wove the cosmos.*
> *Jesus' Apostles caught the fish.*
> *Atoms dance all dances.*
> *By the power of Arachne's web,*
> *the thin strings of the Savior's Apostles' nets,*
> *the atoms dance in everything,*
> *is my safety made.*
> *Protection is laid on myself, my near and dear,*
> *my home, possessions, and projects.*
> *The protection keeps out negativity and harm,*
> *but welcomes goodness, love, and any other positive force.*

The last two lines of the chant are because protection is not the same as isolation.

Arachne is a Goddess who takes the spider's form. She spins all of creation, which is Her web. So it is by the power of everything that exists that your protection is made. This is reinforced by Jesus' Apostles' nets and the atoms' dance. More power!

If you are surprised to see the name Jesus here, in a witch's spellbook, you're about to learn about old-fashioned magic: nowaday Wiccans often view their religion as a rebellion against oppressive Christianity. But we exist in our own right, and did so long before Christ walked the earth.

Jesus brought a good and holy message that many Christians live by today. Unfortunately, many others have corrupted Christ's message, making it one of intolerance, bigotry, and nasty, punishing, life-suppressing oppression. Nevertheless, witches of old have always gleaned power and wisdom wherever it was available. Christ has an amazing message of love, power, kindness, and even life-affirming fun.

So in this spell we draw on the power of Christ's love and great wisdom. If anyone thinks this is sacrilegious—Christ is a God who wants us all safe and happy. He was a carpenter—practical, down-to-earth—so would not mind a practical, magical use of His Apostles' nets.

I talk to Jesus. Although I am not Christian per se, as a Pagan I talk with any beneficent God. And Jesus tells me that although, ultimately, I belong to the Goddess, He doesn't mind helping when it's relevant.

When sewing is done, sprinkle the paper with water into which you've put a pinch of salt. As you sprinkle say, "I bind the dance within." This fixes the protective weave in place, making it secure.

The threaded paper now goes in your special place (see chapter 4). After a month (if putting the paper in your special place did not mean throwing the paper away already) dispose of it however you choose—because that's about how long the protection will last. If you want to renew it, do the spell all over again.

It's easy to be overly concerned about doing a spell exactly right. Forget it! When I was sewing my web, I had to restitch along a line I had *already* sewn in order to get to a place I could start a *new* line. I didn't think, "Oh, my, is it okay to stitch twice in one place?" Please don't fuss. Enjoy!

Protection Against Evil Spirits

This subsection of the section "Protection" focuses on how to avoid negative spirits and what to do if you run into one. First of all, Glinda's bubble alone, with or without one of the above magics or protection elsewhere in the book, may be all the magic focused on protection you ever need to avoid bad spirits. But safety also requires common sense. At the beginning of the book, I admonished, "If you're concerned, don't do it!" Let's take that further now:

* If considering a certain spell gives you a queasy, guilty, or "Bwah, ha, ha, I'll show them how powerful I am!" feeling, don't do this spell. It'll be trouble.

* If another teen witch comes up with lots of lame (read *dangerous* or *questionable*) magical ideas, she or he is dangerous, questionable (and ultimately lame, because she or he is a loser, on the way down).

* No matter how deep the longing, don't risk a spell you haven't been sufficiently trained for. Even if this spell is itself wholesome, you can leave yourself vulnerable to negative forces, from the minor to the demonic. (This book trains you for its spells.)

Teen years are a time for experimenting, and witches are individualistic and a bit rebellious by nature. I tell my adult students, "Just pretend to me that you're doing what I tell you." Though no one can perfectly follow instructions, do not worry. We do our best, we end up okay.

Onto another item: the next caution entails self-awareness and humility. But it's simple. You need to just know the following and act on it: every person has his or her own vulnerabilities. I already mentioned this but it needs more exploration.

Your age, gender, locale, personal quirks, and so on make you more vulnerable, and more resistant, to the various negative forces. Be humble enough to respect your particular limits, whether they be age or whatever. Mind you, at my age I'm vulnerable to influences that might roll right off *you*. Don't think I'm being condescending.

Also be patient—with more training, more spiritual development, or simply more years on the planet, you might be able to do things you can't yet.

The next protection is a spell.

PENTACLE OF PROTECTION

If you ever "meet" (psychically see) a bad spirit, or suspect one's presence, imagine a pentacle between you and the spirit. Here's what a pentacle looks like:

Imagine the pentacle is made of blue light, like the blue fire on a gas stove.

A pentacle can be a very effective protective barrier.

A pentacle can also be used to banish negative spirits. In this case, after you imagine the symbol in the air between you and the bad guy, say, "Be gone. The Goddess *alone* lives here. There is no space She does not fill, no place without Her will. Be gone."

Shout it if you want. Say it once, three times, or as many times as feels powerful enough.

One of my students asked me, "Some people leave their body because something traumatic happened to them. Can bad spirits then get into the space that's created?"

Yes. Antidote: do spells to remove your inner blocks to happiness. (And go to "Removing Your Inner Blocks to Happiness," chapter 6, for help with that.) Bad spirits cleave to your misery. Also work on making a better outward life.

If a few months of trying to become happier doesn't make the evil force leave, or the negativity is so huge it's really harmful, get help. See Wiccan Resources to find someone. Don't get taken in by shysters or the misinformed: some people will tell you you're haunted or possessed just to get your money or otherwise take advantage of you; and others—even witches—insist hauntings, possessions, and the like are never anything but metaphors for emotional trouble. Find someone who can tell the difference.

Although hauntings, possessions, etc. *are* real, sometimes it's just emotional turmoil in disguise. A great deal of the time, a "bad spirit" is actually just something like your anxiety, intense fear, or a real-world negative situation. Sometimes, it's hard if not impossible to tell by yourself what the real deal is. For one thing, it's easy to get paranoid and think there are evil beings when there are not.

If you need more information about negative spirits, read up—there are whole books on this topic—dialogue, pray for guidance and/or a teacher. You'll learn what you need. This subsection was a beginning—think home first aid as opposed to a doctor's care. Definitive info on demon protection and the like would take a shelf of books, plus face-to-face lessons. Don't be too proud to find a more advanced witch if you think stronger or more advanced magic than your own is needed.

And remember: protection spells are powerful against *all* negative influences whether they're on the mundane or spirit plane. Protection magic works! So if you're having trouble, use those spells! There are plenty in this book.

Using Magic to Stop Sexual Abuse

The following is a ritual to stop sexual abuse should it be happening to you or a friend. Do not perform this spell for a friend without that friend's permission.

SPELL TO END SEXUAL ABUSE

The first step may be simply to read the section "Reject Physical, Emotional, or Sexual Abuse—You Are a Sacred Child of the Earth," chapter 7. If you think that in *any* way you caused or deserved the abuse, read it. It will show you otherwise! (You should read it anyway—

whether before or after doing the spell—for its useful information.)

Sometimes, when people are abused, they worry that they are somehow like the abuser. They may, for example, think their own aggressive feelings are like the aggressive abuser, or make them like that abuser. This is not true. It is easy to think otherwise, and the abuser may even tell you you're the same. Don't believe it from him or her, and if you think it yourself for whatever reason, tell yourself that you're absolutely wrong.

Even if you think there is something in you that would ever make you sexually abusive, you are not the same. None of us are free of bad urges of one kind or another. We all have them, both great and small, fully blatant and totally subtle. Those feelings don't make us abusers. We just don't act on them.

There is no teeny little bit of you that in any way, shape, or form, directly or indirectly, makes you like the abuser.

Say the following prayer:

Free me of any belief or feeling
that I deserve abuse.

> *Keep me free from seeing*
> *[abuser's name] as me.*

If you're doing this for a friend, both of you must read this section's material that precedes the prayer, then say the prayer—that makes the magic work.

The next step is to write the abuser's name down, then write yours (and your friend's) next to it.

Cut the piece of paper between the names so you now have two separate pieces, on one of which is only the abuser's name. As you cut say, "In Our Lady's name, we are not the same, we are not the same."

Take the piece of paper with the abuser's name on it and throw it away wherever you choose.

Then take the paper with your name on it (and your friend's) and keep it in your pocket for a week. Or put it in your purse, wallet, treasure box, or any other safe place that is a *nice* place. (See "Your Special Place," chapter 4.)

You may wonder what's *nice* about your pocket. It's like you're keeping yourself (and friend) snug and safe, and securely on your own person. You may feel the same or better about your purse, wallet, or somewhere else.

Then go to "What to Do If You've More or Wilder Energy Than You Know How to Handle," chapter 9, because you might need that.

Then for sure do "Grounding."

 Some people think they need to be free of all human imperfections for this spell to work. Good Goddess! We are all very, very, *very* far from perfect. Don't let guilt about your own shortcomings, sexual or otherwise, keep you from doing this spell and anything else needed on the mundane plane to be free of abuse. You, who you actually are right this second, with all your shortcomings great and small, deserve a good life! Do what it takes.

9 You Name It, We Got It: Magical Mystical Miscellany

While no single book, spiritual path, or person has all the answers, witches do have an awful lot of options open to them. I needed a chapter in the book for all the goodies that didn't fit elsewhere. You deserve as many tools as possible to make your life the absolute yummiest. I hope you enjoy.

The Vision Quest and Rites of Passage

While ongoing Wiccan practices—what you're doing if you use this book—help you gain both magical and spiritual power, as well as other-worldly perception and spiritual insights, a *vision quest* is a moment in time—a specific event—geared toward those same ends and developing them a lot in one fell swoop. A *rite of passage* marks—or causes—a life shift or a coming into a new power. Obviously, if your vision quest causes such a shift or power, it is also a rite of passage. For our purposes, I'll use *vision quest* and *rite of passage* as by and large synonymous.

The vision quest, in addition to what I've mentioned, gives you leaps forward in wisdom, self-reliance, courage, identity, ingenuity, resoluteness, confidence, and maturity. Yes, all this happens. Powerful, to say the least. The ancient adolescent used vision quest as part of coming to adulthood.

The pack that you run with can heal Mother Earth or do other great things. A vision quest, whether alone or in the company of your pack members, can make the power to serve others and fulfill the pack members' personal goals a reality. If even only one pack member makes that quest, whether the others know about it or not, the entire pack gains power.

There are many rites of passage for teens. As powerful as the rite of passage is, life just keeps giving us the chances for yet more power. This book's self-initiation ritual and the "Ritual to Celebrate First Menses and Other Passages" are two. I'll point out some less obvious vision quests because if you see them as such you can better perceive, validate, and gain *their* often enormous gifts.

Being of service, discussed elsewhere in this book, provides many rites of passage. Overt ritual does not a rite of passage make; it's whether you grow and change. Owning up when you've done wrong, also discussed elsewhere, is a major adolescent rite of passage. The sense of self, maturity, freedom, and power gained is unparalleled.

Other rites of passage: success with a spell that makes a big, positive change in your life; large accomplishments on the material or spiritual plane; somehow bearing up when you fail on the material, spiritual, or magical plane; standing by your convictions.

Not everyone has to do all rites of passage. I'm showing you options. And there are others, just as important. You'll discover them on your own.

The power gained in vision quests is no small thing. Don't turn up your nose at any that I've pointed out, no matter how simple and unadorned it is. In the movies, you see people do so and we know how those movies play out. Think of how the movies play out when the hero is smarter!

The rite of passage is the more obvious part of a longer process without which that obvious part cannot succeed. You use this book magically and spiritually when needed to make you happy and a good person to yourself and others. Doing so, no matter how well or poorly your efforts pan out, gives you the larger context for the vision quest. It is the process as a whole that actually has importance, though far too few people are aware of that aspect of power and happiness.

Ignore people who give weight only to impressively titled rites or braggarts who say they have the *real* powers. The real powers are gained as described above. You can be like those movie heroes:

victorious in all your glory; believing in yourself; a person who does the right thing.

Think you can't use a rite of passage unless you've used a lot of the book first? Wrong! Go for it; you'll benefit loads. Then realize that you still need to do ongoing Wicca or you may lose what you gained. In fact, your ongoing Wiccan practices *afterward* are equally important as those before the rite of passage. They're follow-through, even if you don't know how.

If your vision quest doesn't seem to have helped much, not to worry. It might take time to show. Plus, it can be a year or two before we realize that we've changed!

Sometimes, men and woman use very different types of vision quests. For women one such vision quest is the ancient menstrual hut. You know the old, stupid, patriarchal taboo about women being unclean during their period? (Ooh, don't let them touch you, or touch your food!)

This nonsense is a bastardization of an earlier, truly beautiful practice that gave women great power—everything I mentioned a vision quest giving! When a woman was on her moon (a Native American expression for *period* that many witches use), she would leave the hustle and bustle of her regular life and community to go to the "menstrual hut." There, she would find solitude and take time for herself. She was not only allowed but expected to indulge in her "selfish" desires: this was her special time to focus solely on her own wants and needs. Interestingly enough, while doing so she was often very useful to her village: by creating what she *felt* like creating, just for the satisfaction the process gave her, she often made things that the community really needed.

She also might enjoy the company of other menstruating women as they all indulged together. Think pajama party, and doing each others' nails.

This solitude and healthy self-indulgence, interestingly enough, nurtured character and wisdom. It also opened her to her magical and spiritual gifts. Further, during menstruation, if a woman retreats this way, her magical power and other psychic abilities as well as spiritual insights can become stronger. This is twofold: she emerges from her special time stronger as a magician, psychic, and wise woman. More, *while* she's in her hut she experiences yet a whole extra depth of both magical and spiritual power. Ritual with other women during menstruation might accomplish some of the same empowerments.

Here is the woman's modern vision quest equivalent: during your period, try to enjoy at least an hour alone-time, during which you indulge yourself and/or spend time on your spells, divination, and spiritual life. Actually, this indulgence is not always a separate thing from your magic and spiritual life. Experiencing menstrual time devoted just to yourself will teach you why! If you want more time—an hour a day when you're on your moon, a whole afternoon at the park enjoying the sun and casting spells, an occasional weekend retreat—these are great if you can arrange them.

This might be a good time to hang out with other women. Many women who spend a lot of time together all start bleeding at the same time of the month, anyway. But, regardless, this can be a good time to bond with other women.

If you suffer terribly from menstrual cramps or premenstrual syndrome (PMS), an hour's worth of a menstrual hut can alleviate the problem. More "hut time" might work even better. This is, of course, not instead of medical attention, should it be warranted.

Now let's look at men. For their vision quests they have traditionally taken on physical challenges, such as the Native American sweat lodge where the heat is so intense it's really a trial. Modern-day equivalents would be a marathon or particularly challenging hike. I do not know if sweat lodges are appropriate for teenagers. You could find out in a local Native American community, or look for an online Native American website or chat group.

Men are usually blessed with a special and remarkable ability to vision quest through overcoming physical challenges that are external. This is their way of honoring their bodies and its relation to magic and spirit. And it gains them *everything* that results from a vision quest! Whereas women tend to be blessed with an ability to vision quest by living *within* their bodies, honoring the body just as it is and moving with its changes in their lives as women. In later years, this includes childbirth for some women, which is, of course, physically challenging.

Speaking of which, I'm not nay-saying women's sports—they're vital. And, women also come to power through physical duress, physical challenges, athletic pursuits, just as men need both solitude and the company of other men to develop their sense of self and magic. There are many ways to come to power that men and women share.

But when we recognize and try gender-based vision quests on for size we gain more and remarkable ways to come to power. I repeatedly see men miss out on these opportunities because they think they need to do Wicca like women, and women losing out because they don't know about the power they have quietly hidden within, whether they're athletic or not. I mean, men could stop thinking they should be wimps in the name of the Goddess and instead create their own destinies. And some women could replace their PMS with the power to live their dream lives. These are only two examples of what's lost if we don't know about gender-based options for vision quests.

But feel free to gender bend and do what works for *you*. That's important!

Guys, the male vision quest I've described is physically taxing, so it's not done as a monthly event. Traditionally the male vision quest was done *far* less frequently than the women's monthly menstrual hut. Try once a year? Once every few? Remember, the rest of the time, your magical lessons, such as are in this book, and life, not only give you the same thing, but make the vision quest successful. Likewise, you physically train for your hike or marathon. Training your body is part of the rite of passage.

If you cannot take on a marathon or long hike, try a daylong hike or other shorter athletic challenge. Then, instead of waiting so long between vision quests, do your day hikes or the likes.

The male vision quest provides a sense of manhood in part because it's a chance to bond with other men. Men also need time alone. There is no safe modern version of the adolescent left alone to fend for himself in the wilderness and thus come to manhood. But that older version combines physical challenge, self-reliance, and solitude, and we've covered the physical challenge already. Let's deal with solitude: you'll get that on your marathon or hike(s.) If you have a disability that prevents your participation in hikes or the like, or there's no way to hike or marathon alone, remember I am showing *options*. God will show you *yours*. Perhaps yours have to do with being unable to do what many others *can*. Be open, and you'll discover your own rites of passage, and gain special wisdoms in the process.

As for self-reliance, there's more than one way to skin a cat. (No one uses that phrase anymore and I want to bring it back.) Being of service is one way. Life, being the training the Gods give us, will provide others, ones that make sense in the context of your modern life. The youth dropped off in the forest had been trained to cope with it.

Such a challenge for you would be foolhardy and stupid. Life will present you with a challenge that modern living will have prepared you for. Plus *his* challenge was to get him ready for wilderness living. That was real life then. Your real life is now; your challenges need to be in the context of *that*, to prepare you *for* that.

Life is a rite of passage!

What to Do If You Have More or Wilder Energy Than You Know How to Handle

This section deals with your inner power when it's too much for you, whether that energy is magical, sexual, or emotional. Let's start with the magical.

After you do a spell, ideally you should feel really good, happily filled with energy. You shouldn't feel exhausted—again, this is ideally.

However, sometimes afterward you can feel *so* filled with energy that you become uncomfortable. Or energy feels stuck in one part of you, let's say your arms, rather than throughout your whole body.

In either case, blow air out of your mouth toward the sky—in other words, blow air upward—after you say inside yourself, "This excess goes to the Goddess within and the Goddess without." Then be open and you might feel some of the excess drain away into the air. The excess goes to the Goddess within you as well as to the Goddess who is our creator. Men and women both have the Goddess in them.

It might seem odd to call it *Goddess within* when you're blowing upward over your own head. But part of the Goddess within you actually is above your head. We are not just flesh, we are also spirit, which extends past our physical body.

If you still feel the problem, face the palms of the hands down and imagine the excess and/or stuck energy pouring down into the earth from your hands. If that is not sufficient, get down on the floor or ground with your forehead, shins, and forearms along the floor or ground and send more down.

More help needed? Use your imagination to gather the final excess and/or stuck energy into a wee, tiny ball placed an inch below your belly button but deep in, at the depth of your spine.

If you still have more energy or stuck energy, then the Goddess has a job for you. But you may not want to do it right then and there if you're feeling really wound up. It's easy to lose your head with all that energy. But be patient and, in the next few days, figure out what the Goddess wants from you. Good chance it's the ax that goes with the spell you just did. Or She may want you to do something to help someone else. She often gives us energy for that.

Next I'm going to teach you a witch trick that can be used when you have lots of energy that you don't like or can't handle other than an overabundance of energy after a ritual. I am no longer talking about magic. I am talking about, for example, a lot of anger, or sexual power inside you, or any other type of overwhelming feeling that you don't know what to do about. (Sex is healthy, but we don't want to be ruled by it.)

Adapt the technique. Before you blow upward say inside yourself, "Goddess within and without, use this power for the greater good of all. Guide me" instead of the words in the original version. If you need to do more, before you send downward say to yourself, "Mother Earth, take this power, to nurture both you and me so that all is wonderful for both of us." If more is needed, before you collect the last of the energy into the place below your belly button, think, "My power is mine. I am responsible. I will use it once I am ready to use it wisely and well." If there is still energy, as I said, the Goddess has a job for you. Be patient so you know what it is and can do it wisely and well. Again, She might want you to help someone. Or She might want the discomfort to motivate you to discuss with a parent, therapist, friend, or other appropriate person how to deal with the problem better.

A last note about finding peace when you are experiencing difficult energy, whether it's sexual frustration, depression, or anything else: often serenity has to be gained one minute at a time. Try to find peace just this one minute instead of thinking ahead to how hard things will be in an hour or the rest of the week. You can find real peace amid awful stuff this way.

The Witch's Coven: Why, How, When, and Why Not

Coven: *two or more Wiccans who gather in order to practice magic and/or the Wiccan religion.* **Solitary:** *A witch who practices alone.* A given individual might choose to be in a coven at one point in her or his life, then be a solitary at another. Some witches, myself included, do a lot of their magic as solitaries, but are also in covens. I like the combination because I want ritual to be woven deeply into my everyday life—I can't wait to do it only when my coven can gather—but I also love and need rituals done *with* people.

Six reasons to be in a coven:

1. It's fun.
2. The magical power of group magic is enormous.
3. The support and camaraderie of others who practice Wicca keeps one from feeling like a freak just because one believes in and enjoys magic or Fairies or the Old Gods or . . .
4. Coven members can help each other better understand magic, for example the lessons in a Wiccan book.
5. A coven offers moral support during life's challenges.
6. It's fun.

Six reasons to be a solitary:

1. It's fun.
2. The magical power of working alone is enormous.

3. You can focus undistracted on your own beliefs and experiences.

4. You can study and pursue Wicca at your own pace, emphasize your special interests, and easily do a quick spell right when you need it.

5. You've time alone with God to reinvigorate your spirit amid life's challenges.

6. It's fun!

If you want, be a solitary who is also in a coven and have everything one can gain from both approaches.

Not everyone of course has the option of coven work. But I strongly suggest it, should the opportunity arise, at least for a while. One of its strengths is that it might keep you real—less likely to get so "holy" and pie-in-the-sky magical that you think you're the highest of the high-muckety-mucks that ever existed. Working alone can make you a bit grandiose.

On the other hand, the wrong coven could offer some "holy," pie-in-the-sky Wiccan priest(ess) who may fill the group with that grandiose attitude, or at least make the rest of the group feel inferior to his or her oh-so-grand self.

And certainly it is fine to work magic alone. I couldn't bear losing the power and fun of it! Besides, if you're going to really *live* your Wiccan beliefs, instead of being like some Christians who go to church on Sunday but ignore their religion the rest of the week, you can't wait for your coven to gather every time you want to just pray or do a little ritual. Therefore at least a little of your work may need to be alone, unless you feel too insecure to practice Wicca unsupported or just can't get yourself to do it alone.

In any case, never join a coven where anything seems the least bit shady or off. "Celebrate an Initiation and Wiccan Secrets (Avoid Harmful Teachers and Damaging Cults)," chapter 7, helps you recognize cults and nasty Wiccan groups.

Creating a coven is simple. You say "Let's be in a coven." Okay, if you want more, develop a secret handshake. It'll give you something to laugh about, and you ain't a real witch yet until you can laugh at yourself about being one.

Some people want to be in a coven only with a best friend, or a few very close friends. Other people gather with friends who are sufficiently trusted but not necessarily bosom buddies. Still other people get to know each other by being in a coven, but, of course, this isn't safe if the person or people involved are total strangers or suspect.

Some covens gather as needed, or wanted, others once a month—perhaps on the full moon—and others every month and a half. It's totally up to the group—my coven meets an hour to an hour and a half once a week, by phone.

We use three-way calling. We want the chance to meet, and reap the benefits thereof, every week. A little phone meeting makes this possible. Many witches, however, don't like, or can't do, that short a meeting, let alone enjoy it by phone.

Of course, you can gather for Wiccan practices without being an actual coven—for example, I do a lot of rituals with people in class to teach them how, and also have gotten together with a person or group just once or twice because we had a specific need or mutual interest. Perhaps a coven might have a guest for a session or even for a while; this might be done just for fun, or to help with a problem, or as a way to see if the guest and the coven feel right about continuing *as* a coven.

One needn't commit to a coven forever. The group can decide they'll exist for a specific length of time—e.g. a year, two years, until graduation, until a certain goal is achieved—or they might simply say, "Let's do this as long as we feel like it, then stop." Or they might decide to be in the coven for a month, two, three, as a trial run, in order to see if, in fact, they want to *be* a coven, then go from there.

Meetings might be one hour, a whole evening, a daylong trek, or any variation you might come up with. Activities could include doing spells in this book, studying parts of this book together and discussing them, visits to metaphysical stores online or in-person, or a simple potluck. I suggest the latter because sometimes witches just need to get together with each other simply to hang out and be themselves. In any case, my suggestions are just that. Use them, reject them, create other activities if you want. And here are more ideas.

Figure out which spell a coven member might need for a certain situation she or he is in. Clean up a beach of its litter as a way to

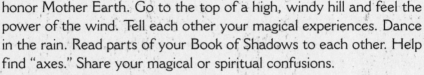

honor Mother Earth. Go to the top of a high, windy hill and feel the power of the wind. Tell each other your magical experiences. Dance in the rain. Read parts of your Book of Shadows to each other. Help find "axes." Share your magical or spiritual confusions.

Of course, some of these things combine with each other as a matter of course. But even those activities can be specifically chosen as an activity for a meeting, and much gained thereby.

Finally, while some covens may last ten to twenty years, others may disappointingly die after a week. Bless yourself and the members of a failed coven for trying, don't hold on to indignant resentment (use "Spell to Remove Inner Problems" and/or talk it over with your folks and friends), and don't walk away from a good friend just because you're not suitable coven mates. Even if your coven attempt ends in a big fight, or brings out someone's worst traits, try not to think "Well, if (s)he acted like that, I guess I was blind before this, and (s)he was never any good anyway." Perhaps those negative traits you saw only come out in certain situations, and once the coven disbands, so will the problem—unless you hold on to resentments or don't forgive. Or maybe this is a chance to love someone, faults and all. It is an important part of the spiritual life to accept people despite their flaws. Otherwise, given the fact that everyone is *so* far from perfect, you end up mighty lonely, off in your "I can't accept anyone's faults" ivory tower. (Damn! So often, as I write this book, I think "I

wish adults would read this. We need it, too." I know some supposed
adults who are still stomping around in so-called moral righteousness,
complaining about what so-and-so did five years ago in their covens!
The loss of friendship is a terrible thing, and sometimes we don't realize what we've missed out on until years later, if ever. Furthermore,
those indignant adults are so busy being angry and "right" that they
miss out on life and love. Don't be like them.)

A closing joke: how is a coven different from a church? . . . . There
are brooms parked outside!

Okay, that was bad.

Money Is Sweet!

Money's good! Bucks for a great date, the bass guitar you've been
eyeing in a store window—nice. Money's also part of our most basic
survival. And it pays for the things that help us feel secure, such as
health insurance.

In the following spell you ask God for money. Some people might
object, primly announcing, "God is not Santa Claus." Blah, blah. As
I've said elsewhere in this book, my Gods are *Pagans*—They do not
think wanting material goodies is a sin. They are thoroughly delighted
to help us acquire abundance.

Anyway, Santa Claus is a holdover from a male Pagan God. Ho, ho, ho to that prim naysayer. My Wiccan friend, Kathi Somers, prays to Santa Claus year-round. And when my coven mate, Thom Fowler, during the planning of one of the coven's rituals, suggested asking Santa for whatever we want, I was game and we had a great time.

MONEY SPELL

1. Decide the minimal amount of money you need. I say *minimal* because you don't want to shut out receiving more than that. And this spell, as you'll see, will allow more to come, perhaps even causing it. Whether it's a lump sum, or an amount you want over time, write the figure down.

Don't be greedy: your figure should be the minimum you need to do whatever it is you have in mind. Within that minimal can be luxuries galore, mind you. Do go for the amount of money that'll allow those luxuries! The whole cosmos will conspire to help you receive it. You are the child of the earth and sky, of the stars and cosmos. But, as Matthew Fox shares in his book, *Original Blessing*, there are enough resources for everyone to have bounty, but not enough if some people are selfish.

And if you're greedy, the cosmos will either thwart your spell or allow its success so you can learn better (and you'll likely be miserable as a way to learn!).

2. Do two fun things, ideally within a week after you write down

your desired amount of money. (Some ideas follow.) But let it take however long it takes. So if you're slow to get around to it, whatever the reason, just move on to the next step when you're ready.

Everyone's idea of fun is different, but here are some ideas:

Rent a favorite DVD or video. Take a bubble bath while singing the theme song from *SpongeBob SquarePants*. Play football. Go out dancing. Cut up a chocolate-caramel-with-nuts candy bar, name all the pieces, then say "Bye-bye" to each of them before they leave for a holiday (destination: your tummy, by route of your mouth). Put on music and dance for five minutes in your bedroom. Water the garden. Cast a fun spell. Make a homemade birthday card. Eat a food you loved when you were little. Write a poem. Write a slogan you'd like to put on a T-shirt. (Yet another activity would be to print that slogan in a great font and photocopy it on a T-shirt. You can call copy shops to find one with a machine that accommodates fabric. On to more amusements:) Put colored streaks in your hair. (There are colors that wash out with one shampoo. That way, you needn't raise too many eyebrows or live with something that might only suit you for a day or so.) Read a fairy tale. Go to a museum or monster truck rally.

If you choose an activity that's more time consuming, feel free to count it as one or two activities.

If you're in the middle of trauma right now you may feel it's over the top of me to ask you to have fun. You might be right.

If so, go through the motions for the sake of the spell. The act of at least *trying* to have fun or, if it suits you better, going through the motions sets up internal currents that make the next steps of the ritual effective, as well as creates an external flow of goodness to you which the money can ride in on.

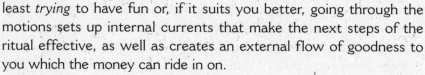

Spell aside, I've learned that play, pleasure, and humor can some-how happen in the middle of a day it seems Stephen King scripted. And that's when they may *need* to happen if you're to handle truly horrible times with any semblance of hope and clear-headedness.

Give it a try and you may find, despite your expectations, that you are able to play, and that it helps you with your problems by giving you a break or making you feel more hopeful, or freeing your mind from worries long enough that solutions come to mind.

In *any* case, it'll help you with the spell.

3. Ask God for whatever amount you wrote down adding the words "at least." Say "Please give me at least $80,000" or ask Her in your own words, whether elaborate or simple, lengthy or brief, poetic or plain.

4. Now do two *bad* things. Well, I don't mean *actually* bad. ("What is it with my spiritual teacher? First she tells me to have fun, but that I don't really have to have it. Then she tells me to do something bad, but not really in truth bad. Huh?") What I mean is those things that people enjoy *pretending* are bad, like eating ice cream with twice as much chocolate syrup as could possibly be reasonable. Or things that some people have wrongly told you are bad, like doing something nice

for yourself instead of never giving yourself any fun or goodies. As was the case with the two fun things, if it takes you forever to get around to this, don't worry. For one thing, your inner blocks to prosperity, whether conscious or not, might stop you from moving on with the spell, and need some time to work themselves out on an unconscious or even conscious level.

If however you find yourself never getting around to finishing the spell, at this time or any other point, you might want to see if something inside you is going on about money and keeping you from finishing. For example, maybe you don't think you deserve abundance. Or you've been told that you shouldn't care about material things. Or you fear success. If you find something, cleanse it away in "Spell to Remove Inner Problems."

5. Optional but good to do if possible: use the nostril breathing in "Waking Up Magic," to help you focus for the following step.

6. Below are words spoken by the Goddess to you. Read them slowly:

> *The earth conspires. Shsh, can you hear her? All the plants*
> *conspire. Shsh, can you hear their rustle? Do you hear the*
> *stars singing to you, you who are another star, a soul*
> *companion to the earth and sky?*
> *Do you see the conspiracy of all things to love you, or are*
> *you blind?*

It matters not, my child. Nor do your powers, weaknesses,
   good points, or faults, my beloved child. All that matters is
   that the weave is mine and I enfold it around you, waft it
   through you; in fact, it is *you.*
Abundance is yours, you can be sure.
I love you.

7. Say, "Thank you, Mother, for your unconditional love. You give me everything, simply because you love me." Some might think that because these spells involve internal work or external acts that don't seem magical on the surface, the spells are not *real*, but metaphors. I hate metaphor disguised as magic. It bores me. I'm not criticizing it. Each to his own. And if you see this book as metaphors, I support that. I'm saying it isn't fun or effective for *me*. Anyway, real magic, with its glittery feel and power to work miracles, is a natural part of being human; it is in our hearts and souls and bodies; so we must use our own beings as a magical tool, the most potent of all.

8. Now make an offering to Her. Options:

* Put a flower in a vase. (You don't have to let anybody know that what you're doing is an offering unless you want.)
* Go into your backyard and pour a tablespoon or so of water on the ground along with about a tablespoon of any food.

* During a meal, after you've consumed everything but approximately a tablespoon each of food and beverage, eat and drink them knowing that you're doing it as the Goddess' stand-in.
* Do something nice for somebody. It can be a single, quite small act.
* Pull out one strand of hair—I said *one*. It doesn't hurt, if you pull quickly. Then go for a walk subtly dropping the hair on the ground anywhere outside. If you want, also spit once on the ground.
* If your nails need cutting, do so and when you dump them in the wastebasket think to yourself, "For you, Mother."
* Say in the quiet of your own mind, "Mother, I offer you this moment of my time." Then, sit for a minute doing the nostril breathing in "Waking Up Magic."
* Make this prayer, "May all beings find happiness," three times over a week.

Don't forget your ax. You could look for an after-school or weekend job, borrow money, tell someone you want it for your birthday, forsake eating out for a bit and save that money, brainstorm with a friend about a way to earn cash just for a week or so, pray for ideas about the best ax to use or ask your folks for ideas.

Academic Success

Want to go on to a college program that will train you to be a symphony conductor? Maybe instead *your* dream is not so much about the career per se but about earning oodles of cash so that you can vacation all over the world and own a second home in France.

Or perhaps you look forward to studying for a degree in education because you know you'd love to teach kindergarten. Or maybe your idea of the future is just getting a passing grade the next few months so that your folks don't ground you for life. Whatever makes you want academic achievement, below is a ritual for improving your scholastic career.

The spell helps you concentrate when doing homework. (You'll see later the ritual has many other uses, but let's stick to concentration for now.) Concentration is hard sometimes. For one thing, some of what we have to learn is incredibly boring, yet still demanding—let's face it.

And you might as well learn to deal with it now because you won't escape this when you get older. I *choose* to be a writer. But the hours of tedium required—proofing typewritten pages, correcting galleys, researching for book proposals, on and on and on—make me on almost a daily basis shout the cry of almost every pro-writer I know: "I hate writing! I hate it! I hate it!" I also love it, love it, love it. But I can have the fun of doing what I love only if I accept the tedium involved. Hopefully, high school years prepare us to deal with our later career frustrations. Because, let there be no delusion, all jobs have a great deal of exasperation involved. And it's worth it if you, aside from that, love your work, the cause for which you do that work, or the cash work brings you.

Sadly, some schools do not teach well. (Understatement.) But unless you can change to another school, you still have to do the work to move onto your college or career.

So:

SPELL TO CONCENTRATE DURING HOMEWORK OR OTHER EXACTING ACTIVITIES

This spell can be done immediately before sitting down to study, or just when you've time for magic. Orange is the color of concentration. Get an orange—as in the type you eat. Cut the orange into four pieces.

Slowly eat the first piece, focusing on its taste. There's magic in that taste whether you feel it or not! As you eat, recite silently, "I take in the bright fire of my Divine Father. It illuminates my mind."

Savoring the second piece, think, "My Father's focus is sharp like a sword. That blade edge and point is mine."

Slowly eating, and enjoying the third quarter of the orange, think, "My Father is the wind that clears my mind and feeds my spirit."

As you eat the last piece: "My Father sits by me, in every molecule of the earth, watching over me, guarding me, guiding me, as I tend to my work."

Then, add, "Thank you, Father."

You can use this spell as often as you like. But, after one use, you might not need it again for a while.

And, once done with an orange, you can "refresh" the spell with four sips of orange juice, and the recitation. If the "refreshing" doesn't work, try the orange again.

This spell helps you concentrate *whatever* the upcoming activities are—sports match, quiz, dramatic performance. So once you do the spell, it brings focus to all your activities.

Variation: Memorize the spell's four lines about our Sacred Father, plus the thank you. Use them instead of OJ to refresh your focus.

The orange spell can also be used to help you get through the school day when the problem is other than lack of focus. If you're having trouble with a difficult teacher, violence on school grounds, or anything else, try the spell. If you look at it, you'll see it gives you all sorts of inner powers that would help with any situation in school, as well as protect you. Blessed be!

Mother Earth's Bounty No. 3: Divination—A Personal Vision

The following allows you to develop your own way of viewing life. It also is a form of divination, something essential to a witch. *Divination* means psychically gaining information about the past, present, and future as well as spiritual guidance. A few of the ways divination is accomplished are: Tarot cards, a crystal ball, intuition, clairvoyance, clairsentience. (As clairvoyance is clear-seeing so clairsentience is clear-knowing.)

Finding a personal vision, that individualized approach to hearing the Goddess, demands long, disciplined study, just as a traditional interpretation of Tarot does. Here is a lesson:

It is possible to practice divination—and thus garner spiritual wisdom as well as knowledge about past, present, and future events—using whatever is on hand, wherever you are. It is also possible to do so in your own unique style. Here's how: A historical perspective of divination is the first thing that's needed. It is a time-honored understanding that the natural world surrounding us serves us as both a mirror and a guide. This must have been the first and oldest form of divination. In the sense that if one saw certain types of clouds, one knew it would rain.

We learn who we are and who we must strive to become by watching nature. The seasons turn, from a time of flower and fruit to a time of darkness and cold; this mirrors our own passages. And fruit-bearing trees rest from their labor in their winter-barren sleep, serving as role models that teach us that there is a time for labor and a time for rest. If you were troubled and found yourself at the beach, you might notice how the ocean slowly, ever so slowly, tears down the cliffs. This observation might give you the patience you need in your time of sorrow, so that you feel more accepting and peaceful.

Use the patterns of nature for spiritual guidance and as role models. Use the ancient technique of finding oneself, materially and spiritually, through nature. It is a very natural way of finding insight and counsel.

Try the following:

RITUAL OF NATURAL DIVINATION

Go to a natural spot and ask the Goddess, "Please show me a picture of myself, of who I am today, and help me understand it correctly." Let your eyes fall where they randomly happen to. Now study what you see. You've been given a portrait of yourself that will reveal something that you need to know about yourself. Look at the object, scene, or person your eyes fall upon as if you were looking into a mirror. As the natural world around them mirrored the ancient witches, so this moment will mirror you. Every moment offers a unique aspect of the natural world, and we are as much a part of that world as a tree or river, and as subject to the same laws.

Don't worry about any traditional interpretations (i.e., meanings that are repeatedly taught in books) of what you look at in this exercise. If you know customary interpretations, save that important knowledge for other times. And don't worry about being "right." What's important is what *you* see. You need to trust your own eyes and contemplate these questions: In what way is this scene (object, person) in front of me a picture of me? What are my strengths and weaknesses as shown in this portrait?

If the scene confuses you—"What does a billboard have to do with me?" (Yeah, you're supposed to be in a natural place, but advertising springs up *everywhere*.)—or perhaps seems an abstract configuration rather than something that could in any way be construed as a mirror or a person, look at it as if an artist had created an interpretive painting of your present state of mind, or of how you have been behaving lately. Perhaps you are being shown a picture of your inner landscape. And if there are several people where your eyes fall, you might, either intuitively or deductively, choose one to represent yourself. Or you can decide to view a whole crowd as representative of you.

Don't be discouraged if you learn nothing about yourself from this exercise, or if you can't quite pick up the knack of psychically reading yourself this way. It takes time. The important thing is to do the exercise, because this will open you up to guidance and bring you closer to your deep self. And that is why you did the exercise in the first place. Most likely, if you continue to do the exercise you'll get the hang of it.

A note of caution: take what you read with a grain of salt—or, better, take it with the whole salt lick! Expertise in any field, whether athletics or divination, takes time. For now, enjoy the *process*, and use what you are being told as something to *consider* as a *possible* truth rather than as a certainty. Even the most skilled Tarot practitioner rejects a great deal of what his or her cards say—the *most* skilled!

If you get negative info that's accurate—for example, this mirror of you reflects you as being too stubborn with your sibs—that's a good thing! Self-knowledge allows us to change so that we can be our happiest, most fulfilled selves. The universe never gives us negative info of any sort through divination except to show us what we need to change, avoid, or overcome, inside or out, to create the present and future life we want. Of course, I'm talking again about *accurate* info, not an inaccurate negative reading.

If you seek consistently accurate and useful guidance, you need to study and to practice this skill so that it improves—just as a physician studies and practices a long time to perfect the skills of diagnosis. This one exercise won't make you an expert on reading nature—it's a lifelong study.

But this exercise can serve as a great beginning and improve your other divination forms, such as Tarot cards, tea-leaf reading, palmistry, and clairsentience, should you have them. (An improvement in, for example, one's accuracy with tea-leaf reading may not seem connected with having performed Ritual of Natural Divination, but experience has taught me otherwise.)

Used often, this exercise can offer insights into yourself and life. Most important, it will help you find your own inner voice and vision of life, which is the real goal of divination. It is always to be used as a means to, rather than a substitute for, your own vision of life and the future; divination should never be exercised as a mindless following of invisible spirits or the like. If divination deafens you to your own opinion, you will get a bad reading and need to stop using this tool for a bit.

Here is an easy way to adapt and expand on the above exercise. Instead of doing this exercise in the country or in a nature spot within the city, read in a truly urban landscape. When doing so, don't look only at the nature in the city; *wherever* your eyes fall—on a tree, car, or shopping cart—might be your guidance. Read paper clips if your eyes fall on them when doing this ritual at your desk.

You can also read for things other than pictures of yourself; make requests like "Goddess, I've a great opportunity coming up. Please show me a role model of the absolutely best way to handle it" or "Goddess, please show me a role model to help me through this bad day (or problem) I am having and help me understand that role model correctly."

Enjoy! Divination is exciting and fun.

How to Find Magical Tools in the Mall

Everything—*everything*—has magic. The trick is to know that. And, if you didn't already, as of this paragraph you do.

The next few pages discuss the magic at the mall—or wherever you might find the items I'll mention. (Hey, maybe they're in your dresser drawer.)

When you find a magical tool such as the ones in this section, you can use the ritual on it that you find at the end of the section if you would like.

People often unknowingly buy good luck charms. Bob wanted to go on a ski trip but couldn't afford it. Nevertheless, he bought a ski hat, just to wear in his daily life, because he liked the style. He unconsciously felt that buying the hat would make his ski trip dream come true. He was right.

Sandra wanted long hair. She knew it would take a few years for it to get to the length needed for a hairstyle that epitomized what long, beautiful hair meant to her. But she purchased a barrette that's the perfect adornment for that hairstyle. Wearing the barrette, or keeping it in her drawer, not only made her feel a little like her hair was already long and perfect, but also, without her knowing it, magically gave her the resolve she needed: she closed her ears to people who said she would look awful with long hair; she ignored schoolmates who declared "Short hair is the thing!"; and she stuck through a particularly unflattering length her hair had to grow past. You should see her flowing tresses now!

So if you have a wish, look in stores for something that either symbolizes that wish or that you would use were your wish fulfilled. Either will work as your charm. See the box for examples. Be cre-

What You Wish For	Lucky Charm
Money	Wallet
Fun	Body glitter
Camping trip	Postcard of a state park
A new romance	Valentine's Day card
An audition to be a model	The perfect lipstick
Academic achievement	A graduation congratulations greeting card

ative and find your own lucky charms (No I do not mean the breakfast cereal!) for *whatever* wishes you have.

Moving on, choosing an item according to its color is another way to easily shop for magical tools. Below is a list of colors, each with the attribute(s) it brings into your life. But before that come examples of common everyday items that are, or might come in, that color. Though I'll give several examples, all you need is one colored item for your magic!

* nail polish
* barrette

* clothing (it needn't be everything on you; one item, even underwear, does the trick!)
* coffee mug
* marble
* hair color—a temporary color that washes out immediately is an easy, temporary spell
* pillow cases
* if a fabric store is near you, any color's magic is yours. Buy ribbon in your desired color, then either wear it as a choker, or around your ankle when you want its magic.
* bead (fun: put it on the ribbon choker?)
* notebook with a cover your desired color
* greeting card that you keep for yourself (it needn't be totally your chosen color; the overall effect is what counts)
* vase
* purse
* wallet
* pen (the ink needn't be the color you want)

As to which color does what:

Green draws money. It also brings peace of mind, and it heals the body. (Never use magic in place of a doctor, though. That doctor is your ax!) Instead of what's on the common everyday magical item list, you also have the option of a green plant.

Light blue heals a troubled spirit. Yellow lifts the spirit, bringing a sunny disposition. It also helps dispel negative influences around you.

Red's magic is that it brings you more energy, if you're tired. It also gives one determination and a zest for life. Instead of choosing items from the above list, one might purchase a piece of jewelry with a garnet or garnets in it. Or how about red lipstick? Orange helps you to focus and concentrate on whatever task is at hand. It also helps draw people's attention to *you*. Re lipstick: It needn't be a glaring orange. Orangey will do.

Purple will give you power, when you need self-confidence to face a challenge, or you want the discipline to see something through. How about lavender-colored body lotion?

Awareness and intention go a long way in Wicca. We've touched on awareness—the knowledge that magic exists in each thing we see—so let's deal with intention. You might want to use a ritual on your purchase, to help "wake up" its magic (it's already working, but this'll make it work better). In other words, by using ritual, your intention to increase the magic exerts its power. All you have to do is use the ritual, "Waking Up Magic," and adapt as follows: when reading its instructions and using the chant, substitute the word "color, symbol, object" or the like, as is appropriate, for the original "jewelry, adornment, stone, metal" and the like. And change the instructions in step 7 to: wear the item, carry it on you, or keep it near you, to reap its benefits. If it would be inconvenient or inappropriate to always wear or keep the item on or nearby—who always keeps a sweater on or a cup with them?—just occasionally have it on you or near. After step 7, the spell continues on as is, except with the aforementioned word substitutions. So read all the way to the end of the section to get the whole spell and get it right.

Privacy

Mmm, privacy. The peace and quiet to fully focus your attention and ponder a whole new wardrobe or a whole new life! Enough time—and the right place—to enjoy whatever activities float your boat. Your possessions respected so they're not rifled through by mischievous or prying family members. Freedom from annoying—or even unsafe—attention so you can go about your business undisturbed. Whether it's for fun, safety, or work we all need privacy.

PRIVACY SPELL

Pour a glass of water. Blow into it, one time. Then take a sip of the water.

Now the water is ready to help you have privacy.

If you wish to be left alone, anoint your forehead with the water. If you want to have the time and/or place needed for you to be undisturbed, you can instead or in addition sprinkle a bit of the water on your feet.

If you have a place where you like to hide things, or a diary you wish your siblings would not read, or . . . put a dab of the water around said place, or on the diary.

When you're done with your sprinkling or anointing, drink the water as you recite silently or out loud

> *My power*
> *my self*
> *my place.*
> *A circle of power*
> *with nary a face.*
> *Invisible power*
> *and no one debates.*

Repeat this ritual as needed.

Make a fresh batch of water each time you need it, though you *can* use the water on several items and/or places, as well as on yourself, each time you "brew up" a batch.

Here are mundane steps (axes) that can help you attain privacy.

Ask your parents for a locked box in which you can keep things away from siblings. Explain that it's not for hiding anything bad but that you are seeking privacy.

Brainstorm with friends for better hiding places.

Set aside a special time just for you. Plan for ten minutes a day, or an hour a week, or whatever, that is your time to be uninterrupted so that you can do whatever you want: Daydream. Read. Do ritual. Masturbate. Write poetry. Thumb through your Book of Shadows to see if something jumps out at you that you need to remember right then.

If you need the privacy to study, try the library.

If the issue is more serious—for example, someone is physically threatening you at school—do the spell and talk to an adult. Or if your privacy's violated by any sort of abuse in your family, do the spell and find the relevant sections in this book for axes.

If your parents are not abusive but nevertheless are badly intrusive people who will not allow you privacy no matter what, even if you sit down and talk with them, here are some thoughts.

Find the privacy in your own mind. Use the nostril breathing in "Waking Up Magic," to find moments of inner calmness—that's an inward privacy. And the knowledge that someday you'll have your own place is a real ax. Keep remembering that all bad situations pass.

How to Answer Inane Questions About Wicca

Okay, so, here's the scenario: you're into Wicca, going merrily along your magical way, and someone suddenly asks you the most inane question about your witchcraft. Your jaw drops.

Below are responses to dumb or otherwise offensive remarks. Some of my suggestions, I will admit, should not actually be used. I wrote them to let off steam and suggest you do the same, by sharing said suggestions with Wiccan friends or by imagining the wicked pleasure you would take were you to actually use the equally wicked responses.

After you've done that, realize that spouting the "wicked responses" would cause more trouble than it's worth. And, in fact, it would not feel as good as it did in your imagination. You'd end up more frustrated than ever.

There, now that we've proven how terribly terribly mature we are, we can proceed.

Question: "Do you worship Satan?"
Answer you can't use: "Why, were you thinking of giving me an introduction?" You might also consider, but then forgo, "How dare you suggest your Satanic practices to me! I'm going to tell everyone what you're up to!"

While neither response will help you be happy, they both *do* put the burden back on the asker. So here is an effective way to do that and thus deal with someone who is, basically, asking if you are evil: "It really hurts my feelings that you think I'm capable of such a terrible thing." Deliver this with a straight face, verbatim. Memorize it so you're ready with it when you need it. Say it sincerely, and look hurt. Fact is, it *does* hurt when people make such accusations. Yes, it is often due to ignorance or fear, but it still hurts. And all the long-winded explanations about Wicca being a *good* religion won't make half the impression that this short, sweet statement does. Say what I suggest and you've said "Wicca is ethical" more clearly than any massive verbal spouting ever could.

Do *not*, I repeat do not make the remark angrily, defensively, or with added explanations. Otherwise you do not attain the desired outcome, which is to show the goodness of Wicca and put the burden on the fool who elicited your need to respond in the first place!

Do it my way and the fool has to focus on the pain they've caused. Or at least we can hope. Nothing's *fool*proof.

Moving on:

Question: "Do you kill babies (say 'The Lord's Prayer' backwards; practice black magic . . .)?"
Answer you can't use: "Why, were you thinking of teaching me how?"

The proper response is the same as for the first question. And with that:

Question: "Aren't you worried that because of witchcraft you will lose your soul (go to hell; get God angry; be led away from Christ . . .)?"
Answer: "Thank you for your concern."

Alas and lackaday. We will have been neither wise nor effective if we angrily jump up and down, waving our finger in the face of the errant questioner, as we shout, "You've got to be kidding! Are you kidding? Of course, you're kidding!"

Instead we have to be polite and can't point out that the questioner, for his or her part, is being *rude*. However, courtesy is not the same as being a doormat:

When someone, through fear, bias, or religious ignorance, asks an insulting question, the details of which are not part of the Wiccan way—an angry, repressive God, hell, the salvation of the soul—you can gently say, "Thank you for your concern."

If the person asking is not close to you, stop there! Ha! You've got them—if you have delivered your line calmly and you don't add a word. Smile, then change the topic. It is not a stranger's right to pry.

If you care about the person, or they are in a position of authority so that you have to offer more, add the following—*immediately*, so they don't think your initial remark a wisecrack—in a sweet, truly sincere voice: "A punishing God, the salvation of souls, hell . . . is not part of the Wiccan belief system. We believe in a God who is loving (souls that do not need saving, a God who loves Her children so much She would never condemn them to torture)."

Again, do not say this angrily or defensively. If you do, you've lost your ground. Say it as if the person has asked a perfectly civil question.

From there, it depends. A religious bigot will not let you drop it. Say courteously "I prefer not to discuss it." If they ask why, don't fall for it! A response *would* be discussing it.

Should the person insist, just keep repeating variations, always pleasantly, never angrily:

"I don't want to discuss it."

"Are you ashamed?"

"I don't like talking about it right now" (then, a pleasant smile).

"C'mon, tell me."

"I'd rather not" (followed by another sweet smile).

Notice that not one of these answers adds an iota of info. You never really respond to *anything* they add. Because as soon as you do, you're engaged in debate about your religion.

Finally, there are parents, other family members, and the like, who are truly concerned and you can't put off. Nor should you. Have them read my "Letter to Parents." It is below. Also, check out "What to Tell Your Family, Friends, and Community About Wicca." It includes a discussion about families who are close-minded.

All the suggestions above, in the current section, are probably irrelevant when dealing with them, and, in fact, will likely make life hell for you. Please, apply the above responses elsewhere!

A last inane question: "Isn't magic just a way to control others unethically (run away from real life, a delusion . . .)?"
Answer: "No."

Hee, hee, hee. By now I think you know: say it nicely and don't add another word.

Unless, of course, you really like the person. In which case, pause graciously, with a pleasant smile, while what you said sinks in. Then tell them what magic is to *you*. Also, saying, "You know, for some reason a lot of people seem to think that but it's not true at all," then sharing *your* experience of what Wicca is can be a great way to answer a lot of questions if they're asked by well-intended open-minded people who just haven't ever talked to anyone who knew the real score about Wicca. As to others:

I regret that the above handy-dandy guidance about dealing with fools has its limits. There's no way to cope with all possible inanities. If I wrote a whole book of questions and responses, some fool would only read it and plan *new* stupid things to ask. More to the point, you and your life don't come from a cookie cutter. Sigh.

For more ideas talk with friends. Go online. Read additional books. And most important, ask the Goddess, "Tell me what to say." For one thing, She might tell you to pause before answering, so that you can collect your thoughts as well as become calm. She might even suggest you say, "Hm, let me think it through first, so that I give you a good answer. I'll call you tomorrow." This gives you even more time to get calm.

Yup, that Goddess! She'll guide you every step of the way.

Letter to Parents

You're a concerned parent. You love your child(ren) and, with every fiber of your being, want to create happiness, safety, and morality for your offspring. You want to be sure your loved ones receive the best possible information, tools, and influences available. In addition, you check up on what your child is up to because we can't let our children live unprotected in this incredibly dangerous world. With all that in mind, I invite you, please read this book. I believe you will discover it not only helps a teen be her or his happiest, most fulfilled self, but also teaches a moral, productive way of life. Nowadays, spiritual teachers seem to forget to teach spirituality. I am of the ridiculous notion that it is my *job* as a spiritual teacher to help instill spiritual values. I have done my best to also include the kind of down-to-earth, practical advice young adults need to navigate this crazy world.

There are many misconceptions about Wicca. If you don't already know the facts about Wicca, I hope you'll be open to learning it is an ethical, joyful, and growth-enhancing approach to life.

Let's next look at sex: You'll notice in this book that I am neither for nor against teens being sexually active. For one thing, I am at a point in life where I am rethinking issues of sexuality at a very deep level, evaluating some of my most fundamental premises. Also, I've seen great harm come both from the imposition of sexual abstinence on teens and from teens being sexually active.

You may ask, "Why are you writing this book if you can't yet take a stand?"

Adults who take an arbitrary stand rather than admitting their own confusions provide a bad spiritual role model for children. They cannot learn to admit their own confusions when their religious instructors will not. Won't teens dig in their heels and refuse to look at things from new angles unless we let them know that we must do it ourselves? This is, while we're on the topic of sex, especially vital when it *comes* to sex.

In any case, I am pro–sex education because I detest ignorance. It destroys lives. I want young adults to be healthy and happy. They cannot do this in ignorance.

No child should be punished by, for example, HIV for his or her mistakes. Nor should accidental pregnancy happen because of foolish choices. Whether we believe teens should be sexually active or not, they need to be informed of the facts.

If you yourself are against teen sexuality, you may be happy to know that studies show no data supporting the belief that sex education causes an increase, or earlier onset of, sexual activity, and in fact delays or decreases it. Makes sense to me: if you have the facts, you are less likely to jump in over your head.

Please continue to check up on your child through her or his journey through the world of Wicca. Like any community, it has its share of good and bad. There are Wiccan practitioners whom I wouldn't trust with my house pet let alone another human being. But the percentage of such people is no greater than in any group and as such please monitor your child(ren)'s forays into the Christian, Buddhist, or any other religious community.

Especially look through the Contents and Table of Spells. There you'll see material that may address additional concerns you have about your child reading this book. I bless you for meeting your job as a parent head on by taking the time to read this letter.

Back to my teen readers. You read the letter yourself, didn't you? You peeked. . . . If you hadn't, I would have been worried about you!

Inane questions—check! Letter to parents—check! Let's move on to the next aspect of talking about Wicca with Cowans (non-Wiccans).

What to Tell Your Family, Friends, and Community About Wicca

It can feel great to say, "I'm into Wicca. I love it. It would be wonderful for me if I could tell you some of what I've learned. May I?" Getting to share an amazing experience—"Wow, I did this ritual the other night that rocked. Do you want to hear about it?"—can set a grin on your face and make you feel oh-so-fine. Or you might want to tell someone, "I really like learning about the Goddess but sometimes it confuses me. Can I explain to you and see what you think?" There's a million and one good reasons—fun, serious, and in between—to tell someone about your Wiccan interest.

On the other hand, there are just as many reasons not to let people know you're into Wicca. It really depends on you, as well as how people around you would react.

There's nothing wrong with being in the broom closet. An enormous number of witches are, and not for cowardly reasons. Sure, I'm "out" big time, but I strongly support the choice of people who aren't, and I make a point never to "out" someone—I won't even leave a witchy phone message on an answering machine because there's no telling if a bigoted relative, landlord, or whoever might hear it and cause serious trouble. My public life as a witch engendered a serious death threat and, thank Goddess, I'm okay, but I lived in terror for a year. Witches do not out each other. (Watch those phone messages.)

A witch chooses his or her battles. And knows from honoring the cycles of nature that there are times to fight and times to refrain. For example, Harold, a teen witch, is quite secretive about his magic. Fact is, his parents are Wiccans and are in on his secret. But all of them are involved in environmental work in their area, which is quite straightlaced. Their devotion to Mother Earth is not lip service; they live their Pagan religion by working hard to care for the planet. (Witches believe the earth and nature are sacred gifts.) Their neighbors think Harold's family odd for their commitment to a healthy environment, and that sometimes makes things hard for the family. But they tough it out because their environmental practices in their personal lives as well as political actions to save endangered species are having an effect in their hometown, and globally. It's worth being thought odd. If, on top of everything else, they came out as witches, their "square" neighbors might think the family *thoroughly* weird and even evil, and therefore totally ignore their important role model and information.

A witch wants to be effective. Stay in the broom closet if it helps you to be a force in the world. And stay in the broom closet for *whatever* reason you want to do so—it's a very personal choice, each situation and every person unique, and requiring wildly disparate things.

So if you are like the many teens who write me about parents and families for whom my above letter would make no difference, consider the closet. Religious fundamentalists, for example, usually think that there is only one right way, and that any deviation from it is evil.

Fundies or not, if your parents are gonna make life hell, you may want to wait until you're independent to practice Wicca, or keep it minimal for now. You can hold your spiritual beliefs quiet in your heart, living them in subtle but powerful ways, like prayer, environmental work, food drives for the homeless, and occasional simple spells.

If you do want to tell someone, you might have them read my letter to begin with. Even before that, perhaps feel them out. "What do you think of Wicca? I hear it's a real religion." If they answer with venom, you may want to forsake further dialogue.

Thing is, as a youth you are more likely to suffer if bigotry occurs because adults have legal control over youth. Be smart!

Don't tell someone you're a witch to impress, frighten, or prove something to someone. It not only belittles your religion, but also makes you look stupid. "Look at me, I'm a witch!" I hate it when Christian fundamentalists rant that way, and it's no better (or *really* different deep down) when a Pagan does it.

More, though, is the issue of religious intolerance. People can suffer everything and anything because of it, from ostracization to physical violence. Bigotry can lead to grave harm and endangerment. Add to that mixture added vulnerabilities because adults have legal control over you. Do not tempt fate by sharing mindlessly what you're up to. Share only with good reason that you're Wiccan, and then do so carefully and cautiously, and in a way that's likely to engender support. Instead of throwing witchcraft in someone's face to defy them or prove yourself, feel them out, have them read my letter, then introduce Wicca bit by bit, showing parts that are easier to understand and seeing how that goes before sharing further.

Two easy-to-understand parts of Wicca: The Wiccan Rede (see page 285) and community service (see "Service, One of the Secrets of Happy People," chapter 6). Be creative about how to talk to the person(s) you want to tell you're Wiccan.

Then, if they're upset, give them the chance to come around. It takes time to overcome years of misinformation. Don't nag or push.

Wiccans are not missionaries—we do not seek to convert and convince. We respect other people's right to believe what they believe.

And if the person can accept Wicca on the surface, you needn't try to shove *everything* down their throat. If all you want is their tolerance, give them just enough for them to feel okay about Wicca. Again, witches don't proselytize, educating only when people ask for it. Of course, concerned adults may want all the details. That's a *good* thing—it shows they care.

Circling 'round so that we end where "What to Tell Your Family, Friends, and Community About Wicca" began, it's great to share your Wiccan experiences. Don't take any of my cautions to mean otherwise. If you want, go for broke with people whom you have felt out or those whom you already know won't freak at the word *witch*. There are so many good reasons to talk about one's witch-life. And sharing your enthusiasm is *not* proselytizing. You may want to share all the nice things you're learning because you're excited about them. Or maybe you want to show a friend a particular spell because it seems exactly what your pal needs. Suggesting something you've found helpful is not proselytizing either. Whether you've written a prayer to the Goddess that you want to show someone, hope that your best friend will try a spell with you just for fun, have a more serious reason, or whatever—we all love to share our lives, and witchcraft is not an exception to that.

Be proud—even if it's silent pride—you're a witch.

Taboos That Really Should Be Taboo

Broken taboos cause *you* major boo-hoos! So let's kick off this section by getting right down to business. Taboo No. 1: hurting others intentionally. (Whenever I mention harm in this discussion, assume I mean *intentional* harm.) Witches hold to a law called the *Wiccan Rede*: Do as you will and harm none. I talk about not hurting others throughout the book, touching on, for example, gossip and revenge. Now let's look at how hurting others hurts *you*.

Trying to hurt someone, whether through magical or mundane acts, embitters your heart, sours your spirit, and poisons your mind. Be mean, whether through magical or concrete means, and it sickens *all* your magic, every spell. As is your spirit, so goes your spells; the more you hurt others the more you hurt your magic. It stops working or backfires on you, causing damage. Clearly, it is no smarter to hurt someone magically than on the mundane plane.

To use revenge as an example, hurting someone doesn't do one little itsy-bitsy tiny minuscule microscopic particle of good for you, anyway! Maybe you'll feel a moment's satisfaction or you'll enjoy planning your enemy's entrapment. But the cost—in pain and perhaps material loss—always exceeds the degree of pleasure.

Here's a fabulous, and acceptable, way to be mean: never think about the person who's wronged you. Seventeen-year-old Rachel did that with someone who had been *awful* to her. It was the best revenge. The person involved got his comeuppance, because while Rachel went about her own business everyone became very interested in what she was doing—putting together an a cappella jazz vocal trio whose first concert was a successful fund-raiser to upgrade the town's public playground—and the meanie ended up deserted. Rachel didn't have to lift a finger against him. How cool is *that*? (←a rhetorical remark, written in the hope it will make me appear incredibly hip).

Of course, *never* thinking about the evildoer is an *ideal*. We can work toward it and hope for the best. And before we can have any success at all we may have a lot of feelings and thoughts to wade through. Unless you deal with that, you only bury the feelings and thoughts so don't really move on from them. Tools herein can help. See "Spell to Remove Inner Problems" and thumb through the text for other ideas.

If thoughts of hatred or the desire to hurt someone plague you, cleanse it or them away in the "Spell to Remove Inner Problems." You can also or instead pray for the person, "May (s)he receive what her/his deepest, most sacred and good self really wants." (Everyone is good deep down, even were it 100 percent buried.) Say this prayer once a day for a few weeks, or at least when you think of it, and your brooding on that person can disappear. Presto!

When focused on harm, we don't have the time it takes to be happy by being good to others and ourselves. Become happy by making your own life good and also look at "Service, One of the Secrets of Happy People," in chapter 6.

Taboo No. 2: hexing. I'm no pacifist. Hexing is magical war. How-ever—and this is a huge *however*—hexing is a dangerous magical prac-tice and I'm going to tell you not to do it:

Hexing is enormously complex magically. Consider anyone who tells you otherwise an amateur or insane or an ego-ridden fool. (Yes, there's always the exception. There's no way to know whether it's the exception without unnecessarily risking your own well-being big time.) Such magical complexity must be dealt with through face-to-face instruction.

Hexing is taboo in almost any situation anyway. War is war—dangerous! You may want to ask yourself the following questions: What happens when someone starts a war? Does the person who started it survive? What sort of losses might be sustained? What hap-pens when someone fights back? What might befall a soldier who is ill-equipped, poorly informed, tired, sleeping, or momentarily dis-tracted? Realize that your answers apply to hexing. Eek.

Also, once started, war is an uncontrollable force. Its chaos can do *anything* to anyone in the vicinity.

And almost every last time someone has come to me asking to learn a hex, they didn't need it. Some readers will now think, "Yeah, but *I* do." We humans always think our situation is different! But I'm not ignoring the painful emotions and terrible situations that lead up to wanting to hex. They're part of why hexing is so very dangerous and complex and I can't explain that in print because, well, again, it necessitates dialogue not monologue. Ditto, trying to explain why it's not needed though it seems otherwise. But I can tell you this: Doing it when not needed = big trouble.

Finally, most Wiccans don't know how to hex safely. They don't understand all the ins and outs but might think they do. I've spent so much time studying the science of magic, and developing Wiccan curriculum, that I know only one Wiccan in the United States with a comparable magical history—he was one of my teachers. I have rare expertise backing up my statement that hex instructions tend to be dangerously incorrect.

Alternatives are available. The Goddess never gives us a limit unless there is another option. Don't ever quit until you find it no matter how impossible it seems or how dire the situation. I speak from experience; I've been pushed to the wall so often and always found a way around the wall.

Taboo No. 3: ritual bloodletting. As popular a contrivance as it is in the movies—"Okay, let's all use the ritual knife and prick our fingers"—it is dangerous, sloppy, and the sign of a wannabe-witch. By dangerous and sloppy I mean both on the material *and* magical plane.

Other than bloodletting's dangers and lack of magical accuracy, the Gods loathe it. There's enough bloodshed in this world without anyone spitting in the face of human suffering by, on purpose, cutting oneself for ritual use.

It is great, however, to use your menstrual blood ritually, like in "Ritual to Celebrate First Menses and Other Passages."

Finally, these are not all of the Wiccan taboos. There are other major no-nos. As you continue your Wiccan journey with this book and elsewhere, you'll be able to find the taboos.

The Myths That We Are: A Cosmic Pep Talk
(Closing Words)

We walk midst other humans, but we are part myth.

Before history, the Fey Folk married humans, and now all of Adam and Eve's children have a drop of Fairy blood in them.

But that is not all of our myth. Some of us, in addition, have a streak of mermaid. Or a bit of dwarf power. Or our Fey blood has come forward, stronger than that of other people, making us live lives that are so *particularly* Fey.

Or we watch the world through the calm eyes of a cat or an eagle. Or whisper to trees, one tree to another.

Or maybe we are simple, earthy humans, and the Fey-touch in our veins gives us a way with plants, or a knowing what will happen in the future.

Or maybe we have a totally different myth—there are as many as there are stars in the universe.

And each of us is a God(dess) of some sort, with special powers and joys—we can glory in our divine stature.

And we struggle, because the mythic life is demanding, it insists we be our true selves.

And we struggle, because we *are* human, and cannot escape from the requirements, realities, and needs of human existence.

"My magical, mythic children," says the Goddess to me, and to you, "Do not reject your human self. Acknowledge your limits. Live among humans as a human. Accept people despite their lack of wings, and fur and mysticism. Accept them so much that you love them, work with them, live with them, do not judge them.

"And develop your human talents. They are part of your destined greatness, destined fulfillment.

"Otherwise, your wings and fur, magic and mysticism, wyrd ways and special powers will leave you lonely and frustrated.

"But embrace all of who you are and you'll learn that your human joys, powers, and feelings equal that of any mythic being. You'll see that human limits can be a chalice, that holds all your potential in place so that you can draw on every last bit of it.

"Embrace all of who you are and whatever your magic self is it will *be* magic, breath magic, love and laugh magic. If you're dragon, your dragon self will fly and fire, if you're plant your plant self will bloom and twine, if star your star-self shall glimmer and be wished upon, if lion you shall rule, whatever your magic you shall fully *be* that magic and meet the other magic creatures in those times hidden between the moments of your human ways, in those moments hidden midst your human days."

Blessed Be,

Your faithful (though foolish) dragon,

Francesca De Grandis

WICCAN RESOURCES

Here's a guide to where and how you can network Wiccan, get Wiccan support, and learn more about witchcraft. I also threw in a few other goodies.

First of all let's deal with what info and help you can get from me and how to get it. My books, website, classes, and professional spiritual counseling sessions are where people can get a spell, advice about the Craft, my thoughts about their specific life situation, networking help, or referrals to axes. By the time I'm done with that, and related correspondence, I can't answer letters, e-mails, or phone requests asking for a spell, advice about the Craft, my thoughts about their . . . However, it is such an honor to hear from you. *Please* feel free to write just to say "Hi," tell me how this book went for you, what you think of the website or would like to see in another book. I'll make a *point* of it to give a "Hi" back at you soon as I can—even if it takes me six months, I'll find the time.

Contact me via *The Wiccan & Faerie Grimoire of Francesca De Grandis*, at www.well.com/user/zthirdrd/WiccanMiscellany.html, which has lots of free stuff—rituals, spells, links, articles. Mongo amount of help there. There are also instructions for how to be on my e-mailing list to receive helpful spiritual hints in my free newsletters, and news of upcoming books, classes, and other events.

When you're eighteen, I'm available as a teacher. I teach Wicca and interfaith spirituality in my area as well as through international teleseminars—classes by telephone. You only need your phone so you can do the training where you live. La.

In the Third Road, we teach teens a type of magic that is powerful yet does not necessitate knowing magic through and through. Why go through a lengthy training to learn all the technical underpinnings of magic just to do the spells you want? Once an adult, you can learn more if you so desire. I can teach you the in-depth ins and outs of magic—think magician-college-level—as well as the training practices that instill the magical finesse needed to apply that info.

I teach adults and teens a totally different type of magic. Once your physical body is fully grown, past a teenager's physical volatility and resulting vulnerabilities, so your psychic body matures, becoming strong enough and stable enough to practice the magical techniques that under-lie Third Road's really strong and highly technically oriented spells for adults.

The form of Wicca I teach adults also further develops their psychic abilities and mysticism.

Though the following are my books for adults, they have info relevant to teens who want to read more about Wicca. *Goddess Initiation* and *Be a Goddess!* both discuss Wicca's wild mysteries at depth. *Be a Goddess!* also further develops *Be a Teen Goddess!*'s discussion about finding power, peace, and self-expression through virtues such as patience, surrender, willingness, instead of falling prey to the bastardized explanations of such virtues that squelch us and keep us miserable. And, if you want more info about balancing supposed opposites, such as combining healthy pride with humility, and how the net result is more magical and mundane power, *Be a Goddess!* explains this. *Goddess Initiation* shows how to soar high but keep your feet on the ground so you don't crash—part of the larger question of balance and of reconciling opposites. Again, being a different type of energy, for grown-ups, neither book has the exact same style of spellcrafting as *Be a Teen Goddess!*—so don't be confused by different definitions, rules, and requirements for those books' spells.

The Modern Goddess' Guide to Life: How to Be Absolutely Divine *on a Daily Basis* has games and quizzes. It's my Pagan humor book for female readers, as a fun way to get in touch with the Goddess within.

When you're eighteen: I act as a spiritual counselor (call it shamanic counseling, pastoral counseling Pagan-style, or psychic readings) by telephone for people all over the world. Appointments are suitable to people of any or no religion. I treat you as a special, unique individual, so you receive what *you* want and need.

Call 814-337-2490 about counseling (or my classes if you need more info than you get on my site and e-mailing list).

To find Wiccan friends, teachers, and support regarding Pagan-related issues: See if your local Unitarian Universalist Church has a CUUPS group. Some of its members might be witches, or able to refer you to some. Also, look on search engines for online Wiccan chats and networking groups. There you can ask if anyone can refer you to someone in your area. If people you contact don't have time to help, realize that there are too few of us trying to help too many. For such folks, the expression "There's often more than one person can manage" can be literally true. Some Wiccans do demanding research to find their teachers or other Wiccan support. Just keep at it. A local metaphysical or occult shop may be able to refer you to networking groups or teachers. (Proceed with caution. The shop may or may not be trustworthy. Ditto online resources or people you are referred to.)

Let me get you started with the Wiccan Web. Here are two sites you may want to check out. I hear www.wiccanmail.com/forums/ deals with all sorts of Wiccan issues. On it, people chat and there's an exclusive teen section. Wyld Wytches Web, at www.wyldwytch.com, was started by a teen (now in his twenties) and hosts *lots* of his writings from when he started the site. The site also has an online newsletter as well as the "Be a Goddess" list. Wyldwytch created this list for folks who relate to my work, so you can talk about it there. You might even meet someone who lives nearby. It's a list for adults thus far, but Wyldwytch is cool about teens joining. Since the list focuses on my work, I need to be clear: I'm not involved in the list or site and don't personally know who joins; I am not vouching for any of the resources in Wiccan Resources, so, when you look into them, use your common sense.

Forget obscure chants: think smoky samba and wise-guy paganism in the Goddess Spirituality music CD, *Pick the Apple from the Tree*. Phone Serpentine Music, 800-270-5009, to order or go to my site.

At www.well.com/user/zthirdrd/sacredtoys.html there's more fun Goddess paraphernalia—sacred toys for *modern* witches—coffee mugs as holy chalices, witchy T-shirts instead of ritual robes.

GUIDE TO AXES

The first axes in this guide are books. A witch is smart, sizing up each situation then deciding how to *best* use, change, or, as a friend of mine added, celebrate its energy. One uses an overt ritual to do this if needed. But one should never waste one's power, nor choose anything but the best means to an end. Often one can more effectively use or shift energy without ritual. The etiquette books *Miss Manners' Guide to Excruciatingly Correct Behavior* (1989, Warner Books) and *Miss Manners' Guide to Rearing Perfect Children* (2002, Scribner) are a sure help in this. *They offer solutions to everything from awkwardness at a funeral to awkwardness at a dance.* And if your parents didn't give you all the tools you need to navigate life, use the child rearing guide to rear yourself a bit! Also, real courtesy is not about empty form or feeling better than others but about genuine concern for people's feelings and well-being. What could be more practical spiritually than a book of guidelines for such caring ways to act?

Problems in relationships, whether with parents or romantic partners, can be mitigated and even overcome by courtesy. I'm not suggesting you suppress your feelings and be fake. I am a big one for being real and acknowledging your feelings even when they are not "nice." But that is truly a different issue. And I am not telling you to be courteous if someone is coming at you with a chainsaw! But witches understand that sometimes when you take the shape of something—in this case the shape of a loving, kind, and calm person—your insides start to truly be that shape as well. Buddhists call this "Right action makes for right mind."

If you cannot be courteous (and there's no Texas massacre scene going on) use the purification ritual, "Spell to Remove Inner Problems," to cleanse away your inability to do so.

Next book: *I Am On My Way Running: Women Speaking on Coming of Age*, edited by Lyn Reese, Jean Wilkinson, and Phyllis Sheon Koppelman (1983, Avon), with its poems and other works by women from around the world, can be an inspiration for a teen woman, help her collect her thoughts, and show her she is not alone or freakish in her experiences.

Dating and Sex: Defining and Setting Boundaries by Judith Peacock (2002, Lifematters Press) is about a lot more than its name shows. For example, it touches on breakups, how to help your family appreciate a date that they disapprove of, and navigating the bigotry and other problems you might meet in an interracial or same-sex relationship. The book is small and note that I wrote *touches* on. Nevertheless, the book is worth reading.

I don't agree with everything that Judith says. In fact, though I suggest resources, services, and products in this book, I may not agree with everything about them. Nor am I saying to you, "You can absolutely trust this resource, service, or product." My suggestions and referrals are starting-off points for your research; from there make your own decisions. Realize that despite my research you might run up against a bad person. When you use something I recommend, check it out thoroughly, weigh and measure all the information it gives you, discuss the info with someone you trust, and understand that you may receive incorrect info from a source I've mentioned. You, not I, are responsible for the results of your usage of my recommendations.

Often, a book or service may only give you a small piece of the puzzle. Or a resource may have a lot of good stuff but one can't stop there. Check other sources because otherwise it may not be clear that you're only partially informed. To get all the information one needs one has to keep finding resources and educating oneself. That's the nature of research. And that is the case with Peacock's book.

Male teens will find a lot of *The Girl's Life Guide to Growing Up* by K. Bokram and A. Sinex (2000, Beyond Words Publishing) relevant. This excellent guide to life addresses a huge number of topics with gobs of tips. From sibling rivalry, to the new stepparent, to being shunned by your crowd, as well as how to communicate in a variety of situations, this is good stuff. Don't be put off by some of it being for younger people. Now that I've covered books, here are a few ways to be of service:

Yes (Youth for Environmental Sanity) at www.yesworld.org offers youth jams—young people can gather, gain leadership skills, and discuss environmental issues.

Help other kids through Childreach, which helps needy children in developing countries (and has no religious affiliation). You can sponsor a child for not too much cash. Info's at childreach.org or call 800-556-7918, Monday through Friday. Maybe you and your family or coven could pool some bucks to make this even cheaper to do.

With any of the resources below, if a person you contact can't help, always ask who else you might get in touch with.

To learn how to use a condom properly so that it helps you avoid pregnancy and sexually transmitted diseases (STDs) call 877-472-SFSI. This national, free service can give you any other sex education you need.

Teenwire.com is a similar resource, if you need the birds and bees explained to you or want expert answers to your sex questions, whether they are about the nuts and bolts of avoiding pregnancy or peer pressure to have sex.

A teen can phone the CDC National STD and AIDS hotline at 800-342-2437 or 800-227-8922 and receive all the information an adult would. The hotline tells people about STDs and how to protect yourself or partner from them. Or go to their website: www.ashastd.org. Their services are free and confidential.

Next topic: Finding a counselor. Adrienne Amundsen, Ph.D., tells us: "There are *many* ways to find a counselor. Of course, if your parents are sympathetic you can ask for their help. You can also ask your doctor to give you names of people to call. Either make an appointment with your doctor to do this, or just call the doctor's office and ask. You don't need your parents' permission. Or ask a school counselor—they may be able to *be* your counselor or give you information about where to go. You can look in the Yellow Pages under:

* Psychologists
* Counseling Services
* Mental Health Services
* Social Workers
* Crisis Services

* Psychotherapy
* Clinics
* Marriage, Family, and Child Counselors
* Social Services
* Alcohol and Drug Treatment

"Also the phone book will likely have listings for 'Family Service Agency' or 'Catholic Social Services' as well as Community Mental Health.

"Many communities have teen drop-in centers. Ask your friends, or look for flyers at places where teens hang out. And of course the Internet is a *great* resource—just type in any of the phrases I suggested for the Yellow Pages, or 'Teen Services [your city]' or 'Adolescent Services' or 'Clinics.'

"People in these places understand the kind of issues teens face. They will be prepared to help you solve worries you have about payment, privacy, and what you can talk about without your parents knowing. Generally these services are totally confidential. Only if you are in immediate life-threatening danger might they want someone else to know, and if your parents themselves are posing the danger, these agencies will not put you in further danger by bringing them in or telling them. Often these services are free."

Next issue: The National Clearinghouse for Alcohol and Drug Information can be contacted at P.O. Box 2345, Rockville, Maryland 20847, or at 800-729-6686. They have no religious affiliation. They can mail you free info about what drugs do. Basically, the same info is at freevibe.com. Their information specialists educate callers.

Alcoholics Anonymous (A.A.) is an organization of alcoholics trying to become and remain sober. You can be any age, religion (or lack therof), sexual preference, race, class, type of alcoholic, or anything not covered in this list, and join. There are Pagans in A.A., but there are also religious bigots. It's a real hodgepodge of people. So act accordingly. A.A.,

N.A., Alanon (see below) and all such groups, are like any place—filled with the best and the worst people. Proceed cautiously and don't quit just because someone's a jerk or worse. Don't let *anyone* stop you from using the tools you need to be happy, including the Anonymous programs. A.A. groups are free, and all over the world. To find a group in your area, call A.A. General Service Office 212-870-3400. Or, ask your local directory for a local A.A. phone number. If no group's nearby, the General Service Office can explain alternatives. You are never too young to be an alcoholic. Their website, www.aa.org, has local contacts.

Narcotics Anonymous is similar in structure to A.A. but is comprised of addicts. You needn't be a narcotic user to join—marijuana, whatever, you're in. Go to www.na.org for free literature and local contact info, or call local info for local N.A. helplines.

If your life has been affected by someone else's drinking, Alateen will help you get your own life together whether the drinker(s) stops drinking or not. Call 888-425-2666, give them your city and state while you're on the phone, and they'll find a meeting for you right then and there. They can also send free literature explaining the Alateen program. At www.al-anon.alateen.org you can find some explanations about Alateen, get contact info in your area, and buy their literature and books.

Overeaters Anonymous helps people who overeat or have other food problems, even some types of anorexia. For local meetings go to www.oa.org or call 505-891-2664.

The following contacts are usually sensitive to the possibility of a child being abused even worse for reporting abuse. So if you're AT ALL worried that this would happen, you should make this absolutely clear to whomever you speak with.

If an abused or neglected kid calls Child Help USA, 800-422-4453, they can do crisis counseling, refer you to a support group, or tell you of an advocacy group in your area that can step in hands-on. They also help with residential placement for abused and neglected kids. Their website is www.childhelpUSA.org.

I know damn well that, both funding and politics being what they are, often a helping agency's abilities are not what we—or they—would like. Keep trying to get the help you need, read and reread anything in this book that helps you think you can overcome seemingly insurmountable obstacles and life's worst situations, and don't ever quit. You'll triumph.

If you are abused physically, sexually, or emotionally, or neglected, National Domestic Violence Hotline, at 800-799-7233, can explain your options, make a plan to keep you safe, or do a crisis intervention. This group refers you to local services and there aren't always enough local services to go around. Again, don't stop trying. Their website is www.ndvh.org.

The National Sexual Assault Hotline (sexual assault includes parental incest) at 800-656-4673 is free, twenty-four hours a day, and automatically connects you to your local sexual assault center. Centers vary regarding their services but all can give you counseling right then and there.

ACKNOWLEDGMENTS

Special thanks to all the teens who shared your stories, hopes, needs, and problems with me—over the years, you told me what should be in these pages.

Gads of Goddess-y gratitude to the following folks: the Teen Wicca Tribe has given me some uproarious fun and amazing healing. Both blossomed into the inner power I needed to write this book. My agents, Elizabeth Pomada and Michael Larsen, as always, have been the best. My editor at Citadel Press, Bob Shuman, both understood and supported my ideals for this book. Blessed be! The following adults and teens are among those who filled out a Wicca questionnaire to help me determine what this book needed: Robynne Elena Blumë, Adrienne Amundsen, Ph.D., Carrie Vadnais, M.A., Janus Laughingbear, Zia Bleasdale, and Thom Fowler. Adrienne and Carrie went on to read the manuscript and their psychological expertise made the book a hell of a lot better. Kush and Phoebe Wray's support of my work and life is endlessly patient and loyal. Deborah Stafford guards my back. Bob W., Danyea S., Deborah D., and Sage Moonstone did typing and other office necessities. About twenty pages of this book were written at Geyserville, California's Isis Oasis, a retreat center—owned and run by Loreon Vigne—that has continually provided me with a joyful, safe, and healing haven. The Pink Bunny Tribe keeps me literally alive with their humble care. My students and readers, old and new, continue to make my work possible and worth all the problems—especially Dawn Walker and Kathi Somers. Without "the fellowship" I'd have nothing; with it all possibilities are mine. And my Divine Mother and Father love me via every atom of the cosmos.